HER FIRST LOVE

"Why did you leave?"

She opened her mouth to answer, but he cut her short.

"Please don't give me the answer you gave your parents."

Her heart pounded in her ears. "I really just wanted to see what was out there."

"So you took off without leaving a note or anything."

"I was afraid that if I told you where I was going, then you would follow me."

"If I had, would it have made a difference?" His gaze bored right through her. It was as if he could see every part of her, every emotion, every thought, every atom of her being.

"Yes," she whispered.

When had he moved so close? She could easily touch his face, run her fingers along his cheek, test the wiry curls that made up his beard. And she did. He felt just as he had all those years ago. How could she remember that? She didn't know, but it was there all the same.

"Hannah," he breathed and moved closer still.

He was going to kiss her . . . and there was nothing she could do about it. Not that she wanted to . . .

Books by Amy Lillard

The Wells Landing Series
CAROLINE'S SECRET
COURTING EMILY
LORIE'S HEART
JUST PLAIN SADIE
TITUS RETURNS
MARRYING JONAH
THE QUILTING CIRCLE

The Pontotoc Mississippi Series
A HOME FOR HANNAH

Amish Mysteries
KAPPY KING AND THE PUPPY KAPER

Published by Kensington Publishing Corporation

Return to the charm of the Regency era with

GEORGETTE HEYER,

creator of the modern Regency genre.

Enjoy six romantic collector's editions with forewords by some of today's bestselling romance authors,

**Nora Roberts, Mary Jo Putney,
Jo Beverley, Mary Balogh,
Theresa Medeiros and Kasey Michaels.**

Frederica
On sale February 2000
The Nonesuch
On sale March 2000
The Convenient Marriage
On sale April 2000
Cousin Kate
On sale May 2000
The Talisman Ring
On sale June 2000
The Corinthian
On sale July 2000

Available at your favorite retail outlet.

HARLEQUIN®
Makes any time special ™

Visit us at www.romance.net   PHGHGEN

A Home For Hannah

Amy Lillard

ZEBRA BOOKS
KENSINGTON PUBLISHING CORP.
http://www.kensingtonbooks.com

To Kay and Vera, who helped raise me.
I wouldn't be where I am today without y'all.

(Did I get that right?)

Chapter One

There should have been more—balloons, fanfare, *something* to herald her return. But there was only the proud burgundy and gold sign that declared Hannah Gingerich McLean was back in Pontotoc.

She eased her car slowly through the town. It was nearing sundown and no one was about. Pontotoc was the kind of town that rolled up the sidewalks after supper. Once upon a time she had hated that small fact. Now it was more of a comfort than an annoyance. There were fewer people to witness her shame. When she'd left so many years ago, she had vowed never to return. It seemed like this was her year for breaking promises.

She sighed and turned to look at Brandon, slumped against the door, lips parted as he slept. When he was like this he still looked like her little boy, her baby. The one person she loved most in this world. Not the surly teenager who had taken over his body, but her precious angel.

"Hey." She touched his leg. "We're almost there." Pontotoc wasn't their final destination, but Randolph, the small community just south of town. There wasn't much in Randolph—just a water tower, a post office, and a community center. And home.

Brandon stirred. "Kay," he mumbled. "Why are we coming here again?"

Hannah took a deep breath and murmured the lie she had almost come to believe. "It's time you met your family here."

"I thought they didn't 'approve.'" He used air quotes around the last word, but didn't open his eyes.

Her family didn't approve, but she was counting on love to win out. Once upon a time she had been *their* precious angel.

Well . . . that wasn't exactly true. Her twin sister, Leah, had always been the good child, while Hannah had been the handful, never quite fitting in with the rest of the community. Never quite accepting their ways. Willful, rebellious, contentious. But this was different.

"I've explained this," she said, her voice heavy with patience. "My *grossmammi*—grandmother—fell and broke her hip." At least that part was true. "Now my mother needs help with things until she gets well." It was as good of an excuse as any.

"Whatever." Brandon sighed and braced his Converse-clad feet on the dashboard. Any other car and she would have chastised him. But this was his car, a beat-up clunker that Mitchell had bought Brandon as a last-ditch effort to make amends. But as usual, the effort was too little, too late. And a little too soon. Brandon wouldn't be able to drive the car for another year and a half. At the time Mitch had presented him with the car, Hannah had been furious. Now she was grateful for the transportation. Without it, they would be on foot.

She peered over the steering wheel, trying to find her way. It was better by far than dwelling on the past. Past mistakes, past heartache, past lies.

But there was no escaping. She was driving into the

past even as she called it a step toward the future. She shook the thought away and studied the landscape once more. Even in a tiny community like Randolph the vegetation changed. The tree line grew or was cut down. Flowers were planted, died, and bloomed once again. The turn was coming up, and she didn't want to miss it.

"I thought you said we were almost there." Brandon squinted through the bug-speckled windshield as Hannah veered to the left. A little farther on Topsy Road, then she would turn down the gravel road that led past the Gingerich drive. But she would have to watch carefully. After all this time, they had probably paved the lane through the Amish settlement.

Hannah eased the car down the lane, not allowing herself time to wonder what her *mamm* would think, her *dat*. Or the bishop. Gravel knocked against the bottom of the car. Going faster than twenty miles an hour was more than impossible. Driving slow gave her the extra minutes she needed to take it all in. It had been such a long time. Over fifteen years.

She spotted the fence before the road and the sign made of slats of siding, carefully hand-lettered to state that local honey, goat milk soap, jellies, jams, and storage sheds were available for sale. The weathered barbed wire stretched across the land, holding in goats and people alike. How could it be that after fifteen years the sign was still the same? The fence the same. The road still gravel. Nothing had changed.

And yet everything was different. Or maybe it was just her. She had been so glad to see the last of this place, with its run-down houses and dust that seemed to coat everything no matter how many times she swept and mopped. Theirs was one of the most conservative sects, not even allowing indoor plumbing or slow-moving triangles on the backs of their buggies.

She turned off the motor, then sighed. She knew everyone in the house had heard their arrival. The sound of an engine wasn't the most uncommon sound in a Plain community, but at this time of day . . . It would only be a matter of seconds before someone peeked out the window, came out onto the front porch to make out the identity of their unexpected visitor.

The thought made her heart pound, her mouth dry, and her palms damp. What was she doing here? Just . . . what?

"Is this it?"

She nodded, unable to get a word past the lump in her throat. She could only imagine what it looked like through his eyes. She had grown up here; some of the best times of her life had happened right there on that front porch. But those were all wrapped up with the worst times. All the times she couldn't understand the rules or the benefits in living such an austere life. All the times she had snuck out to meet Aaron.

Aaron. Now there was another memory altogether.

"It looks so . . ." For once Brandon seemed at a loss for words.

"I told you; they are very conservative."

"Yeah." He nodded slowly, but didn't take his gaze from the house before him. Like most in the area, the house was white, plain, and covered with siding. The barns and outbuildings were protected with the same corrugated tin, though in a deep red. Only the orange dust that floated so freely about took the edge off the contrast.

Once again the truth of her situation slammed into her. How was she going to make it through?

Surely there was another way. She should be able to come up with some plan that would keep her from having to crawl back home on her hands and knees. The car's engine gave one last knock, as if it had traveled its last mile. She'd had to crawl back almost literally. And there was no other course of action she could take. Mitch had seen to that.

But there were things she could have done. She should have written more. She could have waited for a response. She should have made certain that she and Brandon would be welcome instead of hoping against the odds that love would overcome objection, even after all the years that had passed. But just how did a person say, *I have no place to go. I need to come home, can I stay?* And what would she have done if they told her she wasn't welcome?

"Let's get this over with," Brandon grumbled and opened his door.

Hannah didn't bother to correct his attitude as she got out of the car and turned toward the house.

A plump, barefoot woman in a plain green dress and a gray apron stood on the porch holding open the door and staring at Hannah as if she had seen the Lord Himself come back. Her hair was covered by the traditional Amish prayer *kapp*, but what Hannah could see of it was gray. She didn't remember it being that gray.

"Hannah?" The word was barely a hopeful whisper.

"It's me, Mamm." She took a couple of steps toward all the things she had left behind so many years ago.

This was the moment she had been dreading and anticipating. She took two more steps toward her mother, the house. Then she stopped, wrapped her fingers around Brandon's arm, and steered him forward. She tried to convince herself she had done that to introduce him, but she needed him by her side. The one steady in her life right now.

She almost stumbled as her father came out onto the porch, settling his hat into place as he peered at her car.

"Abner," her mother said, her clear voice still barely above a whisper. "It's Hannah. Our Hannah has come home."

Her father grunted once, then jumped off the porch and strode purposefully toward the barn. He disappeared readily into the shadows.

He didn't even glance toward them as he walked past.

"Nice, Mom," Brandon muttered under his breath.

But Hannah didn't have time to comment before her mother rushed toward her and enveloped her in the loving arms she had missed so much. The familiar scents of vanilla, homemade soap, and honest sweat filled her senses and all else fled from her mind.

"Your letter said you were coming home, but I dared not hope."

Tears stung Hannah's eyes. The last few weeks, months, had almost been more than she could stand. Her legs went weak with the relief.

She had missed her mother more than anything else. But the *Ordnung* was clear about such matters. Hannah couldn't live under Amish laws, so she had left, and in leaving she had sacrificed her contact with her family.

Mamm set her away, but retained the hold on her arms. "Look at you." She brushed the hair back from Hannah's brow. "So *Englisch*."

She knew she looked nothing like the girl who had left. She had cut her chestnut-colored hair first thing and never let it grow past her shoulders. Mitch had liked it lighter than nature had determined, and Hannah had kept it heavily highlighted to appease him.

Not anymore.

Her clothes weren't the fanciest she owned. She was

accustomed to going around in top label pantsuits and designer heels. But when she packed her bags she grabbed her comfies from the back of the closet, those clothes she wore only when Mitch wasn't around.

Mamm pulled her close for another quick squeeze, then turned toward her companion.

"This is Brandon," she said. "Your grandson. Brandon, this is your grandmother." How uncomfortable to introduce them after fifteen years.

The sting of her father's rejection and the awkwardness of the evening subsided as her mother put her hands on Brandon's shoulders. "Let me have a look at you. You're the image of your mother, you know."

To Brandon's credit, he didn't roll his eyes. He even let her pat his cheek and fuss over him a bit.

To her mother's credit, she didn't say a word about his long hair or the ring in his lip. But Hannah could see the questions she had about both.

"Hannah?" A hesitant voice sounded close by, and she turned her attention from the long-overdue interaction between her mother and her son to the young woman who approached. "You made it."

"Gracie?" She couldn't hold back the tears any longer as her cousin took her turn to greet her. Though Gracie had been only ten when Hannah and Leah had left their Amish home, Hannah would have known her anywhere. Same big blue eyes that seemed to swallow up her face, same sweet dimples and unassuming disposition. "Oh, Hannah! I'm so glad you're home."

"I'm glad too." And she was. Glad to be home, glad to have her son at her side. If only her father were as happy. "Dat," she said, glancing toward the barn.

Her mother wiped her eyes with the end of her apron and shook her head. "Give him time, Hannah Mae. Now come on in the house. I'll get you something to eat."

* * *

Hell. That was the only way to describe it. He'd fallen asleep in the car, and he woke up in hell. Dusty, run-down, and sad, but hell all the same.

Brandon rubbed his eyes once again, hoping that when he was good and awake things would look better, but he knew that wasn't going to happen.

His mother didn't talk about her childhood much. Not like his friends' parents did. Now he understood why. Geez! How did people live like this?

"Are you coming?" Mom stopped, one foot on the first of the wooden steps that led to the weathered porch.

She couldn't be serious, but she seemed to be. They were really going to stay here?

His new grandmother was standing in the doorway, the screen door open as she waited for his response.

Unbelievable.

Somehow he put his feet into motion and followed behind them.

The inside of the house was dim, only the dying sun from the windows giving light to the rooms. What he could see of it was clean and smelled like the pizzeria that was down the street from their apartment in the city. He figured that was bread or something else baking in the oven that had surely come straight out of the Clampetts'.

The whole place might be out of the history books, but it seemed okay enough. The scent of lemon detergent mixed with the yeasty aroma to form a blend that was both homey and welcoming.

But this isn't your home.

Like he needed a reminder.

He shoved his hands into his pockets and eyed the room around him. *Sparse* and *crowded* were the first two words to enter his thoughts. And a far cry from their Nashville home. There was nothing on the walls, all the furniture looked to be made out of only wood, and there was no carpet on the floor.

But it's clean and sort of inviting.

He pushed the voice away. He didn't want to see any good in this move. His mother had told him that it was just a stopping point until they could get his father's estate settled, but after seeing her hugging his grandmother, he was beginning to think otherwise.

People seemed to materialize from nowhere. The woman who had met them outside had followed them in. Now another girl not much older than him approached, her eyes sparkling.

They were all dressed the same, with funny little caps on their heads, dresses, and aprons. None of them had on shoes.

He couldn't imagine his mother ever wearing such an outfit or going around barefoot, but if she had truly grown up here he supposed she must have.

He shoved his hands a bit deeper into his pockets and tried to make himself as small as possible. He was tired and angry and not ready to meet all these people. Couldn't they put this off until tomorrow?

"Brandon, this is your aunt Tillie."

Apparently not.

"Hi." He gave a quick shrug. The woman looked a little like his mom, with the same color eyes. But her hair was darker, more of a coffee sort of brown, instead of the streaky reddish blond his mother faithfully kept up.

"Are you hungry?" his grandmother asked. He didn't even know what to call her. Had he ever heard his mother actually say her name? He couldn't remember.

Like he cared. All he wanted was to be out of here as quickly as possible. Yesterday.

Mom shook her head. "I'm fine. Brandon?"

He shrugged again without taking his hands from his pockets. "Whatever."

His mother and grandmother stared at him as if he had just walked off an alien spaceship, but he didn't care. He didn't want to be here, and he wasn't about to pretend otherwise.

"Eunice? Who's there?"

His grandmother looked back to Mom. "That's Mammi."

"I'll go." His mother glanced to him as if he should volunteer to go with her, but no way. He'd had enough of meeting people he never wanted to know for one day.

"Whatever," he said again and flung himself down at the kitchen table.

"I have pie."

He turned to look at his grandmother. His aunt hovered behind, along with the woman named Gracie. He heard the door open as someone else entered the small house. So weird to meet these people and find out that he was related to them though he had just now seen them for the first time. He was practically an adult!

"And cold milk."

He shrugged one shoulder. Pie sounded awesome. But he didn't want to appear excited. So lame. "Sure. Whatever."

She gave him a questioning glance, then moved around the kitchen that looked as if it belonged in a museum exhibit. Tillie and Gracie slid into chairs across from him. They propped their chins on their hands and watched him like spectators at a baseball game while he pretended not to notice. Or to care. His grandmother puttered around, and before he knew it, she slid a piece of pie and a large glass of milk in front of him.

"Thanks." He sat up straight and picked up the fork resting on the edge of the plate.

"*Danki*." His grandmother smiled.

"What?" he asked around his bite of pie. Blackberry. Yum. But he wasn't about to say too much. No sense letting everyone know they could get to him. Now, if it had been an apple pie . . . "Is that like Amish for *you're welcome*?"

"It's Dutch for *thank you*," Tillie said.

He took a gulp of the milk. It tasted a little weird—not bad like it had turned or anything, just different. "Dutch?"

"Pennsylvania Dutch." His grandmother gave a quick nod, then moved away as his mother came back into the room.

Weird. He thought they were German.

Mom sat in the chair next to him, releasing a sigh as she eased down. She looked beat, but he wasn't about to show concern. She was the reason they were in this mess.

Brandon took another large bite of the pie. It was so good. Maybe even the best he had ever eaten, but he wasn't saying that out loud. He didn't want his mother getting any ideas about staying. Three weeks and he was out of here. That had been the agreement. Well, sort of. She had said they needed to move, that the house where they lived would have to be sold. Something about unknown debts and bills and an estate in probate, whatever that meant. He'd looked it up on the Internet, but it was boring adult stuff. He should have cared more about it since it somehow affected his life, but he couldn't muster even the smallest interest in understanding it. He'd made up his mind. He was giving this whole thing three weeks—that was fair as far as he was concerned—but once that time was up, he was out.

Unless this was all some kind of joke and his mother would start laughing at any minute claiming that she had "got him."

Yeah, that had to be it. Just a joke. A late April Fool's prank. Never mind that it was August. His mother was never really good with that sort of thing.

"Once you finish your pie, we'll get our bags from the car."

Just his luck. She wasn't kidding. This was no joke. His dad was gone, his home was up for sale, and he was stuck in Amish Land.

Perfect, he thought as he scooped up the last bite of pie. *Just perfect.*

Chapter Two

Hannah stared up into the darkness where the ceiling should be. She had forgotten how dark it got out here once the sun was completely down, once everyone had gone to bed. There were no lights in the house to show the way, no streetlamps or security lights outside. Only the moon gave any reprieve from the darkness, but even its light couldn't make its way into her room.

Above her, the roof creaked and moaned as the soft wind made its way under the corrugated tin to rattle around in the rafters. Not so long ago such a noise would have sent Brandon scurrying into her room wanting to know what all the strange noises were. But these days he was too big and tough to scurry anywhere, scared or not. Just when had her baby turned into such a . . . well, she didn't have a word. *Teenager* was all she could say.

Once she had come out of the adjacent *dawdihaus*, her family had descended, her brothers, Jim and David, and Jim's wife, Anna. David was a couple of years younger than Hannah and Leah, while Jim was a couple of years older. Both had joined their father's business of building storage sheds for Amish and *Englisch* alike. Both had built houses on the adjacent land, though David had yet to find himself a bride. They seemed genuinely happy to see her, though her father stayed in the barn until after she and Brandon had retired to their room.

Across the darkness, Brandon snored softly as he slept. He had rolled his eyes at the thought of having to share a room with his mother, but Hannah explained as best she could. There was only one spare room. He either slept in one of the twin beds in the sewing room or on the hard couch in the living room.

Hannah rolled over and punched at her pillow. She had gotten accustomed to her memory foam pillow, but when it was time to go, some things had to be left behind. Her neck would be stiff in the morning, but it was just another of the adjustments they would have to make.

So many adjustments. And just like always, her thoughts circled around to Brandon once again. Mitch's death had come as a shock to them both. Shocking to learn that he had died in an explosion aboard a yacht she hadn't even known he had bought. Even more shocking was the fact that his twenty-two-year-old assistant was found dead alongside him. Then all of that was topped off with the debt he had racked up, the unpaid bills, loans, and mortgages. Now everything was wrapped up in the legal system. She couldn't even pretend to understand it all. Her attorney assured her that things would settle down eventually. Everything she and Mitch owned together would be sold or auctioned off to pay the outstanding debts—the house, the cars, the apartment in the city. He all but promised that once everything had been liquidated, she would have enough to modestly start over. She could only hope. And pray. Though she wasn't sure God was listening to her these days.

She sighed into the darkness. She hated the nights. That was when the thoughts crowded in and refused to let her sleep. During the day she could pretend that everything was just as she planned. That everything was going to be just fine. But at night it was a different matter. And here, in the home where she grew up . . . all the lies she told herself seemed even bigger, the obstacles that stood in her way greater than before.

She had no idea how long they would be here, or even how long they would be allowed to stay. Conservative Amish sects didn't take to their members leaving, then casually coming back. And with an *Englisch* son in tow? She'd be lucky if they even had a week before they were forced out. Hopefully that would be enough time to come up with another plan, someplace to stay as she waited it out. The attorney had said this ordeal could take months. But she didn't have that much time. She only had days to figure out what she could do. Days filled with family and reconnecting and more memories than she cared to think about.

"Time to get up." Hannah gently shook her son's shoulder, ignoring how young and innocent he still looked as he slept. Despite his long hair and that awful lip ring, he still was her baby.

She hated the lip ring, but it had been his rebellion against Mitch's stern treatment of him. She had used reverse psychology, hoping that if she didn't make a big deal out of it, he would grow bored with it and it would disappear. So far no luck, but she still held tight to her hope.

"Brandon." She gently shook him again.

"Wut?" he muttered, not bothering to open his eyes.

Poor guy, he'd had a tough couple of days. If they had been home, she would have let him sleep in, but they weren't at home. Now was the time to win her family's favor, no matter how long they were staying.

"Time to get up."

He rolled over and flung one arm over his eyes. "What time is it?"

"Time to get up," she returned.

He pushed himself up in the bed and glanced out the window, rubbing his eyes as if he couldn't trust them. "It's still dark out."

Welcome to Amish country. "Everyone around here gets up before the sun. Now come on and let's get something to eat."

He scratched at his chest through his shirt and mulled over her words. "Kay." He pushed himself out of bed, still tousled, as he padded barefoot toward the door.

"Wait. You can't go out there like that." She pointed toward his plaid pajama pants and black shirt emblazoned with the name of his favorite rock band.

He looked down at himself, then back up to her. "What's wrong with what I'm wearing?"

"It's different here. Just get dressed first, okay?"

For a moment she thought he might start an argument, but he grabbed his clothes and motioned for her to leave the room. "I would go to the bathroom to get ready, but wait . . . there isn't a bathroom."

She would give him that dispute. Living without Internet, cable, and electricity would be bad enough. But without indoor plumbing . . . ? She knew she was asking a lot. Yet what choice did they have? "Come to the table when you're dressed and ready."

"Fine," he blustered, turning away as if she were already gone.

"And Brandon?" she started. "Come ready to pray."

Pray? He scoffed as he pulled a clean T-shirt over his head. He had almost grabbed one with a skull on it, just to see what his conservative family members would think of it, but decided against it. He was angry with his mother for bringing him here, but he understood that they had no place else to go. No sense pushing it beyond the limits.

Instead he found a plain one, black, and a pair of jeans. It was the best she would get from him today.

He shook back his hair and pulled it into a plain band. He read once that dukes and pirates called the style a *queue*. He liked the idea; it sounded a lot better than *ponytail*. He smoothed his hands over his hair, hoping it looked okay. But there wasn't a mirror in the sewing room where they had slept. After all the surprises that kept coming about this little vacation in Amish Land, he shouldn't be surprised.

With a quick shake of his head, he started from the room.

He followed the smell of sausage all the way to the kitchen. The first thing that struck him was the noise. Not crazy noise, but comforting noise. It made him think of his friend Carlos and his family. So many people lived in Carlos's house that there was never a quiet moment, not even in the middle of the night. But the sounds were happy, warm, family.

In a separate room off from the kitchen, a large table was loaded down with biscuits, sausage, a large bowl of scrambled eggs, a pan of fried potatoes, fruit, applesauce, some type of peanut butter spread, and more jars of jam than he could take in with one look.

"There you are." His grandmother bustled over. "I was just about to send your mother after you."

She was?

"Come sit down so we can get started."

Almost every chair was full. His grandmother, his grandfather, his aunt Tillie, the woman named Gracie he'd met last night, his mother, and his uncle David were all waiting for him to sit down.

He cleared his throat and took his seat, the one between David and his mother.

Mom elbowed him gently in the ribs, then nodded pointedly toward her father at the head of the table. He had his hands in his lap and his head bowed. Brandon looked around at the others. Everyone was sitting in the same pose. Was this what she had meant when she had said "come ready to pray"?

She dipped her chin, and he bowed his head, sure that was what she wanted from him. He lowered his eyes, and no one spoke.

Geez. What was taking so long?

Brandon blew out a quiet sigh, then everyone shifted in their chairs. His mom nudged him again, and Brandon lifted his gaze. Movement had started around the table once more. Family members were passing biscuits, butter, and jams. But what about the prayer?

It seemed it was over, if it had ever begun.

Someone passed him the plate of sausage. He took a couple of links and passed it to his mother, only then realizing that everyone had been waiting on him, and no one had eaten until everyone was seated at the table. Weird. Beyond weird. But also kind of nice.

He accepted the pan of biscuits from his uncle and stacked a couple on his plate. He looked down at his meal, complete with fried potatoes and eggs. He might have had to get up before the sun and get dressed for no reason, but he could get used to a breakfast like this.

"Dat!"

Aaron Zook closed his eyes, took a deep breath, then turned away from the skillet full of ham to look at his oldest daughter.

Laura Kate came across so much more grown up than

her almost nine years as she pursed her lips at him. "I don't want to go up North."

"Who said anything about going up North?" He didn't need to ask. There was only one person.

"Andy."

"Please go outside and send your brother back in."

"Is he in trouble?" Laura Kate's eyes were alight with something akin to satisfaction.

As much as Aaron hated the look, he understood. Ever since Lizzie had died, Andy had grown increasingly cantankerous, almost surly in his attitude, especially where his sisters were concerned.

"Go get him, please." Aaron was not getting into this discussion with his daughter at such an early hour. The sun was barely up. "Then help your sister get in the eggs."

"*Dat.*"

Aaron shook his head at her tone. Where had *her* attitude come from? He certainly hadn't encouraged it, but he had to get a handle on it. If only Lizzie were still alive. She'd know what to do. "After that we need to get the trash to the barrel. It's burning day."

"Did you hear what I said?" Her blue eyes were serious behind her wire-rimmed glasses.

"And did you hear me, daughter?"

Her lips tightened in an all-too-familiar way. And he couldn't help but think back to a beautiful summer day, much like today, with a chestnut-haired girl with sweet hazel eyes and a similar stubborn expression. He pushed those thoughts away.

He hadn't thought of her in years, but that didn't mean his memories of her were any less potent. They were always there, just waiting for some little thing to push them to the front of his mind.

"But, Dat, I—"

"You have exactly three seconds to get out of this house

and do your chores before you have to muck the stalls in the horse barn this afternoon." He turned back to their breakfast, but could hear her aggravated sigh and angry footsteps as she stomped from the house.

He should have been more careful in talking to Abner Gingerich in front of his children. They were growing up so fast, understanding more and more of the world around them. Or was it simply that they had, at some point, started paying attention?

All his life, Aaron had been good with animals, especially with horses. Somehow, they just seemed to trust him, to do what he wanted of them. There wasn't a horse in Mississippi he couldn't train with kind words and gentle touches. He had a gift, the elders always said. A gift for training horses, but no heart for farming.

But this was Lizzie's father's land, handed to him through her. Since she'd passed, he hadn't seemed to be able to grow much of anything. But for the last year, he'd held on, tried to make the best of it. Through an unpredictable winter, a brutal summer, and the trials of raising three children by himself. He felt like he was losing on all accounts. And that left him only one option: remarry and find his family the mother they needed so very badly. Maybe if he picked careful enough he'd find a widow with at least one teenage son to help him farm the land. But the idea held no appeal.

He had prayed, and now he had a different opportunity. Seemed there was a fellow up in Ohio who'd pay a man a fair day's wage to train his horses. This fellow had heard about Aaron's gift and wanted him to consider the job.

And he was. Despite Laura Kate's reservations about moving away from Mississippi, to Aaron, moving to Ohio held many opportunities—and not just those of a job he would love. Just the thought of working with horses all day every day made his heart feel light and his stomach quivery with anticipation. But there was more to think about than just himself. There were his children. And he'd never much been out of Pontotoc.

"Dat! Dat!"

Essie, his youngest, came flying through the door, leaving Laura Kate to keep the screen from slamming back into place.

"Laura Kate got the eggs." Essie pointed to the basket her sister carried. "And I got the milk," she added, her dimpled smile warming him from the inside out. His youngest daughter was as whimsical as his eldest girl was serious.

In fact, all of his kids were as different as three could be, yet they all favored him with dark hair and blue eyes. Essie's hair was a mess of fuzzy curls, a gift from some way-back relative on Lizzie's side of the family tree. Essie could chat the legs off a table, while Laura Kate spoke with confidence as she bossed her sister into compliance. Heaven help them all if she took a turn. Andy was growing more sullen every day. If asked, Aaron would have said that of all his kids, his daughters would need a mother most, but he was beginning to suspect that Andy was the one who needed the gentler touch. Aaron did the best he could, but he wasn't able to be all the things his kids needed at all times. He was used to being busy and working hard. But the last year had worn him out.

The more tired he became, the more appealing the Ohio job was beginning to look.

"Breakfast is ready." He barely got the words out before Andy pushed into the house, carrying the milk that Essie "got."

Laura Kate set her morning gatherings on the table, then went to the basin to wash up, her sister not far behind.

"Use the soap, Essie," he said without even turning to face them.

"*Jah*, Dat." Her voice held just enough exasperation that he couldn't help but smile.

Aaron dumped the ham on a plate and put it, along with a pan of biscuits, on the table.

After a few minutes of washing, drying, and silent prayer, they were all seated and the house was filled to quiet with the sounds of eating.

"Dat?"

"*Jah*, Essie?"

"Andy said we were movin' to the North. That ain't true, right? Me and Laura Kate, we told him that couldn't be true."

"Well now," he said, all the while looking at his oldest. "I'll tell you like I told Andy: when the decision is made, I'll let you know. Until then, I'll not be discussing it."

"But, Dat—"

He lifted his hand to stop her protest. Remarkably, she fell silent. Or maybe not so remarkably. Essie never gave him much trouble. Even after Lizzie had passed. Laura Kate had become the mother, bossing her siblings to the point of annoyance. Andy had become withdrawn. Only Essie had kept her sunny disposition and sweet attitude.

Or as clear as he could remember. He hadn't spent near as much time with them before Lizzie's death as he had in the last year since.

"Now go on and eat," he said. "Before you're late to school."

"Dat, it's just across the road." Essie bobbed in place as she chewed a bite of ham. He knew that under the table her legs were swinging furiously. The girl could not sit still.

"That's another thing," he said. "No coming home at lunch. Take your coolers like your brother."

Laura Kate and Essie started to protest. But he couldn't allow it. It was a bad habit, them running across to eat lunch at the house when they should be with their schoolmates. He had caved so many times after Lizzie's death that it had become a bad habit in need of breaking. And today seemed like the perfect day to do that.

He shook his head. "I'm going over to the Abner Gingeriches'. And I won't be home until well after dinnertime."

Laura Kate gave a stern nod. "*Jah*, Dat. I'll make sure Essie stays at school."

There was no grumbling as the decision was made, but he could tell they weren't happy. It was for the best, he told himself. He had coddled them long enough. "Make sure you stay there yourself."

"*Jah*, Dat."

After the kids left for school, Aaron hitched up his buggy and started toward the Gingerich place. He had known Abner all his life. There was even a time when he thought Abner would be his father-in-law, but God had different plans for them. Yet just because Hannah had jumped the fence to the *Englisch*, well, that didn't mean he and Abner couldn't be friends. He admired the man, looked up to him for both advice and direction. Aaron's own father had passed, and his father-in-law had moved back to Ethridge, leaving him to lean on Abner.

But Abner couldn't give him the answer to what was best for his family. He had only told Aaron to pray about the situation. Pray and listen for God's answer. Maybe the future was in Ohio, or maybe it was here in Mississippi, married to someone like Gracie, Abner's niece. Aaron had prayed. He had prayed that God's will be carried out. He had prayed for the wisdom to know the direction to take his family. And he had prayed for answers to his many questions and peace in his heart. It was all a man could ask for.

But so far, there had been no answer, leaving him just as confused as he was before.

A strange car sat in the yard off to one side as Aaron pulled his buggy into the Gingeriches' drive. The license plate on the back declared it to be a car from Tennessee, and he wondered if perhaps someone in Ethridge had hired a driver so they could come down and visit with the Gingeriches. It was nothing to see cars parked at the various houses. Drivers, tourists, even the occasional visitor from out of state. But something about the car sent his heart pounding in his chest.

He shook away the trepidation that crawled down his spine. It was nothing. Just a car. He was so wound up trying to make a decision about Ohio that his thoughts were all in a jumble. He had been praying so hard for God's will that he was seeing signs where there were none. Signs that didn't pertain to him at all.

He parked his buggy alongside the car and tied his horse to the fence. Abner, Jim, and David must've been watching for his arrival, for the sound of the saw stopped, then they all ambled out of the workshop. Seeing the three of them side by side, all dressed in matching blue shirts, their feet bare even on the wood shavings in the workshop, gave Aaron a sense of peace. The sight of them made him realize everything was going to be okay. It was as if the hand of God reached out to ease his anxiety.

"Hello," Abner called, raising a hand in greeting.

Aaron waved in return, then met them halfway across the gravel drive.

"You come about that mare?" Abner asked.

Aaron nodded. "I had a little time this morning. Thought I would take a look at her."

Jim and David shared a glance that had unrest rising in Aaron once again.

"You have a visitor?" He nodded toward the car in the drive.

"You could say that," Jim said.

The three men looked so serious that for a moment Aaron worried that some sort of tragedy might have befallen the Gingeriches.

"No sense in beating around the bush," David said. "Hannah came back last night."

Chapter Three

Aaron could only blink as the words stumbled around inside his mind. Hannah was back. Hannah. His Hannah? No, not his. Not really. Though once upon a time he had thought of her just that way. Then she had decided that the *Englisch* world held more opportunities than their small Amish community, and she disappeared without even saying goodbye.

He cleared his throat, trying to get a handle on his mixed-up emotions. A hundred questions flitted through his thoughts, each one demanding to be asked first. What was she doing here? How long was she staying? Why had she come back now? Was she staying? They just kept coming.

"Hannah?" The one word was all he could say. Yet of anyone in the community, these three men knew what she had meant to him once upon a time. He could see it in their eyes: they didn't know how he would react to the news she had returned. "She's not . . ." he started, but was unable to finish the question. "I mean, how did she . . ." Again the words failed him. But the Gingerich men knew what he was trying to ask.

Jim shrugged. "We don't know. She came back last night. Brought her son with her. Mamm talked to her more than anyone."

"We just thought you should know," David added.

"*Danki.*" At least that word he could manage. Hannah had a son.

Of all the days that he could've come out to look at the mare . . . He glanced toward the house, but didn't let his gaze stray for long. He swung his attention back to the man before him and gave a resigned nod. "How about that mare?"

Hannah dried the last plate and handed it to her mother to put in the cupboard.

Mamm smiled and hummed a little under her breath.

She knew her mother was glad to have her back in Mississippi, if only for a time. But her father was another matter altogether. He wouldn't speak to her or acknowledge her in any way. He wouldn't even look at her. She had been thankful that he let her eat at the table with the rest of the family this morning, though he acted as if the chair were empty. It wasn't like she was under the *Bann*. Not yet anyway. She had left during her *rumspringa*, before she had joined the church. But now that she had returned, she would be expected to kneel and ask forgiveness. She would be expected to repent her ways, join the church. Her father was just looking ahead. She could find no fault in him with that. It was simply the way he had been raised and what he had been taught his entire life. But how was she supposed to explain to the people she loved most in the world that she had wanted to know more about the world outside their little community? And because of that she had to leave? There was no easy answer. And though she felt as if she had handled things incorrectly, she couldn't find another way that would spare her family such heartache. "Give him time, Hannah Mae," Mamm said.

Startled out of her thoughts, Hannah swung her attention back to her mother, only then realizing she'd been staring out the window at the dusty driveway, at nothing.

She nodded, but not before the sound of a buggy pulling down their lane met her ears. She tried to judge how close it was by listening, but she wasn't sure. Back in the day, she could guess when a buggy would arrive at the house within five seconds. But no more.

The driver pulled the buggy to a stop and nimbly hopped out. Hannah's breath stilled in her lungs. It had been fifteen years or better, but she would've known him anywhere.

Aaron Zook.

Her heart gave a painful pound. Excitement? Trepidation? All that and more.

He waved, and Hannah instinctively raised her hand in return. But he wasn't facing her direction. A few heartbeats later and her father and brothers came into view.

Hannah watched as they talked. Every move Aaron made was as familiar to her as her own. In fifteen years she hadn't forgotten the way he ducked his head when he talked, the way he propped his hands on his slim hips, the way he moved with such smooth grace.

Oh, she had tried to forget. But like so many other things in her life, that task proved impossible as well.

Anger bubbled inside her. She hadn't even been home a day and she was already facing ghosts from the past. Dealing with her father, dealing with Brandon—why did she have to deal with Aaron too?

"What's he doing here?"

Her mother moved to stand beside her and looked out the window. "That's Aaron Zook."

"I know who he is." Hannah took a deep breath to calm her anger. She held up one hand at her mother's startled expression and tried again. "What is he *doing* here?"

Her mother shrugged and moved to wipe down the plain wooden table that sat in the middle of the kitchen. They used it as a workstation and snack spot, like Brandon with his pie the night before. "Your father bought a new mare. She seemed okay at the time, but she's proving to be a little more cantankerous than he had originally thought."

"And he needs Aaron?"

"*Jah*." Her mother nodded. "That boy is good with horses."

Aaron Zook was more than good with horses. He always had been. But he was also more than a boy. That was for sure.

"What's on your mind, Hannah Mae?"

She continued to watch him through the kitchen window. He turned to look at the house just once. Hannah resisted the urge to step back so he couldn't see her, but she knew he couldn't make her out. "He got married," she whispered.

What did you expect?

She had known when he started dating someone after she left. But she hadn't heard that he'd gotten married. Yet his beard testified otherwise.

"He has three kids too," Mamm continued.

Why did the thought of Aaron happily married with a sweet little family send pains shooting through her belly?

"She died."

Hannah whirled around to face her mother. "What?" Somehow she had lost the thread of the conversation.

"Lizzie. His wife. She died."

"He's a widower?" It was the first question Hannah thought to ask, but not the only one that popped into her head. He had married Lizzie Yoder.

Shortly after Hannah had left Pontotoc, she thought she might return. But her brother, Jim, sent her a letter explaining how Aaron had taken up with Lizzie Yoder. The only reason Hannah had had to return to Mississippi was gone, and she hadn't come back until now.

"You should go talk to him," Mamm said.

Hannah took another step back, away from the window, as if to distance herself from the man who probably didn't even know she was there. "Oh, no." She couldn't go talk to him. What would she say? That she was sorry for leaving? That she was sorry about his wife? That she was sorry she wasn't staying?

Returning to Pontotoc permanently was completely out of the question. Too much water had passed under the bridge, as they said. Too much time had passed. Too many obstacles stood in her way. And she had Brandon to think about.

She glanced over to where he sat, phone in his nimble fingers as he texted with one of his friends. She was amazed he could get service out this far, but she knew he wouldn't have it for long. Once the battery died, he wouldn't have any place to charge it except the car. And when the phone went, she knew what little patience he had would be close behind. But until then, she would let him rest. Tomorrow they had to make plans.

"He's a mighty good man," Mamm said, giving a pointed nod in the direction of the driveway.

Hannah didn't have to ask who she was talking about. She opened her mouth to respond, then shut it once again.

What was there to say? Aaron was a mighty good man, but one thing was certain. He was not the man for her.

"Whoa, girl." Aaron wrapped the lead around his hand once more and urged the mare forward. He could see why Abner had bought her. She was a beautiful creature, chestnut-colored with a white blaze on her face and a sooty-colored nose. Her mane and tail matched its dark color, but all four feet were stark white.

She snorted, her eyes wild, still but calming, slowly. With each second she seemed to trust him more. But they had a long way to go.

"It's okay, girl." He raised a hand to stroke her neck. But she pulled away, rearing up on her hind legs as if she could sense his thoughts of another. He wiped all traces of Hannah from his mind, but he knew that the thoughts wouldn't stay gone for long. "Everything's okay," he continued.

And maybe if he told the horse and himself that enough times he would believe it. Why had Hannah come back?

He pushed the thought away. He couldn't calm this mare with another woman on his mind. That was the thing about horses and women. He could only court one of them. And right now Star was the one deserving of his attention.

The horse seemed to sense the very moment when Aaron regained his mental footing. She tossed her head one last time, her inky mane flying in the wind as she settled all four feet back on the ground. She blew out one last snort, then ducked her head toward him.

He wrapped his hand in the lead once again, then gently tugged Star toward him. She came slowly but willingly, her big head bowed as she bumped into his shoulder.

"See," he murmured softly to her.

She lifted her head, though her eyes had lost that wild gleam.

It was nothing but fear. He could almost feel it coming off her. He hadn't asked, but he would suspect that she'd had many owners, maybe even two or three in the last year. Horses were sensitive animals. They were loyal and true. He could only imagine that being sold so many times could damage the horse's sense of duty, damage how they viewed the world. Kind of like his being rejected by the girl he had thought he would one day marry.

And just like that Hannah was in his thoughts again. She tended to crop up at the most inconvenient times. He did his best to keep thoughts of her at bay, especially when training. But Star seemed to trust him now, and didn't mind him sharing his energy with another.

The chestnut lowered her head once more and bumped his shoulder with the spot between her ears. He laughed, realizing what she was after. He stuck his hand in his pocket and pulled out two sugar cubes.

"You deserve it for all you've been through." He chuckled as she gently took the treat from his open palm. He didn't give sugar cubes often. Just this first time. And as their training continued, the treats would consist of carrots and apples, but for now he wanted her to know how special she was to him and how special she would be treated at the Gingerich house.

More than anything, Hannah longed to shut herself in her room, or sit down next to Brandon and immerse herself in a digital world. Anything but face the issue straight on, which meant that was exactly what she needed to do.

She took a hesitant step toward the door. Then another. And another, until finally she was standing outside the horse pasture.

Aaron looked up as she approached. He stopped, gave a quick nod, then slipped the bridle over the horse's neck. He stroked her affectionately as she bumped her forehead against his chest. He chuckled, gave her a couple of sugar cubes, and patted her rump to send her on her way. She trotted off, black mane rippling in the breeze.

"And here I thought you had a talent greater than merely bribery."

He stopped, the smile suspended on his lips. "Hello, Hannah."

"Hi, Aaron." What else was there to say?

He simply stood there as she approached, neither moving toward her or away. She wasn't sure if it was a good sign or not.

Wait . . . there were no good signs and bad. There were only the two of them and a past that was so far behind them it seemed as if it had happened to someone else.

"Your brothers told me you were here."

She nodded. She stopped when their toes were almost touching, soaking in his presence. He was the same as she remembered, the very same. And yet he was so different. His hair was still the same mass of soft, dark curls that stuck out from underneath the brim of his straw hat. His eyes were still the same smoky blue; his smile with one dimple, its crooked slant, and the chipped tooth he had gotten at their first singing were all the same. And yet he was bigger, stronger. He seemed capable and able. He had grown into a man.

"I figured as much." She felt as if she had to say something, but the important words wouldn't come. It had been years since she had talked to him. Years and years and years. There was so much to say, and yet nothing. How could she tell him that her leaving wasn't his fault? That age-old "It's not you, it's me." But in this case, it was true. Hannah hadn't been satisfied with Amish living. She'd

known—just known—that there was more out there. More
to life than Pontotoc, Mississippi. More to life than the
simple existence her family pounded out each day. She had
to go see about it. She had to see if she could find a little
bit of that *more* for herself. She just hated that she'd had
to leave Aaron behind in the process.

"Aaron, I—" She stopped, and he shook his head.

"How have you been?"

She searched his face, studying his expression, looked
deep into his eyes for any underlying meaning to his
words, but there was none. At least none that he was letting her see. Did he truly just want to know how she'd
been all these years? She had heard word from time to
time about how he was doing, and she could only imagine
that her mother had spoken to him about her and the things
she was doing. She didn't write her mother often, a fact
she wasn't proud of, but she had written often enough to
spread news of the changes in her life, the opportunities
she now had, all the good stuff. But none of the bad. None
of the hardships she had faced in a marriage that should've
been a fairy tale.

But that's over now.

"I've been fine." It might've been the biggest lie she
had ever told. But she had been fine years ago when she
and Mitch had first gotten married, when Brandon was a
baby, and the new hadn't worn off the *Englisch* world. She
had been fine, once upon a time. But lately "fine" was
the farthest from the truth for her. She hadn't been fine.
She hadn't been happy. Not in a long, long time.

"You?" she asked.

She could see the memories, both painful and happy,
cross his features. It was like watching clouds in a time-
lapse video moving across the earth, dragging the shadows
behind. "Good. Good," he said.

Hannah nodded, then shoved her hands in the back

pockets of her jeans. The motion pushed her chest forward, and Aaron's eyes darkened. She hadn't meant to be provocative. She hastily pulled her hands up and tucked them across her. "How is your mother?"

Aaron gave a one-armed shrug. "You know she's not right anymore."

Hannah nodded. "Mamm told me." It was almost the truth. The letter had actually come from her sister Leah, talking about how Aaron's mother, Linda, was starting to change. Something had happened inside her brain, and she no longer remembered things she needed to remember. She needed constant care, Leah had explained, and had moved in with Aaron's sister Amanda so Amanda could look after her.

Aaron nodded. "It's just a matter of time."

Hannah wanted to ask if they had taken her to the doctor. Had they gone to a specialist? Had they gone to Memphis, or even Jackson, to find some sort of diagnosis? But she knew that would never happen. Oh, they would go to doctors. It wasn't like they were backward or anything. But elements of the mind could only be chalked up to God's will.

"I'm sorry to hear that. And I'm sorry about Lizzie, too."

Aaron nodded. "And your husband, as well."

Tears stung at the back of her eyes. Strange tears that had nothing to do with the loss of her husband and everything to do with the man before her. Mistakes piled upon her one by one until she felt as weighed down as if she were Atlas carrying the world.

"Hannah, I'm sorry."

She dashed her tears away with the back of one hand. "You have nothing to be sorry for, Aaron. You were never anything but good to me." With that she turned on one heel and marched back toward the house.

Finding out that her husband had been unfaithful had

been hard. Learning that he had died in an unexpected explosion had been terrible. So why was returning to Pontotoc and facing Aaron again one of the toughest things she had ever done?

Because leaving him had been torture.

Aaron started after her, but held himself in check. Instead he watched her walk away, his mind scrambling to merge the Hannah before him with the Hannah he had known once long ago. They looked the same. Well, almost. She still had the same incredible hazel eyes. But her hair was shorter and bleached out in chunks like the *Englisch* women tended to do. She wore *Englisch* clothes, jeans and a T-shirt with flip-flops on her feet. The Hannah he had known had hair down to her waist, deep chestnut–colored hair like the rich, dark parts of cedar wood. She dutifully wore her prayer *kapp*, her simple *frack*s pinned down the front, and she was always barefoot.

Jah, her eyes were the same color. Her cheekbones, her nose, and a small dimple in her chin, all the same. But when he had known her, her eyes held a spark for life. It was that spark that drew him to her. It was mischievous, playful, and genuine all at the same time. Now her eyes seemed flat, as if the *Englisch* world had squashed all the spirit out of her.

The screen door slammed behind her, and still Aaron remained rooted to the spot. He wasn't going to chase after her. He would have long ago. If she had only asked, he would've gone after her. If she had only asked him before she left if he thought she should go, he would've told her no. He would've done anything to keep her by his side. They had shared one incredible night, a night he had thought would bind them together forever, but when he went to her house the next day, she was gone.

As much as he hated to admit it, then and now, her disappearance just proved that she didn't love him the way he loved her. She didn't care about him, didn't value his opinion or his feelings. He had lived with that bitterness for months, finally reconciling it all with God as part of his journey of life. God's will was a mysterious thing. And it seemed as if He hadn't intended Hannah for Aaron. Then Lizzie had appeared. Sweet Lizzie Yoder had promised to be a dutiful wife. She promised to work the land side by side with him, bear him children, and grow old with him. And yet she hadn't had the opportunity to grow old at all.

He stared at the door another moment, then roused himself from his thoughts. "Abner," he called toward the workshop, "I'll be back tomorrow to look at that horse again."

Chapter Four

Brandon stared at the blank, dark screen of his cell phone in disbelief. He wasn't sure why it was so hard to comprehend that his phone was dead. After all, he was in the middle of absolute nowhere. He knew he was lucky enough to have had service at all as far out as they were. And there were no electrical outlets to plug it into and recharge it.

He hit the top button just in case it had just gone to sleep, but of course nothing happened. Figured.

This was just perfect. This whole trip had just been perfect. Now every bit of entertainment he had was gone. Not that he had been able to do much out here. There were no Wi-Fi connections. He'd figured that out last night. But at least he had been able to listen to his music and play a couple of the games that didn't require Internet service. Now he couldn't even text his buddies back home.

He slipped his phone into his pocket when he would've rather pitched it across the room in frustration. Maybe he could find some electricity somewhere, but until then it would do no good to break it.

Just then his mom came through the door. She looked . . . flustered. It was the only word he could think of—like a bird with ruffled feathers. He watched as she did her best to pull herself back together. She was so intent on her task she hadn't even noticed that he was there.

He shouldn't have felt a bit of satisfaction in the fact that she seemed almost as frustrated as he was. But he did. At least this move hadn't been easy for her either. He still had trouble believing she had grown up here. Not the mom he knew.

"What up?" he said.

She nearly jumped out of her skin, slapping one hand over her heart, her eyes wide. "Brandon," she gasped. "I didn't see you there."

Obviously.

"I'm here." He stood as he waited for her response.

She pushed herself off the door, visibly pulling herself together more quickly now. "I can see that now."

"My phone's dead."

He could almost see the mixed emotions sail across her face. She was such a typical mom. Finally she nodded. "It was bound to happen."

"I guess." He didn't have to say the words for her to know that he was not happy about it. And he really didn't feel like pretending otherwise. Why should he? He'd done everything he was supposed to do his entire life. Well, almost. Not counting his hair and the lip ring and his choice of music, but that was beside the point. He was a teenager. Wasn't that what he was supposed to do?

"Brandon, please." Mom held up both hands as if to ward off this brewing argument. Something in the pose made his anger wilt just a bit. He wanted to be mad. He wanted to raise his fist and rail against the system until something happened, but they were so far out, who would hear?

"Whatever." He propped his hands on his hips as if he hadn't a care in the world. Inside, however, he wanted to run to her, fling his arms around her, and hold on and never let go. How had their life come to this? It wasn't a question he let himself ask often. One minute they were fine, living in Nashville, and the next thing he knew his dad was dying off the coast of Florida. From there it just went downhill. And there was nothing he could do about it.

"Brandon, please," she asked again.

Anger bubbled up inside him once again. That feeling of helplessness. That was what did it. That was the one he couldn't take. There had to be something else they could do, something else. He refused to be helpless. Wasn't this America?

Suddenly he wanted to run. Run and run and run and run like that dumb guy in that dumb movie where he ran clear across the United States. Brandon could do that. He could just take off running and not stop until all of this was over. But when would it be over? Would it *ever* be over?

"Fine," he sneered. "Whatever."

He charged toward her, intent on the door.

She pushed herself away as he stormed through it and out onto the porch. He pulled the door closed behind him with so much force, it rattled the windows on either side. He didn't care. He didn't care if he broke every window in the house. His dad was dead, and he was stuck in the worst place he could ever imagine. Stuck without communication to the outside world. Life was perfect.

Without a glance back, he started across the yard, toward the fields on the back side of the property. With any luck, he would get lost, or mauled by a bear. Did they have bears in Mississippi? He had no idea. But he didn't care. Mauled by a great animal or held hostage without a cell phone. What was the difference?

Hannah watched through the window as Brandon stormed across the yard. He ducked under the large oak tree and disappeared over the small rise between the house and the back fields.

How many times had she taken an identical path when she'd had too much of her conservative Amish upbringing? How many times had she escaped that exact way? Like when her father had found those *Englisch* magazines stuck between the mattress and box spring in her bed. Well, the finding them wasn't the bad part, but when he threw them away, her heart broke in two.

There was something else out there. She just knew it. She had known it her entire life, but that hadn't meant she was going to look for it. She had just needed to know what it was. Some people might be able to go through their entire lives not knowing what they were missing and not missing it at all. She had had to know.

But Dat had thrown those colorful, glossy magazines into the trash barrel and burned them with the other, unimportant things the family had decided not to keep. He had taken them and everything else from the *Englisch* she had squirreled away. He had taken, taken, and taken, until she had no other choice but to go see for herself.

Brandon disappeared over the ridge as she watched, and she resisted the urge to run after him. She'd had enough rejection for one afternoon. She didn't think she could handle much more.

What did you expect?

She'd been hopeful, that was all.

Hopeful about a lot of things.

The rattle of Aaron's carriage grew louder, then faded away until it disappeared altogether.

He was gone.

She eased out onto the porch, just in case, then admonished herself for her unnecessary caution. She just needed a little more time before she faced him again. But time was something she didn't have a lot of. Who knew how long the bishop would allow them to stay? She knew her mother would lead their cause, but her father was a different matter altogether. It was the relationship that pained her the most.

There had been a time when the others teased her about growing up to be a farmer herself. She'd spent so much time with her father, shadowing him as much as the sun did. Even more than Jim had. She had helped him plow, harvest, plant, build sheds, saw wood—anything and everything that he would teach her. She had been ready to learn. That had always been the problem. Her mind was inquisitive, always seeking, searching out new things to learn. But when she felt she had learned what she could of their little corner of the world, she had turned to the *Englisch*. And that was when the trouble began.

How she wished she could go back to those carefree days of tagging along behind her *dat*, the summer sun beating down on the back of her neck not covered by her bonnet. Barefoot and dirty, happy and satisfied. What she wouldn't give to go back. What she wouldn't give to wipe out the last fifteen or so years and change her own fate. Not listen to others talk about how to get out of Pontotoc, how to hitchhike. What to say, what to do, what to wear, all those little details that had been sticking to her mind like beggar lice to the edge of her skirt.

What she wouldn't give.

She stepped down the porch steps and across the rocky, graveled drive. Funny how she'd been gone so many years and yet most everything seemed the same. There might be a different dog lying in the shade under the big oak tree, but there had always been a dog there. The barn might have a new roof, there might be a crack in one of the workshop windows, but those changes were nothing. The overall scheme of things, the big picture, was all just as it had been before. Except for her and Dat.

She pulled off her shoes and hooked them on the fingers of one hand as she picked her way across the drive. Back in the day she could've run across the gravel and not thought twice about it. But that was a long time and many pedicures ago. Now her feet were soft, the skin tender. The going was slow, so much so that she almost stopped and put her shoes back on. She didn't need to let herself have time to chicken out. This was one aspect of her life where she needed to be brave. And she hadn't been brave in a long, long time. But if she was ever going to make up any of the relationship she had lost with her father, now was the time. There wasn't a moment to waste.

The sound of the saw grew louder as she neared the workshop. It was a noise straight from her childhood, as vivid as the memories she carried of people and places. That one sound had been a part of her entire existence. Now that she heard it again, after all these years, with everything changing so rapidly, with the future shaking like an earthquake beneath her feet, her stomach pitched and her hands trembled with a longing for days past. Days that could never be hers again.

The inside of the work shed was dark as she stepped through the doorway. She didn't know why they called it a shed. It was as big as the hay barn, with small rectangle-shaped windows between the top of the walls and the roof that provided light year 'round and air in the humid summer months.

The work continued as she entered, neither her father nor her brothers noticing her arrival. And the smell!

It was as familiar to her as her mother's scent, as Brandon when he was small. Clean and sharp, the smell of cut wood was as dear to her as it was poignant.

She took a couple more hesitant steps into the shed, the wood shavings and sawdust biting into the soles of her feet. There was a time when she wouldn't have noticed the small discomfort; now it filled her with another wave of longing so strong it brought tears to her eyes.

The sound of the saw stopped as she blinked back useless tears.

"Hannah," her brother David said. "What are you doing?"

She should have come bearing water or lemonade, but she had no excuse as to why she had made her way into their domain. None, other than the desire to reconnect with her father. With the past. Water wouldn't help with that, and her father and brothers always had their full coolers at hand. Especially in these hot summer months.

"I-I just thought I would come out and . . . visit." Not exactly convincing, but what was she supposed to say? That she had to try one more time to see if her father would talk to her? Maybe if she approached him in front of others he would cave and speak to her. Maybe even look at her. She had hurt him, she knew, but now more than ever she wanted to make amends. "How is the shed coming?"

She looked to Dat. He inspected the last cut of wood without lifting his eyes even once.

So much for that.

"This is a playhouse for one of the *Englisch* day cares in town," Jim answered.

Hannah nodded, and did her best to hide her disappointment. She would have to see if she could get her father alone. Maybe then he wouldn't feel the need to pretend she didn't exist. Maybe then he could relax a bit and allow the healing to begin.

Maybe.

Tears stung at the back of her throat and rose into her eyes, her vision swimming. "Good luck."

What a dumb thing to say. She turned on her heel and hurried from the shed.

The sound of the saw started up again almost immediately. Her unscheduled visit was just a blip, a small inconvenience to an otherwise perfect day. She had tried and her father had moved on. It was as simple as that.

"Hannah, wait!"

She stopped as Jim approached. He jogged after her as if afraid she would run. Hadn't she done enough of that in her life?

"Give him some time." Jim came to a stop next to her.

Hannah could only nod. But there wasn't enough time in the world to heal some wounds.

They stood in silence for a moment, the wind ruffling her hair. It was a strange sensation. She had never stood here, on this land, with her hair down. Only with it pulled tightly into a bob at the nape of her neck. She shivered despite the rising heat of the day.

"What was it like?" Jim quietly asked.

Hannah gave a small shrug. "I sent letters."

"What was it *really* like?"

Hannah looked around at the place she had called home for eighteen years. Laundry line strung between two T poles, muscadine and scuppernong vines climbing across a similar setup. Red dust, green fields, blue sky.

"Fast," she finally answered. It was the best word she could think of to describe her life these days. "Fast, loud, and busy."

Jim glanced toward the house, where their mother was putting more wood into the water heater connected to the wringer washer.

She knew what he was thinking. Life on an Amish farm never stopped, never slowed down, there was always something to do—but this was different. *Englisch* busy was so different from Amish busy, but to someone who had never experienced both, there was no way for her to explain it.

"Jim!"

He whirled around as David called from the doorway. "Dat said come on."

"Go," Hannah said, giving him an understanding smile. Their father was a hard man.

"We'll talk later," he said, before spinning around and heading back into the work shed.

It was a conversation she anticipated and dreaded all at the same time.

The last thing he wanted was company, but he had it. Brandon assessed the guy about fifty yards in front of him. He didn't look like a man. At least from what he could see. He didn't have a beard or anything. If Brandon had to guess, he would say the guy wasn't much older than he was, if any.

He walked with a loose stride, as if he hadn't anything better to do in the world. Of course, he probably didn't, considering where they were. In one hand he held a fishing pole braced on his shoulder and in the other a small silver bucket. It didn't look big enough for hardly anything, and Brandon supposed it probably contained bait.

The boy walked and whistled a tune that Brandon had never heard before. Who ran around whistling these days, anyway?

Brandon followed behind, not bothering to try to catch up. He really didn't want any company, but then again he didn't want to be alone either. He just wanted . . . something else. Things to go back to the way they were. To go back to Nashville. To have his father back.

They might not have gotten along very well, but he

missed his dad. He did his best to pretend like he didn't, like it didn't matter to him in the least. But it did. It was the shows about father-son relationships on television that had given him hope that one day, when his dad was older and he himself had a family of his own, they would sit back and laugh about the disagreements they'd had as he was growing up. His dad would clap him on the shoulder and smile and tell him how proud he was of the man he had become. Now none of that could happen. His dad was gone, taking any hope of a better, future relationship with him.

The boy started down a small hill. Gouges marked the land, small valleys in the red dirt. Not big enough for anything other than stepping in and twisting one's ankle. He had learned in science that erosion caused such trails and wondered why they didn't plant trees or something to keep it from happening.

There were a few trees around, and what looked like a thornbush. He wondered if it made some sort of berries. But even with the trees around, it didn't seem to be enough to hold the earth in place.

The boy in front of him stopped and started to turn. Brandon dashed behind one of those trees and held his breath as he waited to be found out.

The boy turned slowly as if in some slow-motion video. Brandon held as still as possible. The guy allowed his gaze to sweep over the landscape and Brandon could only hope that the tree hid him well enough from view. It must have, for the guy turned back around, started whistling, and walking once again.

He'd have to be more careful if he didn't want to be found out. And he didn't.

At the bottom of the incline was a rusty pond. Brandon figured that orange water came as a result of all the orange dirt around. But it still looked strange. He'd never seen anything like that in Tennessee. Of course, he didn't have an awful lot of opportunities to go fishing in Tennessee. His dad had never been the outdoorsy type, but Brandon liked the idea of a father-son fishing trip, like that TV show where the father and son walked down the road with their fishing poles.

There he went being stupid again. Even if his dad was alive, Brandon would never have that with him. Not until they were old and he had a family of his own. Now that wasn't ever happening. Just like that his thoughts chased themselves around in a circle.

He crouched down behind a small bush and watched as the guy he had been following set his bucket down and started to bait his hook. He was really going to fish in that water? Apparently so. He acted as if he were about to cast his line into the water, but instead he turned in Brandon's general direction.

"Did you come to fish or just watch me?"

Brandon's heart gave an anxious pound in his chest. He'd been made. Or had he? He could pretend not to hear—or would the guy storm after him? Brandon didn't know. He thought someone had said that Amish were peaceful people, but he didn't know where he had heard that or even who had said it to him. Better not take that chance.

He stepped out from behind the bush and gave the guy his most insolent sneer. "What up?" He tried to play it cool. That was the best thing to do with people he didn't know. Always remain cool.

The guy frowned. "What . . . Up . . . ?" He glanced at the sky as if somehow the answers were there in that endless expanse of blue, then he turned back to Brandon. "I don't know. Is that a joke?"

Brandon jerked his chin back a bit farther, striking a pose he'd seen the cool kids at school do. All the action did was make him have to squint in order to see the guy better. "No, man, it's not a joke. What up?"

The guy nodded sagely. "Oh, I get it. I guess a lot of things. The sky is up. The clouds are out today. Maybe a few birds."

Brandon shook his head. "No, it means like how are things going." Geez, how backward were these people?

"Then why didn't you just ask that?"

"All the cool people say it," he reported.

"I see." The guy didn't look like he saw anything. But he gave another nod and tossed his line into the water. He added some length, then used two big rocks to prop it up so he didn't have to hold it.

"I'm Joshua." He held out a hand to Brandon, even though they were still several feet apart. Brandon hesitated.

"Hannah is your mother, right?"

Brandon nodded, but still couldn't make his feet walk toward him. The boy dropped his hand back to his side.

"Jim is my *dat*." He said *dad* funny, like it ended with a *T* instead of a *D*. But Brandon kinda liked it. It was interesting.

"So, that makes us what? Cousins?"

"*Jah*," Joshua said. "Cousins."

He had a couple of cousins on his dad's side, but they lived up North, just outside of Chicago. His family went to visit a couple of times, but they weren't close. It wasn't like he kicked with them or anything. But he had never known he had cousins on his mother's side. He was almost fifteen years old, and yet he never met his cousin who lived less than three hours away.

"Why aren't you in school?"

Joshua laughed. "I don't go to school any longer."

Brandon eased out from the line of trees where he'd hidden and inched closer toward his cousin. "You don't go to school anymore?" The closer he got, the younger he suspected Joshua really was. At first, he had thought his cousin was eighteen, but now he figured he was sixteen at best. And if he was really sixteen, why wasn't he in school? "Why not?"

"I don't have to go anymore. Once we turn fourteen we don't go to school."

Brandon couldn't help it. His eyes widened, and his mouth fell open. "Are you kidding me?" He asked the question, but his cousin looked serious enough.

"No. Not kidding at all."

"Who's 'we'?" He came to a stop just a couple of feet from Joshua. He looked just like his dad. Just in a smaller form. Not quite as tall, not quite as broad, and definitely not with the serious expression Jim wore all the time.

Joshua shrugged, the loose movement pulling on one strap of his suspenders. Why anybody wanted to wear suspenders was beyond Brandon, but it seemed they all had a thing for them. And blue shirts. And black pants. "All Amish."

This time Brandon managed to hold his expression in his standard "who cares?" form. "All Amish?" Now he knew Joshua was kidding him. There was no way all Amish stopped going to school at fourteen. Wouldn't the government do something about that?

"*Jah.* At least all Amish here. I've heard tell that other places have to go until their eighth-grade year. We go to our fourteenth birthday."

Brandon shifted his weight, still concentrating hard on keeping his expression impassive. "And then you quit?" Maybe if Brandon stood there long enough, Joshua would turn loose of the lie and tell Brandon why he was really out of school today.

"Then we're done, *jah.*"

"And what do you do after that?"

Joshua looked toward his fishing pole, checking to see if he had a bite, Brandon was sure, then turned to face him. "Then we learn a trade from our fathers."

"I don't see your dad around here anywhere." Now he had him.

But Joshua just laughed again. "You don't believe me, do you?"

"It's the craziest thing I've ever heard."

Joshua gave a quick nod. "I suppose to you *Englisch* it would seem sort of strange. Why aren't you in school?"

Brandon shoved his hands into his pockets and looked out over the rusty-colored pond. "My mom's got me in some special program. I'm supposed to do things on the Internet, but I don't think I'm getting Internet out here." He stopped. "Do you know what I'm talking about?"

Joshua rolled his eyes. "Of course I know what the Internet is. We're Amish," he said. "Not backward hillbillies."

Chapter Five

"Tillie, you won't believe what I did." Gracie turned from the cabinet, hands propped on her slim hips.

Hannah sat at the table preparing the persimmons for cooking. Peel, hull, chop. They were canning pie filling today and jam tomorrow. At her sister's calculated words, she set down the knife.

"What was that?"

Gracie appeared not to notice Tillie's stiff words. "I forgot to get another canning pot from Katie Esh."

Katie was their closest neighbor, an elderly woman who had been one of the original settlers in Pontotoc.

"You could go over there and get it now," Tillie said.

Gracie shook her head, an exaggerated motion that sent Hannah's curiosity skyrocketing. What were these two up to? "Oh, no. She's gone to Tennessee for the day."

"*Jah?*"

"*Jah*. She went up there to visit her kin."

"Mary Ann Hostetler said she was going to be canning today too," Tillie added.

"I guess we could go over to Aaron's and see if we can borrow his."

Bingo. Hannah dried her hands on the paper towel and sat back in her seat.

"But that's so far," Tillie protested. "It'll take so long to get over there and back in the buggy. We'll lose so much time."

It wouldn't be long now.

Gracie turned to Hannah. "You could go. In your car."

And there it was.

"*Jah*, that won't take long at all." Tillie's smile was so forced it wavered on her lips.

"Is there any particular reason why I need to go to Aaron's?"

They shook their heads.

"No."

"Of course not."

Hannah stood. "Okay then. It's closer to the Danny Yoders'. Why don't I just go there?"

"No!" they yelled in unison.

"I mean, what with the persimmons already in, Rebecca is probably using hers today as well," Gracie explained.

Hannah was positive. They were setting her up. And they wanted her to go to Aaron's. She wasn't sure why, but she had her suspicions. "If you're sure," she said, palming her keys.

Gracie and Tillie nodded. "We're positive," Tillie said, then shot her the trembling smile once more.

Best to get this over with now.

Hannah gave them a quick nod, then headed out the door.

It was a short little drive to Aaron's house. It was the same one Lizzie had grown up in. Hannah had heard through the grapevine that after Lizzie's death, her parents moved back to Ethridge, leaving Aaron to farm the land in Pontotoc. As with the rest of Pontotoc, not much had changed.

Her stomach sank as she pulled into the gravel drive. It weighed heavy with memories laced with sadness. What-ifs buzzed around inside her head.

At the sound of her car, Aaron came out of the barn. He wiped his hands on a shop rag and waited for her to turn off the engine and get out.

"Hi." His greeting was confident and sure, though his eyes reflected so many questions.

"Hi. Uhum . . . Gracie and Tillie sent me over to see if we could borrow your canning pot."

"Sure. Tomatoes?"

She shook her head. "The persimmons are out of control."

"Right." He started toward the porch and into the house. But he stopped before crossing the threshold. "Do you want to come in for a minute?"

"I'll wait here if that's okay. They're expecting me to come right back."

"*Jah.*" He ducked into the house, and Hannah released the breath she had been holding.

"Hi," a tiny voice chirped from behind her.

Hannah spun around. She had been so lost in her own thoughts that she hadn't heard anyone approach. And she certainly hadn't expected Aaron's children to be home. Well, his girls. Yet there they stood, both of them, grinning at her as if they had a pocket full of candy that no one knew about.

"Who are you?" the older of the two girls asked.

"I'm Hannah." She gave them a reassuring smile. Both had their father's dark hair and smoky blue eyes, and Hannah wondered if his son took after him as well.

"Abner's Hannah?" the younger asked. She elbowed her sister. "I bet she's Abner's Hannah."

"That's right."

"Don't poke me," the older girl said. "I know who she

is." Those pale blue-gray eyes so like her father's studied her like a scientist studies a specimen in a microscope. "How come you're dressed *Englisch*?"

"I moved away." It was the best answer she could think of on the spot.

"You jump the fence?" the younger one asked.

"Something like that," Hannah murmured.

"But you're back now?" the older one asked.

"For a while."

They nodded, their expressions as solemn as priests'.

Just then Aaron came out of the house. The girls jumped as if they had been poked with a stick.

"*Dat*!"

"What are y'all doing home?"

"We came to have lunch with you." The younger sister smiled, showing the space between her two front teeth. She was so sweet and looked so much like Aaron it nearly brought tears to Hannah's eyes.

"What have I told you about coming home for lunch?"

"You said not to," she said. "But—"

"No buts." Aaron propped the canning pot on his hip and gestured with his other hand. "Get your lunch pails and march right back over to school."

"But, Dat—" her sister started.

"Now."

The girls grumbled just a bit, but did as he demanded.

"Bye, Dat."

"Bye, Abner's Hannah."

Hannah smiled at the moniker. "Bye, girls."

Aaron moved to stand on the other side of the drive, she was certain so that he could make sure they got safely back across the road once again.

After a moment, he turned to Hannah once again. "Sorry it took so long. I couldn't find the rack." He handed her the pot.

"I'm impressed that you knew there was a rack."

He shrugged as if it was no big deal, but a flush of pink stained his cheeks. "Lizzie was always canning something." His color deepened as if he hadn't meant to talk about her. At least not to Hannah.

"She was a good wife?" she quietly asked. Why, she wasn't certain. She wanted to know. She didn't want to know. She wanted to tell him how sorry she was that she left and never returned. But what good would that do? She had hurt him, she knew, but he had pulled himself up and started again. She couldn't open those wounds again. Not his. Not her own.

"*Jah*." His voice was as soft as hers. "She was a good *fraa* and a good *mudder*."

"And she made you happy?" That would go a long way, to know that he was happy after she left. It broke her heart that he had moved on. But it would have killed her to know that he had stopped living, that he hadn't been happy.

"*Jah*."

She smiled. "I'm glad."

"What about you?" he asked.

Her. It was the one subject that she didn't want to talk about. "Oh, you know."

Aaron shook his head. "No, I don't."

"It's been a journey," she finally said. It wasn't quite an answer. "But I have Brandon." She swallowed hard. While she had been thinking about how to respond, a huge lump had formed in her throat. It was almost impossible to get words past it.

"He looks like a good kid."

Hannah stifled a laugh. "No, he doesn't, but it's kind of you to say so. He's had a rough time."

Aaron nodded. "I understand. But he has you. And that's a lot."

To her chagrin, tears filled her eyes. She had to get out of there while she was still in control of her emotions. It was a tenuous hold, but it was all she had. "Thanks for the pot. I'll get it back to you in a couple of days."

"Keep it," he said. "I don't do a lot of canning."

Hannah nodded and ducked back into her car. She started the engine, keeping her eyes averted as she put it in reverse and backed up in the side yard. She couldn't help herself. She cast a quick glance at him.

He was standing right where she had left him, watching her prepare to leave. The expression on his face was neutral. She had no idea of his thoughts. She wished she knew what was going on behind those smoky blue eyes.

Why? So she could know that he hated her for what she had done to him? She couldn't bear his contempt. But he was Amish, raised to forgive. Maybe she would see his indifference. She didn't think she could stand that either. That only left him wishing that things could have been different. Loving her still. And she knew that could never be.

He was being ridiculous. But even as Aaron told himself that, he couldn't stop himself. He had thought of nothing else but Hannah all through the night. He could make up as many excuses as he wanted, but the truth of the matter was he wanted to spend a little time with Hannah. Maybe he needed to find out who she really was, without speculation. Or maybe he had simply missed her. Did the why really matter? Not when he was pulling into her parents' drive with no more plans at his disposal than a glass of lemonade on the front porch. Or maybe a carriage ride.

She would probably turn him down flat. After all, she drove around in fancy *Englisch* cars. How could poking around in a buggy be thrilling? But it was all he had.

He pulled his carriage to a stop and looped the horse's

reins around the hitching post. He rubbed his hands down the sides of his pants, feeling more nervous than he had the first time he had asked to take her home from a singing.

What if she told him no? What if she told him yes?

"Hi, Aaron." Abner came from the direction of his workshop. Aaron could still hear the buzz of the saw and supposed that David and Jim were still inside working. "I wasn't expecting to see you today."

Aaron wiped his hands again, but hopefully Abner didn't notice. He didn't want the man to know how nervous he was. Nervous meant this was important, and it wasn't. It couldn't be. No, it was merely two friends catching up on old times. Nothing more. Nothing less. "I came to see Hannah."

Abner stopped brushing the sawdust from his clothes, his eyes centering on Aaron in an instant. "*Jah?*"

Aaron nodded. "You know. Just as friends. She came out to the house yesterday and I . . . I . . . well, I thought maybe now would be a good time to clear the air."

The older man gave a quick bob of his head. "That would be good, *jah.*"

Aaron released a pent-up breath, shook the man's hand, and started for the house. Maybe Abner's hesitation was a sign. Maybe he should forget all about this and just go home. What good was clearing the air anyway?

He climbed the steps to the front porch and knocked on the door.

"Aaron."

She seemed genuinely surprised to see him. But he couldn't tell if she was happy about it.

"I had a mind today to come and see you."

"Yes?" Again her voice was neutral. How was he supposed to know how to proceed if she acted as if his visit wasn't anything out of the ordinary?

He looked into those hazel eyes. Clouds of doubt dulled

the spirit that he had always seen there. But were they doubts about him?

"I thought we might sit and talk for a spell. Maybe go for a ride or something."

She shook her head before he even finished. "I'm not sure that's a good idea."

"How come?" He knew. But he wanted to hear her say it.

"Aaron . . ."

He shifted his weight, moving a bit closer to her. She smelled sweet, like perfume and soap. He wanted to bury his nose in her neck and inhale that scent, make it another memory to treasure when she was gone.

And she would be. He knew that. One day soon she would head out again. How could she stay here after so many years with *Englisch* conveniences? Plus she had her son to think about.

He took a step back. Memories would never live up to the real thing.

Not that it mattered. He had moved on. There were just a few loose ends that needed tying up. Just a few questions. That was all.

"Just talk to me for a bit, Hannah. Is that too much to ask?"

It was a mistake coming here. But now that he had, he needed to see it through.

She sighed and stepped out onto the porch. "I guess I owe you that much."

"Would you like to go for a ride?"

She shook her head again. "I don't think that would be a good idea."

She was probably right. What would the bishop say if he caught Aaron riding around Pontotoc with Hannah Gingerich in his carriage? *Hannah McLean,* he corrected. He had to start thinking of her as Hannah McLean. But even in her *Englisch* clothes with her short hair and no prayer *kapp*, she would always be Hannah Gingerich to him. It was as if he could see past the outside to what lay beneath. Or maybe that was wishful thinking on his part.

"We can sit in the swing, if you want," she offered.

Aaron nodded and followed her to the end of the porch where the swing hung. They settled down next to each other, a good foot between them. She used the heels of her bare feet to set them in motion.

They sat there in silence for a moment, the noises of the farm and the squeak of the chains the only sound between them. Not exactly the picture in his head of them seated side by side, drinking lemonade, and reliving old times. But some of those memories held more pain than good times. And there were others . . .

He cleared his throat. He had told her that he wanted to talk, and yet he hadn't said a word. Any minute now she was going to get up and go back into the house, and his opportunity would be gone.

"Why did you do it, Hannah? Why did you leave?"

Chapter Six

It was the question she had both anticipated and dreaded. Hannah sucked in a quick breath, but she gained no courage, no more clarity than she'd had before.

"I just wanted to see what was out there." She stared out over the pasture. What a scene. Bitterweed with its small yellow flowers and fernlike leaves disappeared down the slope on the other side of the barbed wire fence. The fence posts themselves were gray from their time in the sun. Tiny rust rivers bled down the wood where the wire had turned from the rain. The wind blew through the leaves and, somewhere in the small crop of trees, a bird called to its mate. Peaceful, beautiful, but not enough to satisfy her curious mind. If only she had known then what she knew now. Maybe everything would be different. Or maybe it wouldn't.

"And did you?" His question was so quietly spoken she wondered if she had imagined it.

"Yes."

"And?" he asked.

And what? "It's where my life is."

It's where your life was.

"You broke my heart, you know."

She swallowed back the lump in her throat. She had known, but to hear him actually say it . . . "I seem to be good at that." So many hearts were broken when she walked out—Aaron's, her father's, her mother's, Gracie and Tillie's. And her own. She just hadn't known it at the time. "For what it's worth, I never meant to hurt you."

He nodded, then shook his head as if he couldn't find words.

She thought about telling him of her plans to return. But that was so long ago. What difference would it make now? It would only make her wonder about what-ifs that could never be.

"How long are you staying?" He said it as if he knew she was leaving and had settled himself to it.

Aren't you?

Of course she was. She couldn't stay there. No matter how much she enjoyed connecting with her family. All but her father. Her mother kept telling her to give it time. Yet Hannah knew, he might forgive her in his heart, but he couldn't forget. And he wouldn't leave himself open for that hurt again. In some ways her father and Aaron were a lot alike.

And because she was leaving, she needed to keep her distance as well.

"I don't know."

"Abner said your husband died."

"Yes." There was nothing else to say about it, really.

"I'm sorry to hear that."

What could she say? She stood and made her way to the porch railing, looking out at nothing in particular. "It's okay."

My marriage was over anyway.

But it didn't take away the hurt. It had been a long time since she had loved Mitch, but they'd had a comfortable understanding. And as long as he was alive, there was a hope that somehow things would go back to how they used to be. Or maybe even how she had dreamed they would be. But now that he was gone there was no chance for things to be different. He would always be at odds with Brandon. She would never be what he had imagined her to be. They could never make up, never have what those around them had. Never.

But now she had a chance to start over, to make it right. It was the least she could do for Brandon's sake: to give him the life he deserved.

How are you going to do that with no money, no job, and no skills?

She held on to the hope that the lawyer was right, that there would be enough to start over. She could hope, but she wasn't able to pray. Not yet; maybe not ever.

And if that hope didn't hold out, she didn't know what she would do. She surely couldn't stay here.

Behind her the swing creaked, and she knew the sound well enough to know that Aaron had stood.

"I brought up bad memories. I'm sorry."

She blinked back tears, not realizing until that moment that she was crying. Not sobbing, just tears of hopelessness and frustration trailing down her cheeks. She dashed them away with the back of her hand and blinked again. "It's all right. This whole place is filled with bad memories."

He made a noise behind her. It could have been a sigh, or maybe he just cleared his throat. She didn't turn around to see. "There are more than bad memories here. I pass them every day."

She knew what he was talking about. The schoolhouse where they had gone to school together, the cornfield where they used to hide on summer days when they wanted a little time alone, and that side road next to the cotton gin where they had . . .

"Yes," she managed to choke out. She didn't need to tell him that the good memories were outshone by the bad.

"There's another solution," he said, not asking her to turn around. "We could make some new memories."

She whirled to face him, needing to see his expression as he said the words. "New memories?"

He nodded. "As friends. We could do that, *jah*?"

Hannah couldn't stop her smile. It trembled on her lips, but it held through. "I would like that, but what about . . . ?" She waved a hand in front of herself, indicating her *Englisch* clothes. "I'm not sure how the rest of the community will take us running around together."

He seemed to think about it a minute. "You never cared what other people thought before."

It was true. She had done what she was supposed to because it was expected of her, but she had pushed her fair share of the boundaries. But Aaron didn't deserve the trouble that her presence would bring him. She might not be officially under the *Bann*, but in a district as conservative as theirs, it wouldn't be long before people started to talk and the bishop was brought in. "I'm not worried about me."

He nodded. "I know, but I'm a grown man. Let me worry about that."

Chapter Seven

She was not looking out the window and watching for Aaron to pull down the drive. Well, she was looking out the window, she just wasn't waiting for him. Maybe if she repeated the lie enough times she would even believe it.

Yesterday she had seen him again, that made three times in fifteen years. He had looked so different, yet still the same. At least where her heart was concerned. But no matter how many times she told herself she wasn't looking for him, she still straightened at the sound of the carriage coming down the lane.

As she watched, he pulled his buggy to one side and hopped out with that same lithe grace. Just as he had before, he looped the reins around the hitching post and started toward the barn.

Hannah bit back a sigh. Just what was it about Aaron Zook that made her heart tight in her chest and her mouth dry? Fifteen years was a long time. She should've gotten over him by now. Actually, she thought she had. "They" were wrong; absence didn't make the heart grow fonder. Absence made it easy to forget. Fifteen years away and she had almost forgotten what he looked like, what he sounded like, what he smelled like. She had chalked all that up to being over him. Then one look and it was as if she had stepped fifteen years back in time.

But her mind knew what her heart didn't. There was no going back. There could never be. And she felt drawn to him. Inexplicably drawn to him as he walked toward the barn. How easy it would be to get up, go through the door, cross the yard, and be at his side in seconds. How easy.

"Mom."

Hannah jumped nearly three feet out of her seat. She whirled around to face her son, one hand pressed against her pounding heart. "Brandon," she breathed. "You scared me."

"Obviously." He rolled his eyes. He glanced from her face to the window, then back again. "What are you doing?"

"N-nothing," she stammered. It was true and a lie all at the same time.

"Is that what I'm supposed to be doing too?"

Hannah shook her head, unable to follow the thread of the conversation. "I don't know what you mean."

"Is that what I'm supposed to do all day? Nothing? I mean, there's not a whole lot to do here anyway. My phone's dead. I can't talk to any of my friends. I got nothing. Should I stare out the window too?"

Hannah bit back a retort. She was just shaky and anxious after being caught staring at Aaron. It wasn't like Brandon knew that anything was out of sorts. He simply needed a bit of attention and direction.

"We can play cards."

She wouldn't say his eyes actually lit up, but there was a small spark of interest in there somewhere. "You mean like rummy or poker?"

Maybe she had spoken too soon. "I was thinking more

of Uno or Rook." But both games needed more than two people.

"What's Rook?" Brandon frowned.

Hannah shook her head. "Never mind. Why don't you see what your cousins are doing?" He had told her about meeting up with Joshua and going fishing in the pond. Jim's son was a good boy, and Hannah could only hope that some of that selfless attitude would rub off on her son.

"Can't. He's gone to town with his dad. 'Gone to town'?" he asked. "What exactly does that mean?"

"It means that they went into town." Hannah shrugged. It was something she'd grown up saying. The Amish settlement was just far enough out that going into town was a big deal. Sometimes it could take up most of the day. Brandon had always lived in town. So "going" was never an option.

"Okay," she tried again. "How about you go learn how to milk a goat?" She smiled and gave a nod as if to encourage his agreement.

Brandon frowned at her as if she'd lost her mind. "Please tell me you're kidding."

"Actually, I'm not. Your grandmother keeps several goats. We milk them twice a day, then she takes that milk and makes soap, lotion, and cheese out of it. All sorts of things."

Brandon grimaced. "Lotion? Gross."

That was just about the response she had expected, though she wasn't willing to give Brandon too much leeway in his attitude. They would both be miserable if he spent their entire visit bellyaching about every little thing. Tough time or not, it was past the point of chin up and go forward. "Okay, so if you don't want to milk goats, then I suggest you find something else to do." She used her best "mommy" voice so he knew she meant business.

"Fine," he grumbled. He pushed past her and out of the house.

Hannah watched him stride across the yard and told herself that he would be fine. A couple more days and his online school would start. That would give him a few things to do during the day. Plus he would have to go into town to use the computers at the public library. That would get him off the farm for a bit. And if he continued to spend his afternoons with Joshua, all the better.

In seconds he disappeared behind Jimmy and Anna's house and was off to who knew where. Hannah nearly slumped with relief. At least he was in Pontotoc. There weren't a great deal of things to get a person in trouble in Pontotoc, Mississippi. Especially not out where they were. She wished now she had warned him to be careful, but he would have just grumbled that she was being over-protective. Maybe she was. Maybe she wasn't. Brandon was everything to her, and she wouldn't know what to do if she didn't have him.

She pulled her thoughts off that melancholy path and fixed her gaze on the horse corral. Once again Aaron was out with the mare.

Honestly, she wasn't sure which one was the most interesting to watch. Tall and slim, Aaron moved with such grace, his movements fluid, almost as if he were swimming in slow motion. She couldn't hear him, but could imagine him crooning softly to the horse. And she could definitely see a difference in the beast from the first day to today. She wasn't fighting at her bridle, and she didn't have such a wild-eyed look. At least Hannah didn't think the mare did. The only way to know for certain would be to go out and watch Aaron as he worked. But she would only do that in interest of the job he performed.

She pushed open the door, careful not to let the screen

slam behind her. A sound that loud and sharp would spook the animal for sure.

As casually as she could, she made her way across the yard toward Aaron and the horse. If he saw her coming he made no indication. All his concentration was centered on that mare. And the closer she got, the easier it was to hear the low murmur and see how the words that he spoke soothed the horse as he continued to work with her.

It was unlike anything Hannah had ever seen. Not that she had much experience with horses. She'd had a few run-ins with the gelding they had used back when to pull the carriage. Occasionally Leah had liked to hop on its back and ride through the pasture, but Hannah had never been so bold where the beast was concerned. She hadn't had many more dealings. Oh, she had seen television Westerns where a spunky cowboy was trying to tame an even spunkier horse. Sometimes the results were comical and sometimes tragic. But television couldn't hold a candle to seeing Aaron work live.

She braced her arms against the top of the slatted wooden gate and simply watched.

She could stand there for hours and watch his motion, as graceful and enthralling as a ballet. In fact, it looked sort of like a dance. Aaron would pull the horse closer using the bridle bit in her mouth to get her to come toward him. He tugged gently from side to side, stepping toward the horse. He rubbed her forehead, said something to her, patted her neck, and stepped back. He did this over and over as if showing her the bridle wasn't a bad thing. It wouldn't hurt her and humans were her friends. Over and over he performed the action while Hannah watched, mesmerized.

She straightened as he stopped and headed in her direction. "Good morning," he said. His blue eyes were hooded, hiding the thoughts and feelings plaguing him. Or maybe they were just impassive. Maybe there were no thoughts and feelings. Maybe she was just so fifteen years ago.

It wasn't like she could ever be anything to him again, except maybe a friend. And she decided right then and there: if that was all they could have together, she wanted it.

Hannah dipped her chin. "Good morning. How's it going?"

He turned back to the horse who happily munched what was left of the summertime grass.

"It's going good. Good," Aaron said. He met her gaze, then looked away, back toward the horse. "I'm sorry about yesterday." The words were barely a whisper.

Hannah shook her head. "Don't apologize."

He dropped his gaze to the ground under his feet. "I guess I wasn't thinking. You've not had enough time to adjust. Your man hasn't been gone as long as my Lizzie."

His Lizzie. Hannah shoved the thought away. She wasn't going to dwell. "How long has she been gone?" It was perhaps the one thing no one had mentioned when Aaron's name was brought up.

"Almost a year."

Which meant his time for mourning was nearing an end. Was he contemplating getting remarried?

With three children to care for, he could have gotten remarried right away. But the hurt look in his eyes whenever his wife was brought up made Hannah think perhaps he wasn't ready to move forward from their marriage.

"I don't know what's worse," he finally said. "Losing someone to a terrible accident or watching them waste away and wondering why God didn't go on and take them."

Hannah murmured something, more sounds than words. She cleared her throat. "Accidents are terrible, but quick."

"Like ripping off a bandage?" He let out a small, humorless chuckle.

"Something like that."

He sighed, and she stared off to one side of her father's shop.

"I'm glad you're getting to work with horses. You always loved them so."

His frown captured her attention. "I don't work with horses."

"What do you call this?" She made a flicking gesture with one hand.

"Helping out a friend."

"Oh. I just assumed . . ."

"Lizzie's father farmed peanuts and soybeans."

She remembered that.

"The farm's mine now." And he didn't seem all that happy about it.

"You train horses on the side?"

"Whenever work crops up. But there's not much call for it around here."

She supposed there wasn't. "Thanks for helping my *dat*."

Aaron nodded. "He's good people."

The strange thing about moving away was a person forgot that life where they had come from had continued. Everyone in Pontotoc wasn't suspended in time merely waiting for her to return in order to pick up their lives.

"Maybe you could come for supper one night," Hannah said. "I'd love to meet your children. Officially."

He gave a jerk of his head, somewhere between a nod and a shake. "Maybe."

She shifted in place, more than sad that there had been a time when she could talk to Aaron about anything and everything. Now she could barely get a dinner invitation out without stuttering. They were both uncomfortable, uneasy in this new situation they found themselves in. But it didn't have to be that way.

"I hate this."

Her sharp words brought his attention quickly around. "What?"

"I hate this." She shook her head. "I know we can't go back to being like we were." It was far too late for that. "But we should be able to have a civil conversation without feeling so . . ." She couldn't come up with a word so she just shuddered and made a face. "I mean, I just wanted to share a meal with you." Heaven knew they had shared much, much more.

The moment hung between them, and she thought perhaps he would sadly shake his head and walk away from her and her fanciful notions. Then he grinned. A chuckle escaped. "You're right, of course." He nodded in emphasis. "I guess maybe we should have dinner together."

"Tomorrow night?"

"Don't you want to ask your *mamm*?"

"I don't think she'll mind." Her mother had done nothing but sing Aaron's praises since Hannah had returned. "We'll call it a celebratory supper for your success in training Dat's horse."

"I won't be done with her for a while. Maybe even a couple of weeks."

Hannah shrugged. "That doesn't mean we can't celebrate early."

"I suppose not." He continued to smile, his shoulders relaxed. Now, more than ever, he looked like the Aaron she had known so long ago.

"Say you'll come eat."

"*Jah.*" He ducked his head as he nodded.

"And bring your children?"

"Of course."

Hannah returned his smile, her own tension easing for

the first time since she had set foot in Mississippi. "I'm looking forward to it."

"Me too."

She held his gaze for a moment more, then turned on her heel and made her way back to the house. She could feel his gaze on her as she walked away. How could something like a look feel more like a caress? How could she be so aware of something so simple as him watching her?

She stopped before entering the house, glancing back over her shoulder. Aaron stood just to her side of the fence, still watching her.

She shot him one last smile, then rushed inside, shutting the door behind her as if that alone would remove this connection between them.

"Mamm," she called.

"In here," she returned, her voice coming from the direction of the kitchen.

Hannah hurried over, peeking her head in. "I, uh . . . invited someone to supper tomorrow night."

Her mother turned from the bowl of apples she was peeling. The trees that lined the back of the property could barely produce enough for a decent *snitz* pie. Judging by the size of the fruit in her mother's hands, the apples must have come from the store. "Oh? Who?"

"Aaron Zook and his kids."

The knife her mother had been using clattered to the counter. "Oh, *jah*?" Her voice was tempered, as if she was testing the waters before she committed to her feelings one way or another.

"I hope that's okay."

Her mother retrieved her knife and started peeling apples once again. "Oh, *jah*. Of course."

"I just thought we should thank him for helping Dat with the mare."

"That's a fine idea." But her tone seemed reserved.

"What?" Hannah asked.

Her mother sighed, then she set the apples aside. She wiped her hands on her apron and finally turned to give Hannah her full attention. "I just don't want to see him get hurt."

Him? "What?" It was perhaps the last thing she had expected her mother to say.

"Now, Hannah," her mother started, then stopped with a shake of her head. "You and I both know that you are not staying here. You can go around pretending like it all you want, but the fact of the matter is you weren't cut out for Amish living. I knew that when you were little."

She wasn't cut out for Amish living? She had lived over half her life Amish. Hannah crossed her arms, knowing all the while how defensive it looked. "What makes you say that?"

A small smile played at her lips. "When you were five you started coming up with better ways to do things. What was wrong with using tractors? And the buggies would ride much smoother if they had rubber tires. Why, one time after church . . ." She shook her head with the memory. "You went around to all the women and asked if they thought it would be easier to can with an electric stove."

Hannah stifled a laugh. "I did not."

"You did." Her mother nodded. "Your *dat* was beside himself. He hustled you off to the barn. I just knew you were going to get a spanking, but when you came back out, you said he didn't lay a hand on you. I never knew what he said to you." She moved to the cabinet and pulled down the canister of sugar.

Hannah remembered now. "He told me that we weren't *Englisch*; we were Amish. Amish didn't have electricity, no matter how easy it made things. Then he told me I had better get used to it, because it wasn't changing."

She hadn't thought about that afternoon in years, but

looking back, it seemed like the beginning of the end. "And you think because of that, that I will hurt Aaron?"

You've hurt him before.

Her mother pursed her lips, as if contemplating each word before answering. "He was devastated when you left."

Hannah resisted the urge to roll her eyes and settled herself for a small shake of her head. "Devastated enough that he took up with Lizzie Yoder not even four months later."

Mamm shook her head. "You'll have to talk to Jim about that."

"Jim? My brother Jim? What does Jimmy have to do with this?"

Her mother retrieved her measuring cups before answering. "Lizzie and Anna were sisters. Or had you forgotten?"

"I hadn't forgotten," she said as Mamm started scooping sugar onto her apples.

And Aaron really looked up to Jim. "Are you saying Jim set up Lizzie and Aaron?"

"Aaron had been coming over here for as long as anyone remembered. You took off to who knew where." She shrugged, then sprinkled the apple and sugar mixture with cinnamon. "We all hated to see him hurt."

She could hardly believe what she was hearing. Her own brother had been instrumental in keeping her and Aaron apart. Oh, he hadn't meant to, and he'd done nothing directly, but it was there all the same. She had been more than ready to return to Pontotoc and Amish life, but she hadn't because she didn't think she could see Aaron with someone else day in and day out for the rest of her life. She knew she couldn't. Not with the secrets she carried. So she had stayed away. Married Mitch. And the rest was history, as they said.

Hannah snatched a piece of apple from the bowl. "I'm going for a walk."

"Don't stay gone long. I was hoping you would help me with these pies."

Hannah munched the apple, letting her mother's words sink in. "You're making apple pies?"

"*Jah.*"

"That's Brandon's favorite."

Mamm smiled. "I know, he's been dropping hints for two days. I figured this was the best way to welcome him to the family."

Hannah gave her a one-armed hug. That was her *mamm*, healing the world with food. But there was no amount of apple pie that could repair the rift between her and Aaron. And oh, how she wished there was.

Chapter Eight

Hannah started down the road, all that she had just learned tumbling around in her head. It would do no good to talk to Jim now. The damage had been done. Lives had been forever altered. There was no going back.

The sun beat down on her as she ambled along, no particular destination in mind. Maybe she should have headed over the property to the pond where she had spent a great many sunny afternoons, but she'd had enough memories for one day.

Red dirt dusted her toes and coated the remaining polish from the last pedicure she'd had. The dark purple-black color was supposed to have been elegant and mysterious, but now, chipped and grown out, it seemed a little sad. Too much too late. She should go into town and get some nail polish remover and take it off. That gesture might even help her *dat* on his road to forgiveness. She could only hope.

One foot in front of the other, she walked and kept walking, head down, watching each step. The gravel was uneven beneath her feet, the rocks poking through the soles of her flip-flops. She ought to head back, but going back seemed all she was capable of doing these days. She wanted to push on, no matter where it took her.

She stopped, the analogy of her life stilling her feet in place. She had to keep going. She had to. One day soon she would have everything settled and she could start again. Another chance at another life. How many chances did she deserve? She hoped at least one more. She needed one more to correct the mistakes she had made. One more to give Brandon a fresh start, a do-over he so desperately deserved. One more. That was all she asked for.

"Ho! Hannah?"

She whipped around, so lost in thought that she hadn't heard the approaching buggy. Considering the amount of noise the iron rims made on gravel, that was saying something.

Gracie pulled the buggy to a stop, staring at her through the open front of the carriage. "What are you doing way over here?"

She looked up, suddenly aware of her surroundings. The mailbox in front of her said *Yoder*—one of Anna's brothers, she was sure. Once upon a time the house had belonged to Elmer Beachey. She recognized it immediately. She was miles from home. How long had she been walking?

"Walking." As far as answers went, it was poor at best.

"*Kumm!*" Gracie motioned her over to the buggy. "Get in. I have an errand, and then I'll take you home."

"What kind of errand?" Hannah asked as she pulled herself inside. It had been a while since she had ridden in a buggy, but she climbed inside as if it had only been yesterday. She expected it to be harder. It had been fifteen-plus years since she had ridden in such a cramped space, but it didn't feel tiny. It felt cozy, comfortable, familiar. All the things she didn't want it to feel. Gracie shrugged and set the horse into motion once again. "Your mother cooks for a widower twice a week as an extra job. But since Mammi is down, it's hard for her to leave. I volunteered to come today so she could stay home with Mammi."

"That was kind of you," Hannah murmured. She wasn't even sure why she said the words; that was simply Gracie's way. Someone needed help, and she stepped up every time.

"It's the right thing to do."

Typical Gracie.

"Who's the widower?"

Gracie cast an apologetic look over her shoulder. "Aaron Zook."

"I see." Hannah wanted to demand that Gracie stop immediately and let her out. She could walk home from here. But she was an adult, and she held her seat. There was no need to jump ship, so to speak. Not even three hours ago she had invited him to supper, and now she was trying to avoid him? What was wrong with her?

"You don't mind, do you?"

Hannah cleared her throat. "Not at all."

"Good." Gracie flashed her a quick smile. "With two of us, it should take half the time."

Hannah could only hope.

Walking into Aaron's house that he had shared with Lizzie was . . . unsettling. Part of her wanted to examine every surface and see if she could find any changes in Aaron over the years.

Amish houses and *Englisch* houses were so very different. It wasn't like she could gauge his love for Lizzie by photographs of her all over the place.

Whether or not he was over Lizzie was a moot point. Hannah was still planning on leaving. One day. Real soon. Or so she hoped. It would do no good for her to try to be anything but friends with Aaron.

"Come on." Gracie gestured for Hannah to follow her into the kitchen.

Hannah put her feet into motion and tailed her cousin.

Gracie set about cooking with such ease that Hannah had a feeling this wasn't her first time in Aaron's kitchen.

"How long has Mamm been cooking for him?" *And why didn't she ever tell me?* jumped to her lips, but she managed to bite those words back.

Gracie placed a large skillet on the stove. "I guess just before Lizzie died."

"Before?" She pulled out one of the chairs at the kitchen table and plopped down.

"*Jah*." Gracie handed her a bag of potatoes and the peeler. "If you're going to sit, the least you can do is help."

"And here I thought you were rescuing me from having to walk home. You just wanted free labor."

"Whatever works." Her cousin turned back to the stove. She opened two jars of home-canned tomatoes and dumped them into the pot before turning the heat on underneath.

Hannah peeled the potatoes while Gracie puttered around gathering more ingredients for what Hannah supposed was to be a soup. "Why did Mamm cook for him before his wife died?"

Gracie poured a can of corn in with the tomatoes before answering. "You don't know." She stirred the contents of the pot, tapped the spoon against the rim, and shook her head. "It was so sad."

"What was so sad?"

"Lizzie got sick when Essie was a baby. Cancer." She tsked. "She fought it for as long as she could."

"I had no idea."

Gracie gave a quick shrug. "It's not something we talk about. Are you about done with those potatoes?"

Hannah sat back and gestured toward all the potatoes she had peeled. "How many of those do you need?"

"All of them."

"That many?"

"We only cook twice a week. So we've got a few meals to make."

"I guess so."

Gracie rinsed the potatoes and began dicing them into the pot. She was so quick and efficient it almost made Hannah's head swim. Why hadn't some smart man snapped her up?

Her cousin wasn't exactly an old maid, but with each year that passed, her chances of getting married decreased.

"Why haven't you ever married?" Hannah hadn't planned on actually asking the question, but there it was all the same.

She shrugged. "I guess it's just not in God's plan for me."

But Gracie would make someone a terrific wife. She was amicable and accommodating. Any man would be lucky to have her care for him.

Or Gracie would be so compliant that she'd be swallowed up by the man she married.

Hannah shook the thought away. Everyone deserved the chance to be happy.

Sure Gracie seemed happy enough, but Hannah couldn't imagine her not wanting more. Or maybe that was just her projecting her own dreams onto another.

Hannah and Gracie chopped salad, sliced the bread that Mamm had sent over, and made a pot of soup, a chicken and noodle casserole, and a pork loin with potatoes and carrots.

Then they got into the buggy and started for home.

Hannah had to admit that she was a little disappointed that she hadn't seen Aaron at all. The mere thought was ridiculous. She had just seen him that very morning.

"I invited Aaron to supper tomorrow night."

Gracie half turned in her seat. "You did?"

"I—" Hannah shook her head. "It's been such a long time, you know. I thought that would give us a chance to catch up."

"Catch up." Gracie's eyes were hooded, hiding the meaning behind her words.

"What?"

"I need to ask you something."

"Okay." Why did the statement sound like the world was coming to an end?

"Will you answer me?"

"Not until I know what it is."

Gracie nodded. "Fair enough." She sucked in a deep breath before continuing. "Are you staying?"

"Staying? Like in Pontotoc?" Hannah frowned.

"*Jah.* You've come back, and you're living with the family again, but you are still dressing *Englisch.* Are you planning on staying? Joining the church, becoming Amish once more?"

Hannah opened her mouth to answer, but Gracie cut her off. "And don't lie. Tell me that you don't want to answer, but please don't lie to me."

"I don't know." It was the closest to the truth she could come. She had arrived in Pontotoc planning to stay only as long as necessary. But now that she had been there for a few days, home was starting to grow on her.

Or it could just be the idea of home that was so appealing.

Whatever it was, she was enjoying being away from the hustle and bustle.

"You don't know?" Gracie asked.

"I haven't decided yet."

"Abner thinks you will."

Hannah looked out the window, not daring to meet her cousin's gaze. "How do you know this? He has hardly spoken to me since I got back."

"He's adjusting. Give him a little more time, and he'll come around."

Hannah hated that her cousin knew her father better than Hannah herself did. But she only had herself to blame.

"Don't hurt him," Gracie pleaded.

"Dat?"

"Aaron."

"Why is everyone so protective of Aaron Zook?" She hadn't meant to snap the words, but her head was spinning from the shift in the conversation.

"He's a good man," Gracie said. "He deserves a happy life."

Didn't they all?

"What do you think I'm going to do?"

Gracie gave a quick shrug and turned the buggy onto the lane that led to the Gingeriches' farm. "I don't think you would hurt him on purpose."

"But—"

"If you invite him to eat and try to be friends, and then you leave again . . ." She shook her head sadly. "No one wants that."

"No," Hannah murmured, not knowing what else she could say. It seemed all her family believed that her leaving had been an easy task. They had made up their minds about that years ago, and nothing she could say now would change anything. But if they only knew . . .

Gracie pulled the buggy to a stop and faced Hannah. "I've never left, never even been farther than Tennessee, so I can only imagine what that's like. But when a person leaves, they forget how hard it is on those left behind."

Brandon sat in the shade of the large oak that stood between his grandmother's house and the one belonging to his uncle Jim. As he watched, a buggy pulled to a stop. His mother and Gracie piled out. Gracie was nice enough, his second cousin or something like that. He couldn't really remember the exact relationship. But she was always smiling and always working. In fact, he had never seen anyone work like her in his entire life.

Gracie headed into the house as his mother unhitched the horse and released the mare into the pasture. That was new. He didn't know she could do that. Well, not that unhitching a horse was all that hard. At least, it didn't look so difficult. But he didn't realize she'd had enough experience with horses that she would bravely grab one by the harness and lead it to the pasture.

Across from him a screen door slammed and one of Joshua's siblings stepped out onto the porch. It was a boy, maybe seven or eight, with straight blond hair that hung past his ears.

A dog started barking as a car approached. That was one thing he liked about where his grandparents lived. All the houses were clustered together. It was like a compound or something and made him feel like he was a Kennedy, only poorer.

The car pulled to a stop and a man got out. He adjusted his pants and glanced around as if he wasn't sure he was in the right place.

That makes two of us, buddy.

His grandfather must have heard the new arrival. He came ambling out of the work shed, sawdust trailing behind him like smoke. The men talked for a moment, but from where he sat Brandon couldn't make out a single word. Not that he'd heard his grandfather much. The man had barely uttered two words to him since he and Mom had arrived.

"What are you doing out here?"

Brandon jumped and shaded his eyes as he looked to see who had spoken. "Joshua."

"Did I scare you?"

"Nah, I was just thinking."

"*Jah*. Right." Joshua plopped down onto the ground next to him. "What? Are you out here spying on people?"

"No," Brandon retorted, but it was far from the truth. Watching, spying, it was all in how a person looked at it. Brandon was merely curious. And bored. Very, very bored.

"Want to throw a baseball around?"

Brandon jerked his attention to his cousin. "What?"

"Baseball," Joshua said slowly. "Do you want to throw one with me?"

"Like real baseball?"

"Official MLB."

Brandon shook his head. What did his cousin know about Major League Baseball? But his doubts evaporated when Joshua produced a well-worn baseball and a glove.

"You got another one of those?" he asked with a nod toward the glove.

"I'm sure I can find you one. Are you up for it?"

"Yeah, sure. Whatever." He tried to play it cool, though he was certain the gesture was lost on Joshua. Brandon was up for anything at this point. Though he had always wanted to play ball. He had been on a couple of teams when he was little, those teams where everyone played and everyone got a trophy no matter how lousy they were. But it was soon apparent that his friends were better ball players than he was and that without a little help he would never get any good. But his dad was always too busy to help, and he'd turned to video game baseball instead.

"C'mon." Joshua hooked one hand over his shoulder and motioned for Brandon to follow. Then Joshua disappeared into the storage shed behind the main barn. He stepped back into the sunlight minutes later, triumphantly holding a glove over his head. "I think this one belongs to Libby, my sister."

Brandon was momentarily shamed that a girl had a better glove than he did, but the feeling quickly passed, giving way to excitement over something to do.

"You ever play before?" Joshua asked.

Brandon shook his head. "Not in a long time," he said as he slipped his hand into the glove.

Joshua grinned, obviously enjoying his role as the older, more experienced cousin. "Don't worry. I'll teach you everything you need to know."

There was something comforting about the solid feel of the baseball when it hit the pocket of his glove. The sound, the sting, it was real. Even the smell seemed to transport him to another place. And he couldn't help but wonder what his life would have been like had his father liked him.

Oh, he knew the man had *loved* him, but he hadn't liked him all that much, he was certain. But if he had . . . maybe Brandon would have played ball, or golf, or soccer. Maybe they would have gone on fishing trips and camping trips, done Boy Scouts and all the other things his friends had done with their dads.

His dad always said that he was too busy. But no one was that busy. Not even Johnny Carlisle's dad, who was a big executive with one of the country music record labels. If he could make a game or two a season, there was no reason why Brandon's dad couldn't. But he hadn't. Not even once.

"Brandon?"

"Huh?" He shifted his attention back to his cousin. "What?"

"You weren't paying attention."

He had been. Sort of. "Who's that guy?" He pointed toward the man coming out of the work shed. He was dressed in regular clothes, non-Amish clothes. *English*, he thought the Amish called them, though he wasn't sure why.

"I dunno. Probably came to look at sheds or something. He doesn't look like a gawker."

"A what-er?" He checked his cousin's face just to make sure he was being serious.

"A gawker. You know, one who gawks."

Brandon looked back to the man. He shook hands with Brandon's grandfather and climbed into his car. "You get that a lot?"

Joshua shrugged. "Sometimes. People are curious. They want to come out and see us like we're some show or something. Others want to come out and buy our food and things like it's magical. Most are okay though." He reared back to throw the ball, gesturing that Brandon should get ready.

Brandon pushed thoughts of the man and his shed from his mind, but couldn't help wondering about the others. Were the Amish so different that people went out of their way just to look at them? He'd never given it much thought. He'd heard that there were some in Tennessee close to where he had grown up, but he'd never been there. Would probably never go. But it seemed that there were others who would go just to see if they were real.

Of course they were real. And they were people. Just like him. Just like his mom.

He almost dropped the ball, but managed to recover it before it hit the ground.

His mom. They were more than like her. She was one of them. Born and raised here.

The thought was crazy.

Had people driven out to stare at her the way Joshua was describing? Brandon couldn't imagine. Like, that was his *mom*.

It made him angry just to think about it.

He had only been there a couple of days, but he'd seen enough to know. He'd seen his grandmother returning from her errand carrying a bag of apples. After all the hints he'd dropped about apple being his favorite pie, he knew she was making him one. The thought warmed him from the inside out. Carlos's grandmother made Carlos caramel cheesecake at the drop of a hat. It was just what grandmothers did.

The truth was, they might dress a little differently and talk sort of funny, but they were just people, no more, no less.

Chapter Nine

"You're wearing that?"

Hannah stopped short as Gracie pointed to her jeans and short-sleeved button-down. She looked down at herself, then back to her cousin. "It appears so."

"When Aaron comes to supper?"

"Yes." She smoothed her hands over her hips, doing her best to act calm. This was nothing. Just supper with old friends. There was no need to wear anything other than what she had on.

"You don't want to wear a dress?"

Hannah raised one brow. "An Amish dress?"

"*Jah*. Of course."

"I thought you didn't want me to give him any ideas."

"I thought you said there was nothing to this."

Hannah shook her head. "There's not."

"Shouldn't you wear something a little more appropriate?"

"This is appropriate."

"Uh-huh." Gracie's look was more than skeptical.

Truth was Hannah had been thinking about donning her traditional Amish garb, though she couldn't really say why. Habit? Maybe nostalgia. Or perhaps she wanted to see what it felt like now, knowing what she did, having lived where she had. But that was silly. Nothing would be different. Clothes might make the man in the *Englisch* world, but they meant nothing to the Amish.

"Come on," Gracie said, motioning Hannah toward the kitchen. "Your *mamm* said she needed help setting the table."

Hannah followed her into the kitchen. "Where's Tillie?"

"You've been home less than a week and you're already trying to get out of chores?"

"Not at all. I just wondered where she was."

Gracie pulled a face, then cleared her expression with quick ease. "Out with Melvin."

Hannah grabbed a stack of plates and carried them to the table. "What was the look for?"

Gracie glanced toward Mamm, and Hannah had a feeling the minute her mother was out of hearing range she would get an earful. Gracie felt Melvin was a "bad influence" on Tillie.

But Mamm stayed close, and Hannah had to bite her tongue to keep from asking all the questions vying to be released.

"Hannah Mae, come get this." Mamm gestured toward the large pan of roast and potatoes. Her mother must have thought tonight deserved a special treat. No one cooked a roast in August. It was simply too hot to have the oven on that long. But there it was, a roast with all the trimmings: potatoes, carrots, onions. Hannah's mouth watered just looking at it. And the smell was out of this world. She hadn't allowed herself to acknowledge how much she had missed her *mamm*'s cooking until she returned home.

She might not be able to return to the faith. She might not ever be able to live without the comforts she had become accustomed to. But she could sure try in order to eat her mother's biscuits and gravy every day.

"Did you hear something?" Mamm twirled around, her cheeks flushed from the heat of cooking.

"Hear what?" Gracie asked. She calmly placed a fork by everyone's seat and a butter knife next to each place where adults would be sitting.

"I thought I heard a buggy." She glanced at the battery-operated clock on the wall. "They're early."

Hannah's gaze followed her mother's. Five minutes early. And why was her mother acting like the president was coming to eat?

Scratch that. Her parents weren't exactly political even by Amish standards, so Mamm wouldn't do much different if the president was coming to eat. So why was she giving Aaron the special treatment?

Her mother's gaze fell on her and widened in something akin to shock or horror. "Hannah, go brush your hair. And pull it back. You look so . . ." She trailed off, and Hannah was left wondering if she had lost the words or found them to be more than she wanted to reveal.

"Pull it back?" Hannah asked, backing toward the door.

"Yes. Please. Now go. Hurry. Before he sees you."

Hannah didn't know whether to scream or laugh as she turned and headed back to the sewing room to brush her hair and pull it back as requested. She hadn't given a single thought to defying her mother. It just wasn't in her.

But why did her mother want her to look a certain way for Aaron to come to supper? There was only one answer, and Hannah did not like it.

But surely she was wrong. Surely her mother didn't think that a pot roast and a ponytail could get the two of them back together. Maybe Gracie was right. Maybe she was giving her family expectations that she couldn't uphold.

At least her mother hadn't asked her to put on an Amish dress.

Hannah dragged a brush through her hair, then scooped

it up into a messy bun at the base of her neck. It was as far from a bob as she could come without leaving her hair down. But all this talk of hair and dresses had her on edge. She had invited Aaron to eat with them in order to catch up on the last fifteen years. Not so she could tell him everything. But she wanted to reconnect. Once upon a time she had loved Aaron. Maybe she even loved him a bit still. But she had walked away from everything and everyone. Now the regrets were piling high. Was it too much to ask to right a couple of wrongs?

She didn't think so.

A knock sounded at the front door. Her mother had been right. Aaron had even arrived a little early to boot.

Her heart sped up its beat in her chest. Aaron was here!

"Are you going to get the door?" Gracie poked her head out of the kitchen and pinned Hannah with those shrewd blue eyes. When her cousin looked at her like that, Hannah was certain she had no secrets left to keep. Or maybe she was just being paranoid.

"Where's Mamm?" Hannah asked.

"Changing her apron."

The knock sounded once again. It hadn't been that long since the first knock, so Hannah could only assume that he could hear them talking through the thick wood.

Of course. "You don't want to answer it?" Hannah asked.

The knock sounded again, louder this time, the reverberations almost accusatory.

"Hannah, really. Let the poor man in."

"Fine." Hannah all but flounced to the door and flung it open. But her momentum abruptly ended as she saw him standing there.

"Aaron," she breathed. Okay, if she was being honest with herself, she might be more than a little in love with him. But what Amish girl in her right mind wouldn't be?

"Hi." He gave a quick nod of his head. His son hovered

to one side and slightly behind the rest of the family, while both girls stood demurely in front of their father. "I know we're early. We had an errand to run but it didn't take as long as we thought and there's not enough time to go home and then back . . ." His voice trailed off, and a flush of pink stained his cheeks. Could it be that he was as aware of her as she was of him? Or was he simply uncomfortable? She might not ever know.

"Hannah, are you going to invite them in?" Gracie asked.

"Oh." She hopped back and opened the door a little wider, moving to one side so everyone could enter. She wasn't sure, but she thought she heard Gracie chuckle.

"Aaron." Mamm bustled in from the back of the house. Her cheeks were still pink from the heat in the kitchen, her eyes bright and her apron clean. "I'm so glad you're here."

She greeted the kids in turn, talking to each one of them almost as a grandparent would do.

"Go ahead and have a seat," Mamm offered. "Supper will be on the table in just a few minutes."

Laura Kate took a giant step forward, her hands politely behind her back. "Is there anything I can do to help, Eunice?"

Her mother smiled, that beaming, proud smile such as a grandparent would wear. And it occurred to Hannah in that moment that her parents were very close to Aaron and his children.

What did you expect? You left. He stayed. And in a community the size of Pontotoc, close was the only way to be.

"No, child. But *danki*." Mamm patted Laura Kate on the shoulder, then turned away and hustled back into the kitchen.

Hannah nodded toward the couch in the living room. "Go ahead and have a seat. I'll just go help Mamm."

Gracie took a step forward, effectively blocking Hannah's

escape to the kitchen. "Oh, no, you go ahead and sit with Aaron. And his children. I'll go help your mother."

The whole thing smacked of a setup. But how could that be? Hannah had done her best to make her intentions clear, even as muddy as they were. She didn't know what she was going to do, but she couldn't imagine returning to Pontotoc, donning her Amish clothes for the rest of her life, and remaining there. It wasn't that the idea was repulsive—it just seemed so out of reach. Like the choice that she had already made she couldn't come back from. The choice she'd made had led her down a road so long she could never circle back and be the girl she was before.

Hannah murmured something inconsequential and led the way to the living room. The children settled down on the sofa while Aaron hovered at the window. Hannah herself perched on the hard wooden rocking chair where her mother spent nearly every evening, sewing, crocheting, or reading the Bible. Sometimes all three.

"So, Andy," Hannah started. "How old are you?"

Andy shifted uncomfortably in his place on the sofa and cleared his throat. "Twelve. Almost thirteen."

Hannah smiled, trying to put the boy at ease. "I have a son just about your age."

"Yes, ma'am." He pushed on his pant legs even as he sat on the couch and shifted once more.

"But you don't have any girls?" Essie asked.

Hannah shook her head. "No, I wasn't fortunate enough to have a girl." She had wanted one. How she had wanted a precious baby girl. But that hadn't been in the cards for her. If she had remained Amish, she might have said that it wasn't God's will. But there were times when God's will seemed so far removed from her life she wasn't certain of it at all. Not anymore, anyway.

Laura Kate nodded solemnly. "That's too bad. Girls are fun."

Andy rolled his eyes, but didn't make a sound.

"We don't have a *mamm*," Essie explained.

"I'm sorry," Hannah replied, not knowing what else to say.

Then Essie's face lit up like fireworks on the Fourth of July. "I know. We don't have a *mamm*, and you don't have a daughter. Wouldn't it be great if you could be our *mamm*?"

Aaron nearly choked. He coughed, cleared his throat, and coughed again. Hannah seriously wished he would get control of himself and help her with a suitable answer for that one.

"It doesn't work that way," Laura Kate said with a frown. Hannah could see her mulling over the situation in her head, trying to find some way for this to work out.

Essie sat back on the couch and stuck out her bottom lip. "That's too bad."

"Yes," Hannah murmured. It really was. Essie's idea was simple and pure, but unfortunately that was not how the world worked.

"Okay, everybody. Come on," Gracie called from the doorway. She moved past them to the door. She stepped out on the porch before clanging the triangle to tell the rest of the Gingerich men that food was ready.

Everyone piled into the kitchen. Chairs scraped and silverware rustled as everyone settled in around the table. They had no more settled in before her *dat* and her brother David bustled in.

"Where's Jim?"

Mamm set the last bowl of steaming hot vegetables on the table and took her place next to Dat. "He and Anna were afraid we wouldn't have enough room." She shook her head as if to say there was always room. But even with Tillie missing, the table was crowded.

Hannah looked around at her family and friends, old and new. So many times in her marriage to Mitch she had eaten supper all alone, having fed Brandon and put him to bed before having her own meal.

So many times. Too many times. And through all those years she missed this . . . this controlled chaos that was a big family dinner.

Tears filled her eyes at the thought. She blinked them back and lowered her head as everyone began the silent prayer.

She still hadn't managed to talk to God, but it was almost as if she could feel Him there, hovering around, laying His hands on their shoulders to assure them that all was right and good.

But was it?

She didn't know. Just a few days in Pontotoc and she was already confused. Like she didn't come with enough baggage already. But oh, how she had missed this.

There was rustling around the table as everyone lifted their heads and started to serve their plates. She blinked once more to dismiss the tears and lifted her head with a smile. These were happy times, not sad. A fresh time. A start over. There was no room for indecision, there was no room for confusion. She had time to think about what she was going to do. But really there was no choice at all. She would get the settlement from her husband's estate and start over with Brandon. But maybe this time she would stay closer. Tupelo was beginning to have more and more appeal. And maybe then, these dinners would always be a part of her life.

* * *

Aaron had to admit that Eunice Gingerich was one of the best cooks in the whole community. But that wasn't the only reason why he had accepted the dinner invitation. He glanced up and over to his left, where Hannah sat between Gracie and David.

Why, after all this time, did he still feel she was the prettiest girl he'd ever seen? Even with her *Englisch* haircut and in her *Englisch* clothes, even through all of that, he could see the Hannah he knew long ago. All that was missing was the spark in her eyes. So long ago she had had such a zest for life, living and enjoying each moment for just what it was. He'd known that she had questions about the *Englisch* world and what was going on outside their tiny, close-knit community, but he had never thought she would pick up and leave. Never dreamed that she would go without a word, not a note, no call, nothing to let him know where she was or when she would return. *Abandoned* was too nice of a word for how he felt. It was worse than that. So much worse.

But even through all the pain that she had caused him, all the pain he had endured from loving someone who loved him back but not enough to stay, he cared for her still. Was it love? He didn't know. But the thought of seeing her again made his heart soar. His step was lighter just knowing that he could bump into her in town, on the road, here at her home where he was working to help her father. Just knowing that she was closer brought a smile to his lips.

Apparently he hadn't learned anything from the hurt she had inflicted, so maybe it was love. Didn't they say love was blind? He took that to mean that love wasn't always logical. And it wasn't logical that he would feel this way for her even after fifteen years, after marrying another and having those three beautiful children seated next to him. Even through all that, there was Hannah.

He nodded at something Abner said, only half paying

attention to the conversation floating around him. He scooped up a bite of roast and allowed his attention to settle on Brandon, Hannah's son.

He was a fine-looking boy, the image of his mother through and through, though the set of his jaw and the cut of his chin were a little different. The legacy of his father? What kind of man had Hannah loved? He'd heard rumors around town that Hannah's husband had been unfaithful and had not been an honest man, but Aaron couldn't imagine Hannah with someone like that. Yes, she had a spark for life; yes, she had been a tad unruly; and yes, she was her own person, but Aaron couldn't imagine her falling in love with someone untrue. There was too much good in her to allow it. So why? Why had she stayed with the man all these years? Didn't the *Englisch* get divorced when things didn't work out?

But could he really call Hannah *Englisch*? *Jah*, she had lived with them for fifteen years or better, but she'd been raised Amish, and some things just couldn't be un-learned. Maybe the sanctity of marriage was one of those.

"Don't you think?" Gracie asked.

Aaron jerked his attention up to Hannah's cousin. He'd been caught daydreaming, lost in his own thoughts and oblivious to the conversation going on around him.

"What was that?" He cleared his throat and took a drink of his water.

"Sarah Hostetler."

He really needed to pay attention. "What about her?"

Sarah had been recently widowed and had three small children to take care of. Talk around the community was that she was opening a candy shop in hopes of attracting *Englisch* visitors and Amish alike.

"I was just saying that Mary Hostetler, her cousin, has a work frolic planned for Monday afternoon," Gracie said.

"They need some more men to come out and help hang shelves and make sure all the plumbing works correctly."

She didn't need to say any more for him to understand the question. "I'd love to help, but I can only stay a little while. I need to be home when the kids get off from school." Normally Andy could watch the girls, but lately had become so sullen that Aaron felt the need to stay close to home.

Gracie beamed at him. "That's okay, we're planning this for the afternoon so more of the men can help."

"The kids . . . ?" he started, knowing the excuse would be brushed aside in a heartbeat.

"They can come here." Eunice smiled as if she'd come up with the idea of the century. "Once they get home, hitch up your buggy and bring them over here. Then you young people can all go together."

Why did he feel so desperate to get out of this one? It wasn't that he didn't want to help Sarah Hostetler, but he surely didn't want to spend so much time with Hannah.

That wasn't exactly the truth either. He wanted to spend more and more time with Hannah, and the more time he wanted to spend with her, the more dangerous he realized she was. But he hadn't been raised that way. He had been raised to help when it was needed, and his excuse, although it had been almost good, was now wiped clean. There was no reason for him not to go to Sarah Hostetler's with Gracie and Hannah come Monday afternoon.

"*Jah*, okay." He hoped his tone sounded more eager to them than it did to his own ears. He flashed a quick smile, hoping that would make up for his lack of enthusiasm.

Eunice sat back in her chair and crossed her hands over her middle, a self-satisfied smile curving at the corners of her mouth. "What a fine idea," she chirped. "What a fine idea indeed."

* * *

The sun was beginning to fall in the August sky. Dinner was over, dessert had been served, and the kids had gone out to play with Jim and Anna's children. All seemed right with the world. But Hannah knew how looks could be deceiving. She stepped outside, needing a breath of fresh air to clear her thoughts.

She couldn't say she was exactly upset at the thought of being shanghaied into helping with Sarah Hostetler's new candy shop. In fact, she didn't mind at all. But Gracie's overt attempts at pushing Hannah and Aaron together were barely more than she could stand. And with her mom's efforts added in . . .

She rounded the corner of the house, where she had seen Aaron disappear just a few moments before. She spied him then, standing by the goat pen, pail in hand, pipe clenched between his teeth. The sight of smoke curling up from the pipe caused her to misstep. She never thought about it much, but nearly every man she knew in Pontotoc smoked a pipe. There were a few who didn't, but most did. Where the *Englisch* men had all given up their tobacco and were encouraged daily to do so, the Amish man here still enjoyed a little smoke from time to time. Why should Aaron be any different?

She steadied her feet and kept going. Aaron was alone, and she needed to talk to him. It was now or never.

He must've heard the rustle of her feet in the grass. He turned, even as he dumped the bucket's contents into the goat pen. The goats bleated and called to him as if asking for more even when what he had given them hadn't been eaten. Silly beasts.

"Hannah?" He set the bucket on the ground and took the pipe from between his teeth. "What are you doing out here?"

She stopped, mere feet from him, and shoved her hands into the pockets of her jeans. Suddenly she wanted to trace the curve of his cheekbone, feel the wiriness of his beard, both of which were completely off-limits. But as long as she kept her hands occupied . . .

"I came out here to talk to you."

Now why did that sound so ominous?

"*Jah*?"

Where to begin? She sucked in a deep breath, hoping the words would come in with the oxygen. Sadly, they didn't. "I think Gracie and Mamm are trying to set us up." There. She'd said it. But now that the words were out in the open, they sounded more ridiculous than she could have ever imagined. Inside her head they had sounded almost logical, but now . . . Not hardly.

"Set us up?"

"You know, like trying to get us together."

Aaron shook his head. "I know what you mean. I just don't understand why you think that."

"Gracie inviting you to the work frolic. Mamm offering to keep the kids for you."

"You inviting me to dinner?"

"That's different."

He nodded, though his eyes twinkled with a light she couldn't quite discern.

"I think they're trying to get me to stay," Hannah said. She hadn't wanted to admit those words out loud either. But there they were.

"You mean in Pontotoc?"

"Yes. With the Amish."

Aaron closed one eye, as he did when he was thinking. "Are you saying you think that they are trying to get you and me together so that you'll stay in Pontotoc?"

She shook her head. "I know it sounds dumb. Forget I said anything."

"No, it's okay."

She started to turn away, but he grabbed her arm. Her

skin tingled where his fingers touched her. It'd always been that way. He could talk about taking her hand, and it was as if she could feel the touch before it even came. That was the sort of connection they'd had at one time. Still had.

"I thought it was just me imagining things." He chuckled.

"I don't think so."

"They love you very much."

"I know." And she loved them in return. But staying in Pontotoc was just not possible. Not really. And she couldn't imagine it any other way. "I just thought you should know."

"Thanks for the heads-up."

She looked down at his fingers, still wrapped around her arm, then back up to his face.

"Oh." He released her as if he had only realized then that he still had ahold of her.

The breeze felt cool to her skin, heated from his touch.

"What do we do about it?" Aaron asked.

"This is my mother and my cousin we're talking about here. And probably Tillie too."

Aaron laughed and gave a quick nod. "Right. Not much we can do, is there?"

"No." Hannah returned his smile. "But as long as we know what we're in for."

"Right," Aaron said again. "Then we should be just fine."

"I just didn't want you to not spend any time with me because you knew they were trying to set us up."

"I do want to spend time with you." His blue eyes deepened, and the sheer color made her mouth go dry. She had to get herself together. This was Aaron, and that ship had sailed a long time ago. They had agreed to be friends, agreed to spend some time together, and agreed to catch up on the last fifteen years before she left again.

There was no more to it than that. No matter what her cousin and her mother wanted.

Hannah nodded, and together they started back toward the house. "Thanks for coming to supper tonight. I had a good time."

He gave a quick nod. "Thanks for inviting me."

And just like that, they were back to awkward again. One minute they had been enjoying each other's company as easy as anything, and now it seemed as if a huge wall had been wedged between them, an emotional wall that neither could breach.

It was well past nine o'clock before Aaron had any time for himself; he couldn't decide if that was a good thing or bad. As long as he was busy getting Essie and Laura Kate to bed and making sure Andy brushed his teeth and combed his hair before retiring as well, Aaron didn't have time to think about Hannah. He wanted to think about her almost as much as he didn't want to think about her. She was confusing to him, to say the least. In some ways she was just like the old Hannah and in other ways she was different as night and day. But there had been a time, out by the goat pen, standing there talking to her, and all the barriers between them fell away. Once again they were the Aaron and Hannah of fifteen years ago, talking, laughing together, simply enjoying the other's company without any expectation or demand. How he missed that. But as quickly as it had come, that comfort had disappeared, and Aaron was left wondering where it had gone. Or maybe it was *why* it had gone.

He would be lying to say he wasn't looking forward to spending time with her Monday afternoon. There would be plenty of people around, but somehow he knew it was going to be different. How many times in the past had they gone to people's houses to carry through with a work frolic or singing to the sick or elderly? So many times in their youth, they had gone to help others, elders and young people alike. This would be like that, like old times.

But it's not like that.

"It could be," he argued back. But he wasn't sure how. Did he make it so by simply wanting it that much? And he didn't want it; he knew he couldn't. He just wanted one more glance at how they had been back then. Just one more glance at the beauty they'd shared. There were beautiful things in the world, and then there were beautiful things in the world. Their relationship had been one of those. Not many people had that; not many people even knew it existed. He and Hannah, they'd had everything for a time, only to have it slip through their fingers. And they could never get it back. But if he could see it one last time, he would know it was there, and that might even be enough to get him through his old age.

And Ohio?

Ohio was just another reason why it could never be between him and Hannah. She could stay in Pontotoc all she wanted, but it wouldn't change a thing. Sarah Hostetler might hold the dream of opening a candy shop, but Aaron's dreams were a bit different. If he wanted to live out those dreams, Ohio was the place he had to be.

Chapter Ten

She was sitting on the porch swing, wondering about this moment as she pushed herself back and forth using the heels of her feet. She might still be dressing in her *Englisch* clothes, jeans and T-shirts, but she had taken back to going barefoot as easily as a duck to water.

Her father eased down next to her, and Hannah did her best to hide her surprise. After so many days of him avoiding even looking at her, having him suddenly acknowledge her presence was a bit unsettling.

"I need to know your plans."

Just like Dat; straight to the point.

"I don't really have a lot of plans." It was the best answer she could offer. She was waiting and hoping. Waiting on the attorney, waiting on the judges, waiting on the insurance. Hoping there would be enough money to pay off all of Mitch's hidden debt, hoping there would be enough left over for her and Brandon to start again.

He seemed to think about that for a moment. "Why did you come back?"

She knew what he meant. Why had she come back now? She just didn't know how to answer him. He already knew the large facts—her husband had died, and she was practically penniless—but that was all. No need to go into details that he wouldn't understand and she didn't care to admit. "My life didn't exactly turn out like I'd hoped." That was putting it mildly.

Her father stared out over the end of the porch. She could only imagine what was going on inside his head. "Will you leave again?"

She opened her mouth to respond, but closed it again to gather her thoughts. "I have Brandon to think about." As far as answers went, hers was about as vague as they came.

Her father's gaze shifted to the hangnail on his left hand. "What am I supposed to tell the bishop?"

"I don't know." She swallowed hard, reluctant to say the next words regardless of how desperately they needed to be said. "I just need a little help. I have nowhere else to turn." The truth sent stinging tears to her eyes.

Her father shifted his gaze to the horizon. "The bishop is committed to bringing wayward sheep back to the fold."

It was true. So many outsiders believed that a *Bann* was punishment, but it wasn't. Shunning was a way to bring those who strayed back to their senses. Let them see what they would be missing if they didn't change their ways. Once they returned to a righteous path, then all would be forgiven.

She might not be able to say the words to her father, but she wasn't returning. If he thought there was a chance of her staying and he told the bishop the same . . . then they would definitely allow her the time she needed. More than a couple of months. As long as it took.

"When he asks me tomorrow, that's what I'll tell him." Her father had his own version of the truth solidified in his mind. Who was she to convince him otherwise?

A stab of conscience blazed through her. She would be forced to tell the truth soon enough. But until then . . .

Her father stood. "Better go talk to your *mamm*. You'll be needing a dress for service tomorrow."

Hannah looked down at herself and sighed. A few short months ago, if someone had told her that she would find herself here, in Pontotoc, on this beautiful Sunday morning dressed in traditional Amish clothes in order to go to the bimonthly church service, she would've laughed. She had left this life behind years ago, and though daydreams of returning had crept into her thoughts from time to time, she knew it could never happen. Not permanently. Now yesterday she had all but promised her *dat* she was staying. She could almost see the light of hope in his eyes, a hope that he wanted to believe in more than anything. When the time came and she had to leave again, it would be hard on everybody. But she saw no solution. There was no way to make this better.

She smoothed a hand over her cape and apron. The dress underneath was a somber navy blue, not her favorite color by far, but the one dress she could fit into.

She adjusted the straight pins that held together the bodice of the dress. How she had ever gotten through her days without scratching herself to pieces was a miracle. But if she had done it then, she could do it now. And the one big change? A bra. There was no way she was going out in public without a bra. Not that she was heavy-chested, but she felt exposed somehow. Though she knew she would probably be the only one in the congregation with one on, she just couldn't make herself go without one.

A low whistle came from behind her. Hannah whirled

around to find Brandon standing there, a goofy grin spread across his face. "You look hot."

She gave him a mockingly serious look. "Watch your sass."

He chuckled and made his way into the room, lying down on the bed and crossing one ankle over his bent knee, hands folded behind his head as if he hadn't a care in the world. But they both knew otherwise. "What? You don't like the down-home look?" he asked.

She hadn't worn this look in years. But it had never been the way they dressed that had bothered her. It'd been more about knowledge, convenience, and just simply discovering what was out there. She could've done that in a *frack* and a prayer *kapp*. If she had been allowed.

"We'll be home this afternoon sometime," she said, pinning the prayer *kapp* in place. She tied it loosely under her chin in a neat little bow.

"This afternoon? You're going to be gone all day?"

Hannah nodded. "Church is three hours, then we have a meal, and everyone will stay and visit for a while, so we'll probably be home about three o'clock."

Brandon pushed himself up on the bed. "What am I supposed to do all day without a cell phone, or a computer, or even an MP3 player?"

She shot him an almost apologetic look. "Write a letter."

He flopped back onto the bed, exasperated. She wanted to feel bad for him, but he wasn't having to go sit on the church bench and listen to three hours of Bible teachings in high German. It wasn't the teachings or the language that caused her grief, but the benches were hard on the back. Even for the young.

"You'll survive," she said, then patted his leg and started for the door.

"I take it back," he called after her. "You don't look hot, Mom. You look like a dork."

Hannah chuckled. To him, she probably did look like a dork. He'd never seen her in anything like what she now wore. And it was more than a little strange to be walking around in Amish garb once again.

She stepped out onto the porch and stretched, hoping to pull some of the tension from her shoulders. The day was already starting off warm. By this afternoon she would be drenched in sweat from all the layers of clothing: the long-sleeved dress, cape, apron, and the thick black stockings that covered her legs. How she had survived this the first eighteen years of her life she wasn't quite sure. Must be an acclimation thing. How long would it take her to get re-acclimated? She wouldn't be here long enough to find out.

"Hannah," Tillie called from the buggy. Her little sister waved her over.

Hannah made her way across the dusty drive to where Gracie and Tillie waited in the carriage.

"Mamm and Dat took Mammi to church already. They want to make sure they can get her settled in before the service starts." Tillie's smile grew wider. Hannah could only believe that it was due to her manner of dress. Though she couldn't tell if Tillie was pleasantly surprised or laughing inside at the sight of Hannah in one of her mother's dresses. "You can ride with us."

"Thanks," Hannah said, somehow keeping all the sarcasm from her tone.

Tillie hopped down from the front seat and moved around to the small seat in the rear of the carriage. "You can sit in the front."

"Thanks again."

"Brandon's not going with us?" Gracie asked, picking up the reins but not yet setting the horse into motion.

Hannah shook her head. "I'm surprised that they even want me to go."

"You won't remember what you're missing by staying home," Tillie chirped from the back seat.

Hannah resisted the urge to shake her head again. She might be allowed back to church today, but she could almost guarantee that she couldn't come back in two weeks if she didn't perform her kneeling confession and state her intention of baptism classes.

Hannah didn't answer, and the conversation ground to a quick halt. She wished one of them would say something, for without the easy, everyday chatter, her thoughts were growing bigger and bigger. What was she doing? It had never been her intention to deceive her father, and yet she had. What was she going to do when it was time to leave again?

"Everyone will be so happy to see you," Gracie said, patting her arm.

"I doubt that," Hannah murmured. She looked out over the fields. Funny how things never change. Fifteen years and the crops were the same: peanuts, soybeans, corn, and cotton. Muscadines and tomatoes.

"What about Aaron?" Tillie asked from the back seat.

Hannah twisted her fingers in her apron, then stopped and smoothed the fabric. She was only wrinkling it. "What about him?"

"Did you have fun last night?"

Hannah sniffed delicately. "We had a nice time, yes."

"Gracie said y'all went around the house away from everyone else, all alone."

Gracie's mouth fell open. "I did not."

"You did too."

"I said they went off together."

"What's the difference?" Tillie asked.

"There's a lot of difference," Gracie retorted.

"Don't get any ideas," Hannah interjected. "Aaron and I can only be friends."

"Who's getting ideas?" Tillie said. "He's a widower, you know."

"Stop." Hannah gave Gracie her stern you-better-listen-to-me look, then shifted in her seat to pin Tillie with it as well. Neither girl seemed to take her seriously.

"He was heartbroken after you left." Gracie's voice was soft, but carried as if she had yelled.

"Yeah, so heartbroken he took up with Lizzie Yoder less than four months later." Four very important months.

But if it hadn't been for that, would you have really come back?

She pushed that thought away. "What's done is done," she said. How many times had she uttered those words about Mitch? About their failed marriage? About all the bad choices she had made in her life? Unfortunately, there were a lot of them.

"But now you can have a second chance." Tillie scooted forward and poked her head between them, an excited grin on her face.

"We won't have a second chance. We *don't* have a second chance." She'd almost told them that she was leaving as soon as possible, yet here she was, sitting in the buggy on her way to church wearing an Amish dress. Who was she trying to kid? Neither one of them would listen to her now.

"You should leave yourself open to possibilities," Gracie said.

Hannah studied her cousin. Gracie was a kind soul. And, Hannah thought, as she took in every aspect of her profile, she was quite beautiful. So how come no one had noticed that? How come no one had seen how smart she was? How come no one had swept her up before now?

It was as if Gracie was somehow invisible to everybody until they needed her for something. Hannah had only just realized it now. Anytime there was a problem while they were growing up everyone called Gracie. Too many tomatoes to can, but don't have enough time? Call Gracie. Take a fall and get hurt? Call Gracie. Need help with the kids? The dogs? The chickens? Call Gracie.

Hannah turned her gaze back front, realizing that she was staring. She didn't want to make her cousin uncomfortable. But why hadn't she noticed that before? Why hadn't she noticed that Gracie was the one constant helper in everyone's life? She seemed happy enough about her lot, but Hannah couldn't help but wonder if Gracie wanted more.

And wanting more is what got you into your predicament.

She really needed to get that voice under control. It seemed to taunt her every move now that she had returned to Pontotoc.

"Are you saying that you don't want a second chance with Aaron?" Tillie asked.

"Who said he wanted the second chance with me?" It wasn't exactly an answer, but Hannah hoped that it would be enough to dissuade any more question asking on the trip.

"Maybe we should find out . . ." Gracie pulled on the reins to turn the buggy down Oak Forest Road.

"Don't you dare." Hannah's jaw ached from clenching her teeth to keep from yelling the words.

"Are you saying you don't want us to go talk to Aaron for you?"

"That's exactly what I'm saying." But she had a feeling those words fell on deaf ears. Her cousin and her sister exchanged a look, and Hannah had a feeling even more matchmaking would be going on very soon. But how did she tell them all she was leaving as soon as she possibly could?

* * *

Aaron could hardly believe his eyes. He stood next to the Danny Hostetlers' barn with a group of other men talking about this, that, and the other. Nothing important, just before-church chatter about crops and horses and other things. He was surprised that no one had asked him about his job offer in Ohio. But he supposed everyone had chalked it up to God's plan for his life. When Aaron figured it out, then that would be that.

"Is that . . . ?" Chris Lambert asked.

"It sure looks like it," Jason Menno replied.

Aaron had no words of his own. As he watched, the most crazy, miraculous, unexpected thing happened. Hannah Gingerich McLean climbed out of a buggy.

The navy blue dress she wore and the newly starched prayer *kapp* brought back more memories of her than he had even known he had. Their walks together, fishing at the pond, saying they were going fishing at the pond and not fishing at all. But he pushed those thoughts aside. It wasn't time for that. That time was over, and it was never coming back. She had made her choice, and she had made her intentions clear. This was just a stop on her map. She was like a wild bird that had to be free. She might fly home every so often, but she would never stay.

But his heart didn't get the message. It pounded heavily in his chest at the sight of her. He remembered the old days, their times together. So much had happened between them. So much that drew them together and yet her desire for more had ripped them apart.

"Are you going to say hi to her?" Jason asked.

Aaron shook his head. "I saw her the other day." He explained how he'd gone over to the Gingeriches' to work with one of Abner's horses. He did his best to make the event as insignificant as possible, but the mischievous light stayed in both men's eyes.

"Don't you think it's about time you got married again?" Amos asked.

Aaron shook his head. "Don't even think about it." How could he talk that way? If Aaron ever did get married again, it certainly wouldn't be to Hannah Gingerich. And her returning home, bringing back all those memories, just gave him further cause to move to Ohio. *Jah*, that was what he would do.

Chapter Eleven

Hannah shifted uncomfortably on the bench and did her best to concentrate on the message the deacon was delivering to them. It was a good message about loving your neighbor and helping out when you were supposed to. It was a message of community and togetherness. Was it merely coincidence that he chose to speak about this, Hannah's first church service back in Pontotoc?

Unlike Protestant preachers, Amish elders didn't plan their service out in advance. They didn't search through Bible passages, make notes, and work on getting just the right words for the congregation. No, Amish deacons, preachers, and bishops preached off-the-cuff. So it was most likely intentional that today the deacon felt moved to talk about togetherness.

She reached up and pulled on one of the bobby pins holding her hair. She adjusted it, then pushed it back into place. The bob she had put in her hair was starting to itch. She'd wound it up tight to keep it from falling out. Her hair was so much shorter now that she didn't want any stray strands to distract the people around her. She wanted to blend in as much as possible. She wanted no one to notice her, but of course everyone did. She was the talk of the district. Hannah Gingerich had returned home.

Her mother sat next to her and on the other side of Mamm sat Anna, Jim's wife. On Hannah's left was Tillie, and then Gracie. Five Gingerich women all in a row. As was tradition, the men were on the other side of the room: her father, her brothers, and Aaron, of course.

In the far back, in the section of padded chairs, her grandmother watched and listened. She sat among the other infirm: some elderly, some injured, and one hugely pregnant woman that Hannah didn't know. She thought back to her own pregnancy and decided the woman had to be having twins. Either that, or the baby was going to weigh twenty pounds when he was born. *Poor soul,* she thought to herself.

Once again her gaze drifted to Aaron. A fit of awareness seared through her. It had been easy to forget how handsome he was, how sweet he was, how strong and kind and loving, when she didn't have to see him, or maybe she had just convinced herself it was easy. She never let her thoughts stray to him or the time they had spent together.

But that wasn't exactly true either. She had. One time. That was when she had found out that he was seeing Lizzie Yoder. From that moment forward she pushed him from her thoughts and never let him return. Now that she was back in Pontotoc, it seemed he was all she could think about. Every day, he came out to the house to work with her father's new horse. And every day she fought the urges to run away as well as the ones that enticed her to move as close to him as possible. Just like she told Tillie and Gracie, what was done was done. There was no going back. And she had hurt him bad enough to know that forgiveness would be given, but it would not be absolute.

The congregation stood and sang. Then everyone turned and knelt at their benches to say the last prayer.

Lord, please let this all be settled soon.

She felt like a traitor, an impostor, and somehow like she was home all at the same time. Being back in Pontotoc was as confusing to her as it was to those around her. But if she had someplace else to go she wouldn't have come here.

Lord, please let the estate be settled soon and allow me and Brandon to begin again.

Everyone around her started to shift and shuffle, and she knew that prayer was over. She rose to her feet, realizing how selfish her prayer had been. It was all about her, her needs, what she wanted, with not much thought to anyone else. True, Brandon would benefit from her prayers, but he hadn't crept into her thoughts just then. How long had it been that way? When had she stopped thinking of others and started thinking only of herself? She couldn't remember.

She turned, and from across the room Aaron's gaze snagged hers. They held that way for what seemed like full minutes but could only have been a couple of seconds. Then Laura Kate captured his attention, and the moment was gone.

Thankfully, most of the afternoon was taken up in setting the benches up for the afternoon meal and getting everyone fed, then in the cleanup afterward. She didn't have an opportunity to see or talk to Aaron in all that time. But if she was being honest with herself, she had a feeling he was avoiding her as acutely as she was avoiding him. The thought made her sad.

She shook her head at herself. It didn't matter if he was avoiding her. It shouldn't matter. And it shouldn't make her sad.

"Hannah? Are you coming?" Tillie stood next to the buggy as Gracie hitched up the horse.

Hannah shook her head at herself. She had stopped in

the middle of the yard, halfway from the house to the buggy, a handful of napkins in one hand and the other empty. Just standing there like a statue in the park. She had no aim, no direction. She wasn't thinking about the parallels to her life. It was too much for her to take in.

"I'm coming." She set her feet into motion without another look and ran headlong into something . . . Someone . . .

Strong hands came up and clasped her arms to steady her. She breathed in the familiar scent. Part man, part laundry detergent, part nostalgia.

She planted her feet firmly on the ground. "Aaron," she breathed.

His touch burned through the sleeves of her dress, warming her skin underneath. His fingers wrapped around her arms was like stepping back in time, to the one time when he held her close, so close.

"I'm sorry. I didn't see you there." He released her, and Hannah gave a small shudder, suddenly cold.

"It's all right," she said. "I wasn't watching where I was going."

"You look like you have a lot on your mind today."

It was perhaps the biggest understatement she'd ever heard anyone utter. "A little bit," she said.

Those cool blue-gray eyes studied her. There was a time when she thought he could see straight through her heart, that he knew every thought, every wish, every feeling she had. If that were true, she was definitely in trouble. For he would know that she wanted to lean in, to simply melt into him and not have to worry about everything that was going on in her life. Not this life, here with the Amish, but her real life. Mitch, the estate, the debt.

Aaron took a step back. "Girls, say hello to Hannah."

Laura Kate stepped forward. She looked so much like her father it was uncanny. She was just smaller and in girl form, her beautiful eyes framed by silver-rimmed glasses. She smiled prettily at Hannah—a smile she had seen a thousand times before on Aaron's face. "Hi, Hannah."

"Hi, Laura Kate. Essie." She nodded toward the younger daughter.

"She remembered my name." Essie tugged on her father's hand. Like her sister, Essie was another miniature Aaron. Each girl had just a slight difference from their father's features, but it was so obvious who they took after. Laura Kate wore glasses, and Essie had a small gap between her two front teeth and a smattering of freckles across her pert little nose. They were adorable, sweet and innocent, and Hannah was slammed with the thought that if she had stayed in Pontotoc, those little girls might be her own.

She shook the thought away. *You made the choices you made.*

A moment stretched between Hannah and Aaron, a moment of what to do next. She got the feeling that he might want to stay and talk for a while, but they both knew it would lead nowhere. Still, she was reluctant to set her feet into motion.

"Andy is off—" He waved a hand in the direction of a group of young men. Hannah had no trouble picking out Andy. Like his sisters, he was the spitting image of their father.

"Hannah," Tillie called. "We're waiting."

Hannah turned back to Aaron. "I should go." But her feet still refused to move.

"You should come by and have dinner with us," Laura Kate said.

Hannah shifted her attention to Aaron's oldest daughter. "That would be nice. Thank you." She said the words out of kindness. There would be no dinner at Aaron's house. They might be able to pull off a friendship of sorts, but she had a feeling that dinner at Aaron's would be a little too intimate for either one of them to be comfortable with the idea.

"*Jah*," Essie added. "Before we up and move to Ohio."

Hannah turned her attention back to Aaron. "You're moving?"

He shifted uncomfortably in place. "There is talk of Ohio, *jah*."

Which didn't actually answer her question, now did it? "I see." But she didn't. What was in Ohio?

"But there's not been a decision made yet," he continued.

"That's what you keep saying." Laura Kate frowned.

Anyone could see that his daughters were not enthusiastic about moving. Why was Aaron so bent on going to Ohio?

"I didn't know you had family in Ohio," Hannah said. Okay, she was blatantly fishing for answers, but she had a feeling Aaron wouldn't volunteer the information himself.

"I don't."

"There's a man there who wants him to train horses," Essie supplied.

"Girls," he started, without taking his eyes from Hannah, "why don't you go get in the buggy?"

"But—" Essie started.

"In the buggy. Now," he said.

Laura Kate took her sister's arm. "Come on," she muttered.

Heads bowed, the two girls headed for their buggy, parked nearby. Hannah's heart went out to them. They felt as strongly about moving from Pontotoc as Brandon did about moving to it. Change was hard, and it seemed like they were all facing a change of one kind or another.

"I'm sorry about that," Aaron said.

Hannah smiled. "It's okay. I guess they aren't excited about the move."

Aaron stared out over the pasture as if the answers he needed were somehow written in the sky there. "They aren't. But I think it's time."

"Time?" She was confused.

Aaron nodded. "*Jah*, time to move on. Time to stop living in the past."

The words rattled around inside her head all the way home. Was he talking about them? Or his marriage and life with Lizzie Yoder?

She mentally shook her head. There was no *them*. Anything between Hannah and Aaron had ended when she found out he was dating Lizzie. Or maybe even before, on that fateful night long ago. The night before she left.

No, he had to be talking about his life with Lizzie. Had he loved her that much?

Hannah shook her head again. She was putting *Englisch* values on Amish actions. Of course Aaron loved his wife, but love wasn't always the driving factor behind Amish marriage.

She was just wishful-thinking. Every girl wanted to believe that they were the one their first love couldn't get over. But Aaron had gotten over her. He had moved on, married another, had children.

Yet he hadn't done anything that she hadn't done.

She exhaled, allowing the tension and thoughts to escape her. No sense in dwelling on the past. Wasn't that what Aaron had just said?

"What's wrong?" Tillie asked from the back seat.

Gracie kept her eyes on the road, and Hannah had a feeling it had less to do with driving and more to do with allowing her the privacy of her thoughts. Tillie wasn't so understanding in that matter.

"Nothing." *Everything,* she thought.

Tillie scooted closer. "No one sighs like that when nothing's wrong."

Hannah thought about it a moment. What was the best answer? "Not 'wrong,' really. Just, you know . . ."

As far as answers went, it was probably the worst. But Tillie and Gracie both nodded. Hannah wondered if they really understood, or if they were just being supportive. They were both younger than her, but just by a few years. Gracie was quickly approaching her twenty-fifth birthday, and Tillie hadn't quite reached her twentieth. Neither one had lived as much life as Hannah. Strange to think of it that way. Neither one was married; neither one had children.

Neither one had run off and joined the *Englisch*.

"Was it hard?" Tillie finally asked.

Hannah turned in her seat to better look at her sister. Normally Tillie's eyes were alight with a mischievous sparkle, her lips curved into a perpetual smile, but somehow a shadow crossed over her features, and she looked more serious than Hannah had ever seen.

"Was what hard?"

"Leaving." The one word was spoken so quietly that at first Hannah wasn't sure if she had actually heard it or if it had somehow just popped into her thoughts.

"You mean leaving the Amish?" Hannah asked.

"Tillie, no," Gracie said. Her blue eyes were trained on the road ahead, as though if she looked away something terrible would happen.

"I'm just asking," Tillie said. The shadows on her face deepened.

"What's going on here?" Hannah asked.

"Nothing," Tillie said. "I just asked a question. Was it hard leaving?"

"It was the hardest thing I've ever done," Hannah said. Until that moment she hadn't categorized it that way. She'd never really thought about it that deeply. It was just something she had done. But leaving the Amish had been heartbreaking, exciting, life altering, and so very, very, difficult.

"Did you ever want to come back?" Tillie asked. "I mean, before now?"

"Tillie." This time Gracie turned and pinned her cousin with a stern look.

"I'm just asking," Tillie said, though the words were close to a screech.

Hannah looked from her cousin to her sister and back again. Something more was going on here. Something more than this conversation that was happening right then. "I thought about it. Why?"

"Why didn't you?"

"Lots of reasons, I guess." But that wasn't exactly the truth. If she hadn't gotten the letter from her brother, if Aaron hadn't been dating Lizzie Yoder, or maybe if some other things had been different, she would've returned long before now.

"Because you fell in love with Michael?" Tillie asked.

"Mitch," Gracie and Hannah corrected at the same time.

"Right," Tillie said with a nod. "Because of him?"

"Something like that." Her thoughts drifted back to those days when their love had been new. Or maybe it had just been shiny and different. Whatever it was, she had allowed Mitch to convince her to stay. She had believed in all his plans and dreams. She had allowed him to convince her that their life together would be better than anything she could have anywhere else. And for a time, she supposed it had been. But that time had ended all too soon.

"I wish I would meet someone like him," Tillie said.

"Bite your tongue," Hannah said. "Someone like Mitch is the last thing you need."

"Why? He was handsome and wealthy and sophisticated."

And a liar and a cheat and a terrible father. But Hannah said none of those things.

"Sometimes the things in shiny packages are just ordinary things dressed up to look special," Hannah said.

"What?" Tillie asked.

"I think she means you can't make a silk purse out of a sow's ear," Gracie said.

Tillie's forehead crinkled into a confused frown. "What do pigs have to do with this?"

Hannah and Gracie shared a look, then burst out laughing.

Tillie's frown deepened. "I don't see what's so funny." She sat back with a pout and crossed her arms over herself.

Hannah recovered first, reining in her mirth as she checked on her sister. "Wait," she said. "You're not thinking of leaving, are you?"

Tillie shrugged and mumbled something incoherent.

"Tell the truth, please," Gracie ordered from the driver's seat.

"Wait wait wait wait wait," Hannah said. "Gracie, pull over." They were almost home. And this was definitely a conversation that needed to be completed before they pulled into the driveway.

"Do Mamm and Dat know about this?"

"I haven't done anything," Tillie said, her defenses rising.

"I never said you did," Hannah returned. "But . . ."

Gracie pulled over to the side of the road and, still keeping ahold of the horse's reins, turned to face Tillie.

"Why are you ganging up on me?" Tillie moaned.

"No one's ganging up on you," Gracie said. "But I told you my opinion. Leaving would be a huge mistake."

"I never said I was leaving."

"Then what did you say?" Hannah asked.

"I just wanted to know."

"Are you having doubts?" Hannah asked. She knew all about those. They were the worst. They had crept into her thoughts time and time again. She had assuaged them by standing in the hardware store watching the news cross the television screen, going to the library and soaking up everything she could about the *Englisch* world, those bright, colorful magazines that her father had hated so much. But curiosity could turn into more.

"Just don't do anything rash, okay?" Hannah asked. "If you have any questions, come to me. I promise I'll tell you the truth. Deal?"

Tillie's expression brightened just a smidge, not enough to call happy but definitely out of the frustrated range where it had been. "Deal," she said.

Gracie shook her head. "You should tell her she needs to stay." She turned around, snapped the reins again, and started the horse in motion.

Hannah would love to tell Tillie not to leave, but she knew firsthand that was a choice everyone had to make for themselves.

"Are you mad?" Essie asked as they drove home.

"I'm not mad," Aaron said, but even to his own ears his voice was quick and clipped.

"You sound mad," Essie continued.

"I'm not mad," he said again.

"Isn't it a sin to lie?" Essie asked.

Aaron turned in the buggy and shot his daughter a reprimanding glance. "Sit down, and I'm not mad."

"You sound mad to me," Laura Kate said.

Aaron released a deep sigh. He did sound mad. He was mad. But not at them. Or maybe not *just* at them. He was mad at himself a little too. How had he allowed himself to get distracted by Hannah Gingerich once again?

Face it. She's been distracting you your entire life.

Essie stood once again and leaned over the seat. She was in the back, while Laura Kate took the special place of honor next to him. Andy had leaned his head against the back wall of the carriage and appeared to be asleep. Or maybe he was simply ignoring them. Aaron did his best to rotate the kids' places, making sure everyone got the chance to sit up front. Sometimes he forgot whose turn it was. But they never did.

"Sit down, Essie."

She plopped back in the seat once again. Of all the children, she was undeniably the feistiest. Full of energy, always into everything, but a constant joy all the same.

"How do you know her?" Laura Kate asked from beside him.

"Who?" He feigned ignorance.

"Hannah. She's Abner and Eunice's daughter, but how do you know her?" Laura Kate asked.

"I like Abner and Eunice," Essie chirped from the back seat.

"I do too." He hoped that was the only answer he would need, but that was wishful thinking.

"I think Hannah is nice," Essie added.

"How do you know her?" Laura Kate asked again.

"I've never seen her around here before," Essie said.

"That's because she doesn't live here."

"Where does she live?" Laura Kate asked.

"If she doesn't live here, how do you know her?"

"She used to live here," Aaron said.

"Where does she live now?" Essie asked.

"Someplace in Tennessee, I guess." He didn't know for certain, but he thought he'd heard someone say that she had moved to Nashville.

"Like Ethridge?" Essie asked. "Isn't that where Mammi and Dawdi live? Does she know Mammi and Dawdi?"

"Sort of," he said, feeling somewhat as if he'd been run over by a truck. He didn't have the answers to these questions. Or at least, not any answer he wanted to give Essie right now.

"If she lives over there, why haven't we gone to visit her when we go out to see Mammi and Dawdi?" Laura Kate asked.

Great, now Essie had her sister firing questions at him. "I don't know. Sit down."

Essie settled back into the seat once more. "She's pretty," Essie said.

"*Jah*," Laura Kate agreed. "But it's not just looks. It's what is in a woman's heart."

Amen to that. Hannah was pretty, beautiful even, and once upon a time he had thought he knew what was in her heart. But that had all changed one night. He thought he had done everything right. He thought that if he took a chance, did something big to bring them closer together, that she would know how much he loved her. Yet all he had done was push them apart.

He gathered up those thoughts and stuffed them back into a box he normally kept locked. There was no sense going down the road to the past. It led nowhere. Whatever had happened between them then, between him and Hannah, was over and had been for fifteen years or better. There was a time when he had counted each and every day. But when he realized that Hannah wasn't coming back, he knew it was time to look to the future, a future without Hannah Gingerich.

He glanced around at his three sweet children. They were the future and what he needed to concentrate on. Not past loves, not past mistakes, but these precious kids of his. That was why Ohio was so important. He felt like there was opportunity there. Something more perhaps.

Just like Hannah.

He shoved that thought away. He was nothing like Hannah. He just wanted the best for his kids, opportunities, new faces. Most everyone in these parts had to travel back to Tennessee in order to find a marriage partner. Most everyone was related to a certain point. They wouldn't have to worry about such matters in Ohio.

"How far away is Ohio?" Essie asked.

"Far."

"If it's so far, why are we moving?" Essie asked.

Aaron sighed. "I haven't decided if we're moving or not. And I have no control over where Ohio is located."

"*Jah,* Dat." Something in his tone finally got through to her. Essie sat down, pushed herself all the way back in her seat and crossed her arms, a sure sign she wasn't happy.

Aaron bit back his second sigh. He hadn't wanted to hurt her feelings. It was just that all this talk of moving mixed with Hannah's return had him on edge. And the worst part was, there was nothing he could do about it.

First she was Hannah the *Englisch*, with her blue jeans and fancy hair. Then today at church she was like Yesterday's Hannah in her Amish *frack* and prayer *kapp*. He didn't know what to expect. He never knew who she was going to be.

Or maybe he didn't want to face the fact that the Hannah at church, Yesterday's Hannah, was only a front. She had dressed that way because she was going to church. Had it been any other event, on any other day, she would have looked just as she had today. So *Englisch*, so worldly. So not the Hannah he remembered.

It was better this way, he told himself. The *Englisch* Hannah was the real Hannah, and it always had been. Even when she was Amish. Otherwise why would she have left?

Chapter Twelve

"This is dumb."

Hannah's hands tightened on the steering wheel as Brandon stared out the window. "It's the best option we have."

He turned toward her, pinning her with hazel eyes so like her own. "Really?"

She had no response. Going to the public library in town and using their computers to complete his online school assignments was the best option they had. Aside from leaving Randolph and Pontotoc behind and going . . . where? They had nowhere to go.

And that makes it your only option.

She pushed the thought away, but the sinking feeling in the pit of her stomach was a little harder to rid herself of.

"Brandon, can you please just do this for me?" Why hadn't someone told her these teenage years would be so hard? Or maybe they had but she was so enamored of the young Brandon that she hadn't believed them. Or maybe this terrible situation they found themselves in was taking its toll on the both of them.

That was what she wanted to believe, that once everything with Mitch's estate was settled life would return to normal. Or at least her relationship with her son would even out.

"Yeah, whatever." He turned to stare out the window once again.

As far as answers go, it left a lot to be desired, but it would have to do for now.

She dropped him off at the door of the small library. "Do you have all your instructions?"

He rolled his eyes. "Yes, Mother. I've only done this about a hundred times."

But never from a library computer. "If you have any problems, ask the librarian."

"Got it."

"And leave your phone."

"Why? It's dead."

"Just leave it," she said.

"But—"

"Leave. It."

He took it from his pants pocket and with a perfect teenage eyeroll, he tossed it into the passenger seat. Then he slammed the car door and sauntered away.

Hannah watched him enter the building, then closed her eyes. *Lord, if You're listening, give me strength.* But she knew; He had stopped listening to her a long time ago.

She backed up the car and headed down Main Street. She just wanted to get out of sight of the library in case Brandon decided that if she was out in the car he didn't have to work anymore. Their lives were in complete upheaval, but education was of the upmost importance. She should know. Growing up Amish, she had stopped school the day after her fourteenth birthday. At eighteen she left Pontotoc, then she found out she was pregnant. She married Mitch, and the rest was history, as they say. No GED. No college diploma. Now Mitch was gone, the house was gone, and she could barely balance the checkbook. Not that it mattered; all the money was gone too.

She pulled into the bank parking lot and kept to the corner and out of the way. She needed just a few moments to make a call, then she would head over to the grocery store to pick up a few things for her mother, then back to the library for Brandon.

Brandon's phone was completely dead, and thanks to her ever-shrinking cash fund, she'd had hers turned off weeks ago. She plugged his phone into the car charger and waited while it charged enough to turn on.

Outside the car, the small town of Pontotoc bustled about its business. People walked down the sidewalks shopping in the antique stores and resale shops that lined the quaint street. Not much had changed. There was a Chinese restaurant. That was new. And another shop that sold clothing for teens. The wind rustled in the trees, and cars quietly purred down the street as people ducked into the home-owned eateries there on Main.

It was more than different from Nashville. They were worlds apart. A person could almost hear the grass grow in Pontotoc. In Nashville she couldn't hear herself think. Or maybe it was that she couldn't allow herself to think about all the could-have-beens and should-have-beens. All the what-ifs.

The phone finally charged enough that she could dial the now-familiar number.

"Lipman and Qualls, attorneys-at-law. How may I help you?"

"This is Hannah Gin—McLean. Is Mr. Lipman in, please?"

"One moment, please."

She said another small prayer that he was there, just in case God was listening. She needed to talk to her attorney. She needed that connection with the outside world. And with her limited telephone access, she needed it when she needed it.

"Mrs. McLean?"

She nearly wilted in relief when her lawyer's voice came through the line. "Hello, Mr. Lipman. I was just calling to see if there's been any news about my husband's estate."

Papers rustled on the other end. "I'm sorry. There's been no change yet." His voice was soft and caring and brought tears to her eyes. She blinked them away.

"It's just . . . this is hard." Her voice caught on a sob, and she swallowed it back. This was not the time to break down, but dang it! She wanted her life back. She wanted *a* life back. Something. Anything.

"These matters are seldom easy on any involved," he kindly continued.

"Yes," she agreed, thankful that her voice was clear and not choked with unshed tears. Now was the time to be strong. But she had been strong for so long that the burden was growing more difficult than ever to carry. "I understand."

"As soon as I know something I'll give you a call. I have your number here." He recited a number from her file. It was her old cell phone number.

"That's not a good number anymore." She rattled off Brandon's number. Pontotoc Amish were so very conservative that there was only one phone shanty in the entire district. It sat in the schoolhouse yard in the event that the youngsters needed immediate help. There were no cell phones for business, or phones in the barns. If an Amish person needed to use the phone, they went to their nearest *Englisch* neighbor and asked to borrow theirs.

"It's my son's number. And I can't promise that it will always have a charge, but I'll check it every chance I can."

There was a pause on the other end of the line. "Is everything okay, Mrs. McLean?"

"Yes," she said with a nod he couldn't see. "I've just come home to Pontotoc, and well, my family doesn't have a home phone.

"Pontotoc, Mississippi?" he asked. She could almost see him making a quick note on the edge of her file.

"That's right."

"And you don't have a phone."

"Right again."

"I see." He said the words, but she had a feeling he had no clue as to what she was talking about. Most people didn't know that she had grown up Amish. "I'll let you know as soon as I hear something."

Hannah thanked him and disconnected. She'd figured out the solution to one problem, but she had yet to figure out why she had called Pontotoc home.

This was so dumb.

Brandon looked at the ancient desktop computer and about gagged. He hadn't even known such antiques still existed. Much less that some people actually still used them. Why he couldn't bring his own laptop from home, he'd never understand. Oh, his mother had tried to explain. Something about everything of value having to remain at their house until the estate was finally settled. He hadn't paid as much attention as he probably should have, but sometimes the way adults talked made him want to curl up in a ball and go to sleep.

Then again, if he had brought his laptop he'd still be here, hooked up to the electricity. How people could survive like that in the twenty-first century, he would never know.

He pressed the button to turn on the dinosaur and hoped

it actually worked. How embarrassing it would be to have to get help to turn the stupid thing on! The screen flickered, then came into focus. Wow. Would wonders never cease? He shook his head and logged on to the Internet.

He wanted to check his Facebook account and maybe see what was going on over on Twitter. Snapchat, his absolute favorite, was out since his phone was dead. Another stupid thing about Mississippi. Maybe not Mississippi, but definitely the Amish. What was so wrong with a little electricity?

He resisted the urge to check his social media and instead logged into his virtual school's site. His mom would have his hide if he didn't get his work done. Or worse, she would put him in public school down here. He shuddered at the thought. New school, no friends, no dad, living with the backward Amish. No thank you. The best plan would be to zip through his assignments—then he could play around all he wanted.

He started his algebra work, only momentarily distracted when someone sat down on the other side of the table from him. He glanced up, then did a double take.

"Hi." She smiled, then lowered her brown eyes to something in her lap.

"Hi," he said in return, though his voice cracked at the end. Great. Now he sounded like a squeaky shoe. He cleared his throat. What was she doing here this time of day?

"Are you in online school?" she asked.

Brandon nodded, not trusting his voice to not betray him again.

"Me too." She smiled again.

She was pretty, Brandon decided. Very pretty. Her long brown hair was straight and hung well past her shoulders. When she leaned in to look at something on the computer screen, a lock of it fell forward. It was really long, and he wondered if she could sit on it. Her brown eyes were big and friendly, and they seemed to smile at him even when her lips were still. She had a few freckles across the bridge of her nose. He figured she hated them; most girls did. But he thought they were cute.

"My name is Shelly," she whispered across the table.

"Brandon." Thankfully his voice held out, and he didn't sound like a silly kid. "You come here to use the computers too?"

She nodded. "My mother takes my little brother and sister to gymnastics three times a week. I come in here to work on my tests for school while they're busy."

"Why don't you do it at home?" She looked old enough to stay by herself. He thought the law was twelve, and she seemed older than that. If he had to guess he would say that she was about his age. Fifteen or so.

She made a face, but the expression vanished almost as quickly as it appeared. "My parents try to live off the grid."

"Off the grid?"

"You know, no television, no computers . . ."

"No Internet?" He knew enough about that. But she didn't look Amish. Shelly simply looked . . . wholesome. Sweet. Like someone he would like to get to know. That was, if he was going to be staying in Mississippi long. Which he wasn't.

"What about you?"

He jerked himself from his thoughts. "What?"

"Does your family live off the grid?"

He thought of his super-pie-making, homemade-clothes-wearing grandmother and his scowling grandfather. No electricity, no running water, no phone to speak of. "Uhum, yeah," he finally said. "You could say that."

"Then that's something we have in common."

Bandon nodded. "And you do your schoolwork here. That's two things."

She nodded along with him, that smile still playing with the corners of her mouth. She really was pretty. Maybe this wasn't so lame after all.

"And you got all your assignments?" Hannah asked. She had picked Brandon up from the library, and thankfully his mood had improved. Too bad hers hadn't. Was she asking for so much? She didn't think so, but life seemed to have other plans.

"I should be set until Wednesday. Is that okay?"

Was that okay? It was downright spectacular. "Works for me," she said instead.

"You'll take me back to the library on Wednesday so I can work some more?"

"I can take you into town tomorrow too." She cast a quick glance in his direction. His expression was unchanged, nothing out of the ordinary.

"Wednesday will be fine."

"If you're sure." She shot him another look, but he was staring out the window at the landscape as it whirred by.

"Did you know that you can get a fourteen-year-old driving permit in Mississippi?"

Was that what this was all about? "I didn't." She had never been licensed to drive until after she had moved away.

"Well, you can. There are steps and everything, but as long as I'm enrolled in a driver's ed program I can get a permit when I'm fourteen. Which I am. Plus I'll be fifteen soon."

Hannah nodded, even as her stomach sank. They had so

much going on that she couldn't imagine adding anything else, even his learning to drive.

But that wasn't fair. She had been with the *Englisch* long enough to understand how important a driver's license was to teens.

"What's the rush? You'll be fifteen in a couple of weeks."

"Yeah, but I could start learning to drive now. And then you wouldn't have to worry about taking me into town for lessons."

That wasn't exactly how it worked, but she wasn't going to argue all the details. "I'll look into it, okay?"

He heaved a big sigh, large enough that she shifted her attention from the road to her son. "What's wrong?"

"You always say that. It's just a fancy way of saying no."

Was it? She pulled the car to a stop in her parents' drive and turned to face him completely. "I know how much this means to you," she said. "And I promise to look into it. You just get your work done. Deal?"

That sweet smile broke out, stretching across his face. "Deal." He got out of the car and stopped, his attention captured by the man and beast in the horse corral.

It was the most interest she had seen him give any one thing since they had arrived in Mississippi.

The horse reared up on its hind legs, snorted, then settled down on all four hooves once again.

"How does he do that?" Brandon asked in awe.

"It comes naturally to him," Hannah replied. "Always has."

Brandon shook his head. "But the horse—" He shook his head again. "It's so big. So strong."

He didn't have to finish the thought out loud. The horse could trample Aaron in the blink of an eye. Run away, overpower him, drag him for miles. But she didn't. She blew out a heavy breath and shook her mane.

"Beautiful," Brandon murmured.

Hannah smiled. "I'm sure he won't mind if you go watch."

"Really?" He grinned, looking so boyishly happy her heart melted. When he looked like that, it gave her hope. Hope that one day his shell would crack and she would see her boy again. At least in the man he would become.

"Really."

He wasted no time, heading across the yard and climbing onto the slatted wooden gate for a better look at the action.

Hannah watched him for a bit, then turned toward the house. Hope. It was a powerful thing, and after her conversation with her attorney, it was in very short supply.

Brandon shifted his weight on the narrow, wooden gate, but it didn't take away the sting. His butt was beginning to get numb, but he couldn't leave. He didn't want to. All he wanted to do was watch the man work with the spirited horse.

Everything about it intrigued him. The ripple of the horse's muscles. The calm way the man pulled her toward him, patted the horse's long, strong neck. The way she tossed her head as if to say, "I'll do what you say, but you haven't broken me entirely."

He knew how the beast felt. Everyone wanted to take him and shove him into a mold. They wanted him to be what they wanted him to be. They didn't care what he wanted, how he felt. They didn't listen to anything he had to say. Even his mom. She acted like she was listening, but she wasn't hearing him. And every day he felt more and more trapped.

But the horse . . .

She understood. And the man . . . Aaron? He understood as well. He didn't try to make the horse do something against her nature. He didn't try to control all her power; he allowed her to channel that strength. Yeah, *channel*. That was the right word. All the beauty, power, and grace were still there under the surface. The horse wasn't changed. She wasn't even controlled. She was simply tempered.

Why didn't adults treat kids like that? Why did it always have to be all or nothing? His dad was that way. He wanted things the way he wanted them, and he didn't care if Brandon had anything to say about it or not.

He loved his dad. He was his dad. But they were constantly butting heads. Constantly at each other's throats. Brandon felt as if his father hadn't even liked him. He might have loved him, but he hadn't liked who he was, what he liked, who he wanted to be. But now that he was gone . . .

Brandon pushed those thoughts from his mind and concentrated on the show before him. He bet Aaron didn't treat his kids that way. Not if he was so understanding with animals who couldn't talk. He would be understanding. He would listen. Brandon just knew it.

But his dad was dead now. His mom cried every night, and life would never be the same. To top it all off, he was stranded in Amish Land with no phone, no TV, and no computer except for the ancient paperweight at the public library.

But thinking about the library brought back memories of Shelly. She was like the horses that pulled the carriages: no trouble, always doing as she was told. But all these horses lived side by side, the good ones and the trouble makers. Maybe there was hope for him yet.

Yeah, he liked that idea.

"McLean!" He turned and shaded his eyes as a figure came into view.

"Gingerich."

His cousin waved with his left hand, and Brandon noticed that once again he carried a fishing pole—two fishing poles—and a bucket of worms. "Holding down the fence?"

"Yeah." No way was he telling his cousin how beautiful he thought the horse was. Or how interested he was in her training. If it was one of his friends from back home, Brandon would never hear the end of it. He wasn't sure how Joshua would respond, but he wasn't taking any chances.

"Well, get down from there. We have fish to catch."

Brandon gave the horse and man one last look, then swung his leg over the gate. Fishing sounded like a fine idea.

Chapter Thirteen

"Please tell me you aren't wearing that." Gracie came down the stairs, pointing toward Hannah's standard dress of jeans and a T-shirt.

"You have an unhealthy interest in my clothing, you know that?"

Gracie just grinned. "We are all going over to Sarah Hostetler's. All of us."

"Yeah, and?"

"And you will be the only one there dressed like . . . that."

Hannah crossed her arms and tapped one foot. "Putting me in an Amish dress and parading me in front of Aaron Zook is not going to change anything."

Gracie tsked. "This has nothing to do with Aaron, and everything to do with fitting in while you're here."

Fitting in? "I didn't fit in before I left. What makes you think I can fit in now?"

"Don't be like that. You should change and wear a dress, and you know it."

Hannah gave her jeans one last look, released a heavy sigh, and plodded up the stairs. She wanted to tell Gracie how wrong she was, but she couldn't find the words. Maybe because she wasn't entirely wrong. Maybe she should wear a dress to the frolic. She would certainly get fewer looks since she was dressed like everyone else. And fewer looks meant more would get done. For Sarah. She would wear a dress for Sarah. It was just one more way that she could help.

Aaron pulled into the Gingeriches' drive, barely getting the buggy stopped before his children opened the door and hopped out.

"Bye, Dat," Laura Kate called. Essie waved, but Andy made his way up the stairs without a backward glance.

Aaron returned her wave, then almost swallowed his own tongue as Hannah came out of the house. She was followed by Gracie, but Aaron only had eyes for Hannah.

How could one person look so different and still so much the same?

"Are you ready to go?" Gracie asked. She pulled herself up and wiggled her way into the back of the carriage before Aaron could even say hello.

"Hi." He centered his attention on Hannah. She was dressed in an Amish *frack* again today. His confusion was mounting. Not that it mattered. Ohio. He had to concentrate on Ohio and his dreams and plans for the future.

"Hi," she replied, pulling herself up and into the seat next to him. "Are you ready for this?"

"As ready as I'll ever be," he replied, and set the horse into motion around the circular drive that looped between the house and the barn.

"I'm really proud of Sarah," Gracie said.

Sarah was making right by herself, but Aaron knew how hard working for oneself could really be. He wouldn't want to see Gracie caught up in that. Why she had never married was a mystery to him. He hadn't heard any gossip about her seeing anyone. If she didn't get married she could very well find herself in the same situation as Sarah.

The motion of the carriage pushed him toward Hannah. Their shoulders brushed, and thoughts of Sarah Hostetler fled. Suddenly he was filled with nostalgia. Perhaps that was what this was all about. It wasn't that he loved Hannah still, but that he loved the idea of her, of first love and everything they had shared. He couldn't say that he wished he could go back. He couldn't minimize his life that way, yet he wondered how things might have been different. But there was no going back. God's will had prevailed. What was supposed to happen happened. Yet, he was only human.

Thankfully they were almost to the Hostetlers' farm. He didn't have time to dwell on the problem long.

Several buggies were already parked in the side yard, and another pulled in just behind them. Seemed most of the community had turned out to help. Aaron was glad Eunice had offered to keep his children so he could donate his time. He didn't get to do this much, get out and lend a hand. He'd been so busy lately trying to keep the farm going and take care of the kids, he'd almost become a recluse, keeping to himself and getting out only for church. That sort of life wasn't healthy.

They piled out of the buggy. Gracie smoothed her hands over her prayer *kapp* and glanced around the yard. "It looks like the men are getting ready to saw something."

"Shelves, I would imagine," Hannah said.

"I'll go see if I can lend a hand." Aaron tipped his chin at the girls, then sauntered away.

He had come here to help; so why did he want to get back in the buggy and whisk Hannah away to the swimming hole?

He shook his head at himself. Nostalgia, plain and

simple. He needed to get a handle on it, and quick. Before he did something he couldn't take back.

Hannah was impressed with the setup that Sarah had designed for herself. Hannah's own father had built the shed that housed the new shop. It was a commercial kitchen in the back, with a store-type setup in the front. People could come and watch Sarah make her candy as well as buy the yummy treats. The best part was that Sarah's three small children, all under the age of four, could be near her as she worked.

They painted boards, hung them as shelves, cleaned windows, and helped Sarah organize what would be her opening stock.

"So," Gracie asked midway through the frolic, "when's opening day?"

Sarah wiped a hand across her brow, then surveyed all that they had accomplished. "I'm hoping the day after tomorrow."

"That will be good." Hannah nodded, taking a step back to look at the items she had just neatly lined up on the shelf. "This place will be unique."

"Do you think?" Sarah's confidence had been slipping as the day progressed. When they had first arrived, she had looked completely sure of herself; now she more resembled a young child looking for parental support.

"I do."

Sarah practically wilted with relief. "Okay. Good."

"I think what you're doing is noble," Hannah said. She, more than anyone else at the frolic, knew what kind of courage it took to start over. But planning was one thing, and actually carrying those plans through another.

Sarah smiled prettily. "*Danki*. That means a lot to me."

But Hannah had questions. "Does this mean you're not going to get married again?"

Sarah shrugged one shoulder even as she shook her head. "I don't know what the Lord has planned for me, but I don't want to feel this way again. Like I can't take care of my children. Paul David . . ." She shook her head sadly. "He was a good husband and father, and I relied on him. Because of that, I have nothing to show for myself. I want to know that I can care for my family come what may."

"The church—" Hannah started, but Sarah shook her head.

"This is something I have to do for myself."

Hannah nodded. She understood. She had allowed Mitch to take care of everything, and because of that, she had nothing. All these years, and she didn't have any money in the bank. She had no home, a clunker of a car, no education. How was she supposed to keep Brandon on the right path if she was off in the weeds herself?

It was the first question she needed to answer before she could move forward at all.

Aaron wiped his forehead with a rag and settled his hat back into place. August in Mississippi was hot, and this year seemed worse than most. The old folks said that meant a bad winter, and Aaron would rather have the heat over ice any day.

"Are you about finished here?" Daniel Hostetler came up behind him and clasped Aaron on the shoulder.

He had known Daniel as long as he could remember. They had all run around together, made trips to Tennessee and somehow made their way to the church. Daniel was Sarah's brother-in-law, and had agreed to help today by feeding everyone once the frolic was complete.

Aaron looked to the shelf he'd just hung, trying to

decide if the brackets were crooked or the board was simply warped. Either way, it was a little off-kilter. "I just need to get this last shelf straight, and I'm done."

Daniel nodded. "I could use a hand at the grill."

"*Jah*, sure," Aaron said, even though the thought of standing behind a fire pit in this heat was enough to have more sweat beading under the brim of his hat.

Heat or not, he had enjoyed this afternoon. It was good to get away from his own farm. It was only an added bonus that he was able to help someone in need.

He had heard what Sarah had said to Hannah about needing to feel like she could support her family. He'd never really thought about it before, but Amish women in their community were dependent on their husbands to bring in most of the money. In Sarah's case, Paul David had brought in all their income. Aaron had been fortunate, he supposed. He was able to make a living and care for his children. He didn't have to get remarried for financial reasons, though he knew he should. If only for his children. There were times when they needed more than he could give. They needed a softer touch. Maybe that was why they had raced inside the Gingeriches' house, excited to spend the afternoon with Eunice.

Just one more vote for moving to Ohio. He couldn't imagine marrying any of the eligible women in Pontotoc. Actually, he couldn't imagine getting married at all, but moving and having new people to meet might make the task a bit easier.

He took a step back and eyed the adjustment. The board was warped, that was all there was to it. He straightened it as much as possible, then walked outside.

The exterior of the shed had been covered with white siding. The inside was left unpainted, and though most of it was newly milled wood, there were a couple of boards that had been reused from other projects. He could only hope that the sign at the road would have people turning in, driving down the lane to see what all Sarah had for sale. They were a simple people and didn't try to be anything other than what they were. There were no bright colors, swirly letters, or other gimmicks to get people to turn in. Sarah would need prayer upon prayer to get her business started.

One last look at the work they had put in today and Aaron headed over to the grill, where Daniel already had coals burning.

It might be entirely too hot to cook over an open fire, but he was glad he came out today. He glanced over to where Hannah stood talking to the other women.

So glad.

"Hey."

Hannah started as Aaron dropped down onto the grass next to her. She had filled her plate with a hamburger and beans and had made her way to the shade to wait for Gracie.

She had never expected that Aaron would show up first.

"Have I told you that you look very nice in that dress?"

She looked down at the Amish *frack* she had worn for the occasion. Funny how she had donned the dress and felt strange for about ten minutes. Since then she hadn't given it a second thought. "'This old thing? Why, I only wear it when I don't care how I look.'"

"What?" Aaron frowned.

Hannah shook her head. "It's from a movie."

"Oh." Aaron set his plate on the ground in front of him, then picked it up again as if he wasn't quite sure what to do with himself.

"Thank you," Hannah said.

Aaron looked up and met her gaze, his expression puzzled.

"For the compliment. I wasn't sure if I should wear this today, but Gracie said I should, and—"

As if conjured by the sound of her voice, Gracie rounded the tree under which they sat, looked from one of them to the other, and started backing away.

Thankfully, Aaron's back was to her, and he didn't see her quick escape.

Hannah shook her head. But Gracie scooted away before she could voice any sort of protest.

"Is everything okay?" he asked.

Hannah took a drink of her lemonade and smiled as if all was right with the world. "Of course. What could be wrong?"

He turned to look behind him, but Gracie was already gone. He faced front again, a frown still lingering.

"It's Gracie," Hannah admitted.

"What about her?" He took a bite of his burger and chewed as he waited for her answer.

"I really do think she's trying to get us together."

"Is your entire family into matchmaking?"

"Probably." Her gaze met his, and they started to laugh.

"Why is that, do you suppose?" he finally asked.

Hannah shrugged. "Maybe they think love will make me stay." Maybe she should have used a word other than *love*, but it was already out there, and she couldn't bring it back now.

"And will it?"

Her conversation with Sarah Hostetler rose to her mind. "No," she quietly said. She couldn't allow love to make all her decisions. Love had kept her away, but she knew that there was more to it than that. Like Sarah, she had to know that she could make it on her own. She hadn't been without anyone in a long time. When she had left Pontotoc, she'd had Leah. Then Mitch. Now that he was gone, she was on her own. She had to get back out there and live, knowing that she could care for herself without the help of anyone else.

It was as if a shade had dropped over his eyes. The blue darkened, covered by unreadable shadows. "I see." He cleared his throat. "I mean, I understand."

She shook her head. "No, you probably don't, but that's okay."

"Then explain it to me."

Hannah finished what she wanted of her burger and set her plate to one side. Eating everything on her plate was one habit she had broken years ago. She had saved herself hundreds of calories and miles and miles on the treadmill. "When I left here, I only wanted to see what the *Englisch* world was really like. I wanted to make it there, as they say. But that has never happened. I let my husband control everything, and because of that, I didn't succeed at all."

"And you still want that?" he asked.

"I need to know that I can do it."

He reached for her hand, but pulled away before he actually touched her. "I understand."

"You do?"

He nodded. "I do, but promise me one thing?"

"I'll try," she said around the lump in her throat.

"Promise me that we'll always be friends."

She gave him a trembling smile. "I promise."

Chapter Fourteen

After everyone ate and the mess was cleaned up, a friendly game of kickball started. That was another thing she missed about the Amish. Everyone knew that they worked hard, but they also knew how to enjoy themselves. How many volleyball games, softball games, and other spur-of-the-moment activities had she and Aaron been a part of when they were younger? Too many to count.

Aaron pointed to the game. "Do you want to play?"

No matter how much she tried to keep her distance, it seemed that every time she turned around, there he was. It was as if God was pushing them together. Or maybe that was just what she wanted to believe.

God wasn't trying to get them together; Gracie was.

Hannah shook her head. "I'm worn out. I'm ready to go home, but I can't find Gracie. Have you seen her?"

"No. Have you checked with Sarah? The last time I saw her she was looking for Sarah."

"I'll check." But Hannah had the sinking suspicion that something was not exactly right with the entire situation.

"There she is."

"Gracie?" Hannah asked, craning her neck around to see where Aaron had pointed.

"No. Sarah." He waved her over as Hannah tried to keep level about the situation. If what she thought had happened had actually happened, then . . .

"Hi, Sarah," Aaron started. "Hannah is looking for Gracie. Have you seen her?"

Her forehead wrinkled into a small frown, but it disappeared as quickly as it came. "She just left."

"She what?" Hannah did her best to keep her voice to a normal level.

"She . . . left . . ." Sarah repeated, slower this time. "She asked me to let you know." She cast her glance toward Aaron, then lowered her voice, leaning closer to better be heard. "She had a problem with her dress." The last word was barely audible.

"She did."

Sarah nodded, totally missing the sarcasm in Hannah's tone. "She had Lavina King take her back home so you wouldn't be without a ride."

Hannah managed not to cross her arms and glare down her nose. It wasn't Sarah's fault that Gracie thought this would somehow push her and Aaron together.

Could that really be her plan? Hannah mentally shook her head. No. It was too far-fetched. Gracie could have faked a problem with her dress, but that didn't mean it would force Hannah and Aaron together.

Except that they had all ridden to the frolic together.

She turned to Aaron. "I guess it's just you and me."

He nodded. "It seems so."

Sarah clasped Hannah's hands and squeezed her fingers. "Thank you so much for coming out today. Thank you both."

"You're welcome," they murmured together.

Sarah smiled, then moved away to talk to someone else about to leave.

Aaron sighed. "I guess we should go."

"Yes."

Why did it feel so weird to be walking beside him? They were just riding back to her house. It wasn't like they were on a date. But how many times had they ridden just like this so many years ago? More than she could count. But this time it was different. They were just friends.

He helped her into the buggy, then slid in next to her. Would it be too strange if she sat in the back? Maybe. She rode beside him all the way here, but that had been another matter entirely. Gracie had been in the seat behind them. Sure, Hannah had been very aware of Aaron and every breath he took, but there had been an audience. Now it was just the two of them.

He set the horse into motion. The buggy lurched to the right. Hannah braced one hand against the side of the buggy to keep from falling into his lap.

"Sorry," he mumbled and urged the horse toward more level ground.

Aaron waved to a couple of people as he drove away, and Hannah felt obligated to do the same, though she saw no faces. All her concentration was centered on the man next to her.

She was being ridiculous. Yes, there had been a time when she and Aaron had shared a pure love. But she had ruined that with her curious and impulsive nature. There was no getting it back.

"Do you remember the time that David found the baby squirrel in the woods?"

She hadn't thought about that in years. She smiled with the memory. "And he brought it home because he thought he would start a squirrel farm."

Aaron chuckled. "He built that huge pen for him."

"Then Leah set it free."

Aaron sobered. "Have you talked to Leah since you ret—got back?"

"No." She had been meaning to contact her sister, but she had limited means. Brandon's cell phone was dead the majority of the time, and when it wasn't Brandon had it, texting or playing games.

And then there was the matter of she didn't know what to say to her sister.

They had talked since their argument. But it would be the first time she had talked to Leah in a while.

Argument was such an understatement. Twins shouldn't fight like that, yelling and screaming at each other, but they had that night, and it had changed the course of their relationship forever.

But the real truth was that she hadn't put much energy into contacting her sister. Not since her return. She didn't want to rehash all the mistakes she had made. And though Leah would never say it, Hannah didn't want to see *I told you so* shining in her eyes.

"Sorry. I just thought—" Aaron didn't have to finish; she knew what he was going to say. They had been so close back in the day, but things had changed.

"It's okay." She shot him a comforting smile. "You know, we're never going to get past this if we keep apologizing every five minutes."

"Sor—" He shook his head with a small grin. "Is that what we're trying to do? Get past this?"

"If we're going to be friends, then don't you think that's the best way?"

"I suppose." But he shrugged one shoulder, then grew quiet as if in deep thought.

They rode along in silence, then he emitted a low growl and steered the carriage to the side of the road. Thankfully they were at the mouth of a small side road and were a little more protected than if they hadn't been.

"Aaron?"

He turned in his seat to face her. "If we're moving past this—" He shook his head. "Then there's something I need to know."

Hannah's mouth grew dry. "What's that?"

"Why did you leave?"

She opened her mouth to answer, but he cut her short.

"Please don't give me the answer you gave your parents."

Her heart pounded in her ears. "I really just wanted to see what was out there."

"So you took off without leaving a note or anything."

"I was afraid that if I told you where I was going, then you would follow me."

"If I had, would it have made a difference?" His gaze bored right through her. It was as if he could see every part of her, every emotion, every thought, every atom of her being.

"Yes," she whispered.

When had he moved so close? She could easily touch his face, run her fingers along his cheek, test the wiry curls that made up his beard. And she did. He felt just as he had all those years ago. How could she remember that? She didn't know, but it was there all the same.

"Hannah," he breathed and moved closer still.

He was going to kiss her . . . and there was nothing she could do about it. Not that she wanted to. If he felt the same, then surely his kiss would be the same as well. She had to find out. She needed to know. For the sake of comparison. Yeah, that was it. Just an experiment to test the memory.

Her eyes fluttered shut and his lips met hers.

His kiss was the same and yet infinitely different. When

he had kissed her before he had been a boy, a little unsure of himself, eager and seeking. This kiss was all that and more. Now there was a wisdom in his kiss that hadn't been there before. A wisdom that came with living. And he had lived that life without her.

She wouldn't feel bad about that. She couldn't, but sometimes she wished . . .

Sometimes she wished a lot of things. But she only had here. And now. She only had this moment in time with him. He was moving to Ohio. She had to prove it to herself that she could stand on her own two feet. Just as before, they had different goals, different dreams, even though every breath pulled them closer together.

But for now, she had this kiss . . .

He abruptly pulled away, his breathing as ragged as her own.

"I shouldn't have done that."

Her lips tingled where his had been. She wished he hadn't have done that too, and she wished that he hadn't stopped.

This was more than confusing.

She shook her head, more to rattle her thoughts back into some semblance of order than to say no. The action didn't work. "No regrets," she finally said. "We have too many of those already."

He blew out a breath as if only then realizing that he had been holding it. "Do you? Regret it?"

There were so many things she regretted in her life, more than she wanted to admit. Leaving Pontotoc, that was at the top of the list. And yet it had made her who she was today.

Uneducated, broke, widowed.

She pushed that voice aside. "I have more regrets than you will ever know." But that kiss wasn't one of them.

"What do we do about that?"

"I have no idea."

He looked out the front of the buggy, leaving her to stare at his profile. That alone told her how things had changed. Every time she wanted to believe that they might be able to be friends, she was sorely reminded that he wasn't the same person he had been back then. And now, more and more, she was understanding that the shift in him was all her fault.

"When I see you dressed like that, I tend to forget the last fifteen years." He kept his gaze trained on the road ahead. "No, that's not really true either. When I see you dressed like that, the past and the present seem to merge into one and everything else becomes blurry and gray. Then I find it hard to remember all the reasons why we can't be together."

"I understand," she said, but still he didn't turn to look at her.

"But there's this part of me," he said, his teeth clenched, "there's this part of me that wants to know for certain, no speculation, as to whether or not we still have something between us."

If the kiss they just shared was any indication, then there was definitely something still between them. A lot of something.

"What if there is?" she asked.

He turned back to her then, blue eyes blazing. "Then I can't see throwing it away a second time."

Aaron watched as the emotions chased across her face. There were fear, desire, curiosity, and something else he couldn't name.

"What then?"

It could never be easy. She was *Englisch*; he was Amish.

There was no middle ground to meet in. It would have to be one or the other. "I don't know."

She nodded.

The kiss they had just shared had been more than fantastic. It was the stuff dreams were made of. And he wanted to kiss her again and again until they knew for certain what God had planned for them.

Or would another kiss just muddle his thinking and keep him from seeing God's real plan?

"Can we just see?" he asked. "Give it a try. Spend a little time together. There's no sense making plans for the future if there's not to be a future for the two of us."

But the opposite could be said as well. How could they revive a relationship if there was no way for them to be together in the end?

But he wanted to spend time with her. He wanted to see if these feelings were real or just a trick of the mind.

A car horn sounded behind them. Aaron shoved his arm out the buggy window and motioned for them to go around.

"How will this work?" Hannah asked once the car was out of sight and the dust had cleared.

"Maybe we spend two nights a week together. Supper at your house, then supper at mine." It was a lame idea, but the best he could come up with for now. There would be more work frolics, picnics, and after-church activities to come, but they all had a bigger audience. They should start off slow, with only family witnessing their experiment.

"What about Brandon?"

She was a package deal. He knew that, but he wasn't sure what to do about it. "He can come, of course. If he wants to. But don't make him if he doesn't."

"And your kids?"

"Same thing. In fact, the less we keep them involved, the easier it might be on them if things—" He stopped.

"If things don't work out," she finished.

"*Jah.*" There was always that possibility. In fact, that possibility seemed greater than any other.

What are you doing? Do you honestly think this has a chance?

He did and he didn't, but there was one thing that he knew for certain. If they didn't give it a try, they would never know. He'd spent over fifteen years wondering about could-have-beens. He was ready to see them through.

"Gracie," Hannah called as she entered the house a bit later. Without any more than a quick touch to the hand, Aaron had gathered up his kids and headed home.

Strange, but Gracie, so often right in the thick of things, was nowhere around.

"Gracie," she called again, louder this time.

"Hannah Mae, what is all this hollering about?" Mamm bustled out of the kitchen, cheeks as pink as always from the heat inside.

"I need to talk to Gracie about something." Hannah did her best to keep her emotions under control. She wasn't so much angry with her cousin as she was put out. She had to believe that she and Aaron would find their way together if that was meant to be, and they didn't need Gracie meddling in their lives, making things happen before their time.

She stopped short. When had she started believing in God's will again? Sometime in the last couple of days. Maybe when she realized that she had come back to Pontotoc for a reason. And that reason was Aaron Zook. It had to be. Why else would God have put her through the trials of her relationship with Mitch, if not to give her a second chance with Aaron?

The idea made her light-headed. The last few days had

been some of the best in her life. She hadn't realized the kind of stress she had been under until it was removed. They still had stress in the Amish community, and it was real, but it paled in comparison to the pressures the *Englisch* subjected themselves to.

Now she was here and testing out a second chance with the one person she had never stopped loving. Yes, she could admit it now. Or maybe she couldn't deny it any longer, not after that blazing kiss on the roadside, but she loved Aaron Zook. She always had, and she always would. But she had seen enough good relationships turn bad that she knew it took more than love to keep two people together. Besides, Aaron hadn't said that he loved her. She couldn't get her hopes up before there was some potential.

"Gracie!"

"Hannah, really," Mamm said. She turned on her heel and headed back to the kitchen.

"Gra—oh, there you are."

Her cousin appeared from the direction of the *dawdihaus,* blinking innocently at Hannah. "What's wrong?"

"What are you doing? Leaving me at the frolic."

Gracie gave a delicate shrug. "I had a problem with my dress, and it wasn't like I left you without a ride."

"Beside the point. What sort of problem?"

"Oh, you know . . ." She hem-hawed around.

"No, actually, I don't."

"It was the seams or something." She waved a hand about, her answer vague enough for Hannah to truly know that she was lying.

Hannah expelled a heavy breath. "Listen, I appreciate what I think you're trying to do, but Aaron and I need to work this out for ourselves."

"And did you?" Gracie asked.

"Did we what?"

"Work this out for yourselves?"

Hannah paused for a moment. "We've got a plan. From there we'll just have to see how it goes."

Gracie gave a quick nod, a smile playing with the corners of her lips. "Well, then, you're welcome." She spun around and left the room, Hannah staring after her gape-mouthed. Where had her mild-mannered cousin gone? She might never know, but despite her concerns about Gracie's interference, her cousin had gotten her and Aaron onto the right track. They had made a plan to see if they could continue their relationship once again. That might not have happened if it hadn't been for Gracie.

"Thanks," Hannah called toward her departing back. She might have felt it in her heart, but her tone was far from gracious.

Aaron arrived the next morning at ten o'clock on the dot. Hannah knew because she was watching at the living room window. Yes, she could admit it now, but she wasn't going to rush out and greet him. In fact she wasn't going out to talk to him at all. She didn't want to appear too eager, and she certainly didn't want him to think that she had gone off the deep end.

"Are you watching Aaron?" Gracie asked from behind her.

Hannah jumped in her seat. "Gracie! Quit sneaking up on people."

"I'm not sneaking up on people. Just you."

Hannah turned back around. "Ha. Ha."

Gracie peered over her shoulder. "You are watching Aaron."

No way was she making a big deal out of this. "Sure. Watching him train a horse is like watching a ballet."

Gracie straightened and pulled a face. "I've never seen a ballet."

"Well, they are beautiful. Flowing movements, graceful steps. Even without music they would be breathtaking." And that was exactly what Aaron training Star was: a ballet without music. Breathtaking.

"Are you going to sit here and just watch him?"

Hannah nodded, but some of the beauty had gone out of the day. *Ballet.* If she came back home to her Amish roots, she wouldn't see another ballet. It wasn't like she adored ballet and couldn't live without it, but to know that she could never have that experience again . . . well, it made her stop and think. How many other things would she miss? How important were they to her? Would their importance increase when faced with being without them for the rest of her life?

"What's wrong?" Gracie asked.

Hannah shook her head. "Nothing." But it was far from the truth. She needed to take this slow with Aaron. Coming back to the Amish would be a chore in itself and not something to be taken lightly.

"That look on your face says otherwise."

Hannah mulled over what she could say to her cousin and still tell the truth without giving away all of her fears. "Sometimes I wonder about all the things that could have happened. You know, between me and Aaron."

Gracie gave a quick shake of her head. "You shouldn't do that. Looking at the past will not change anything, and it certainly won't bring you any joy."

But a future with Aaron would?

And what about Ohio? Had he given up that dream? Why, oh, why hadn't she thought of all these things before now? *Because you didn't want to admit the truth.* Coming back home would be trickier than she could ever imagine.

They might still be able to give their relationship a second chance, but they needed to talk over a few more things first. And it would be best if her mind was clear and her thoughts not muddled from the aftereffects of his heady kiss.

Training wasn't going exactly as he had planned. It was widely known that Aaron had a special touch when it came to horses, but no one knew that when he had other women on his mind, the mares tended to fight back rather than comply.

It wasn't like he was allowing Hannah into his thoughts. He lost concentration for a split second, and there she was.

He had been a little surprised that he hadn't seen her all morning. He half expected her to come out and welcome him. But he'd been there almost an hour and he hadn't seen any sign of her. He decided if he was going to see her it would be up to him to seek her out.

Deciding to cut his losses, he slipped the bridle over Star's head and directed her back to the pasture.

"Aaron?"

He whirled around as Hannah came striding across the yard toward him. She looked determined, focused, but she stopped short as if she had only then realized she was practically running toward him. "Hi, Hannah."

"Do you . . . do you have a minute?" Today she was back in jeans and a T-shirt. Had she dressed that way on purpose? Was she trying to confuse him, or was she truly that confused herself? He could imagine how she felt, one foot in both worlds, but he had never stood in her shoes. He didn't know, could only speculate. But her position couldn't be easy.

"Of course. Do you want to walk?"

She turned back toward the house as if the answer were written somewhere there. "Yeah. I think that would be nice."

They started toward the road, the garden on one side and a field of corn on the other.

"What's on your mind, Hannah?"

She shoved her hands into the front pockets of her jeans and shrugged. "Yesterday . . ."

He waited for her to continue.

"Well, I think we may have acted a little prematurely."

He frowned, but otherwise kept pace beside her. "How so?"

"What about Ohio?"

This time he stumbled a bit, her words taking him off guard. He hadn't thought about much else than her, the two of them, and kissing her again. The magic that existed between them, a God-given gift of attraction and love. "I don't know," he finally managed to say. He hadn't been thinking about Ohio—only about Hannah and that spectacular kiss.

They rounded the bend that took them just out of sight of the house. Aaron stopped, needing to look at her as they talked.

"What does that mean?" Hannah asked.

"It means I don't know."

"If I decide to . . . stay," Hannah started, "I won't move to Ohio. I can't. My family is here."

He nodded. "I understand." And he did.

"But you want to move there."

He shrugged. "I've considered it."

"What's holding you here?" she asked.

"I don't know." He looked around at all the familiar sights. "This is all I know. Sometimes I think that's good, and sometimes I think there has to be more."

A knowing light dawned in her eyes. "That's something I can surely understand."

He nodded. Hadn't she said almost the same thing just a few short days ago? "What do we do?"

"We have to decide what we want." She sighed. "You have to decide about Ohio." She turned her face to the blue, blue sky. "I'm not trying to make you choose between me and Ohio. But if Ohio is what you truly want, I'd rather you go before my heart is too involved."

He nodded again. It was really all he could do. It wasn't fair of him to ask her to move. But how could he go to Ohio without her? All last night he had smiled, thinking about the two of them together. A second chance was intoxicating.

But today that elation was gone.

"Do we just take a couple of days and think about it?" he asked.

"Yeah, I guess that's the best way."

"Saturday?"

"What?" She seemed to rouse herself from somewhere far away.

"Saturday. We can take a picnic down to the pond. The kids can play, and we can talk."

"I thought we were going to keep them out of this."

"It's one day, Hannah."

"You're right." She gave a quick nod. "Saturday it is."

Chapter Fifteen

Hannah walked side by side with Aaron back to the house. Her heart and her steps were heavy, even as she told herself this was for the best. She had no business getting involved with anyone. Even re-involved with anyone. There was too much at stake, too much happening in her life, too many unresolved issues.

They could tell themselves all they wanted that they were making a decision, but she knew they were just avoiding the inevitable.

Once back at the house, Aaron hitched up his horse and headed home. He gave Hannah a small, friendly wave and it occurred to her then that the small gesture was indicative of their relationship. Small and friendly. That was all it could ever be.

Hannah watched as he disappeared around the bend, then made her way into the house. Shortly she would have to drive into town to pick up Brandon from his lessons. She should have just stayed in town with him, but she had wanted to come back and see Aaron.

With a shake of her head, she made her way up the steps and into the house.

"What's wrong?" Gracie sat on the couch crocheting something out of a skein of heavy black yarn.

"Nothing," Hannah mumbled. Suddenly she felt tired. So very tired. Maybe even exhausted. She wanted to lie down on the couch, close her eyes, and not wake up for a long time.

"Now, I don't believe that for a minute." Gracie set her yarn and needle to one side and eyed her closely.

Hannah squirmed under such scrutiny.

"Why are you wearing jeans today? I thought you were stay—I mean, starting to enjoy your dresses again."

"This has nothing to do with my clothes."

"I think differently." Gracie fidgeted, but didn't pick up her crocheting again.

"Being here is confusing," Hannah finally admitted. It was more than confusing. When she walked into her mother's kitchen, she was hit with so many good memories, she could almost taste them. Christmas cookies, summer canning, fall canning, jams, pickles, tomatoes. Baking bread and all the other chores she had performed over the years. Except she had never appreciated them at the time. She had done anything and everything to get out of the work. The *Englisch* didn't do such things. If they needed a can of tomatoes, they went to the store and bought one. They didn't plan months in advance, till and plow a plot, plant seeds, water, pull weeds, and watch the plants grow. And they surely didn't pick them, wash them, clean and can them. But the tomatoes were fresh. There was no worry of growth hormones or GMOs, preservatives or pesticides.

Who was coming out ahead on this one?

Being back in Pontotoc was more than memories of her family. There were memories of so much more. But life was a great deal harder in Pontotoc. Could she give up all the creature comforts in order to regain those precious memories of her youth?

But what about you? Don't you need to prove yourself? You've never done anything for yourself. Now's your chance.

"Hannah." Gracie's tone suggested that this wasn't the first time she had called Hannah's name.

"Yes?"

"What's so confusing?"

Hannah wanted to sob with frustration. "Everything." Or maybe that was her life in general. "Aaron . . ." She shook her head. "You know, for a while there I thought we might have a second chance. But I was only seeing what I wanted to see. He's got Ohio, and I've got Brandon."

"I'm not sure I understand."

"It's okay," Hannah said with a sage nod. "I don't understand it myself. But it's over."

"What's over?"

"Me and Aaron. Before we could even give it a chance. We just want different things and have different obligations. Too much stands in our way."

Gracie shook her head with an exasperated sigh and retrieved her yarn. "That's the dumbest thing I've ever heard." A flush of pink rose into her cheeks. "I'm sorry to be so harsh, but really, Hannah. Are you going to let every detail of your life stand in your way?"

If only she knew.

"It's more complicated than that."

"That's what everyone says. And it's only complicated because you say it is. It's only complicated if you allow it to be."

Hannah was struck dumb. Was she letting her own thoughts get in her way? And what could she do about it?

"We're giving each other time to think."

"About what?"

"What we want from our lives, separately and together. We're going to talk about it Saturday afternoon."

"And you're not going to talk about it until then?"

Hannah shook her head. "No. I need time to think."

"About what?" Gracie asked again.

"It's complicated." Sometimes talking to her cousin was like beating her head against a brick wall.

"So you've said."

"You don't think that's a good idea?"

"I suppose it doesn't matter what I think, but if I had a second chance with a man like Aaron Zook, I would spend all my time convincing him that we were a match made in heaven above."

"What's this I hear about you giving up on Aaron Zook?" The screen door slammed behind Tillie as she came out onto the porch.

Hannah rolled her eyes and stopped swinging long enough for Tillie to sit down next to her. "Don't say that so loud. You know how Mamm is."

"Maybe I want her to hear."

"It won't work, you know."

Tillie cast her an innocent look. "What won't work?"

"You can't use Mamm to convince me to see Aaron."

"Can you blame us for wanting you to stay?"

"How can you say that when you are thinking about leaving yourself?"

Tillie ducked her head and held one finger to her lips. "Shhh . . . don't say that so loud."

Hannah gave her a self-satisfied look and started the swing once more. "'Sauce for the goose,'" Hannah quoted.

Tillie's expression turned to one of vague confusion. "I've never understood what that means. Don't geese and ganders taste the same? Wouldn't the same sauce be equally yummy on both?"

Hannah stifled a laugh. "It means what's good for you is good for me." Sort of, but she wasn't going into the gender implications with Tillie. This was enough for one day.

"Well, anyway." Tillie sniffed. "Aaron's a good man, and I can't imagine why you wouldn't want to be with him."

"No one said I didn't want to be with him, sister."

"Then what's the problem?"

"How long do you have?" Hannah sighed. "Mainly, I have Brandon, and Aaron wants to move to Ohio."

"Ohio?" Tillie was on her feet in a second. "He can't move to Ohio. He'll hate it there."

"How do you know? You've never been to Ohio."

"Well, I've heard talk, and he would hate it there. You have to keep him here, Hannah. You just have to."

Hannah didn't bother to tell her sister that she didn't have to do anything of the sort. When Tillie got something in her head, it was hard to get her off track. She had been that way as long as Hannah could remember.

"Hannah?"

She focused her attention away from her feet and onto her sister.

"Promise me you'll go talk to him."

"Tillie, I—"

"Promise me."

Hannah shook her head. "Is this just another attempt to get me to spend time with him?"

"What difference does it make?" Tillie threw her hands into the air in that dramatic way that only Tillie could perform. "He needs to be talked out of it, and you need to talk to him. Sounds like a perfect plan to me."

Hannah opened her mouth to protest, but Tillie cut in. "Just get over there and don't come home until he promises to stay in Pontotoc."

* * *

This was utterly ridiculous. Hannah sighed as she turned the buggy into the drive leading to Aaron's house. What was she supposed to say to him? She guessed the truth might be the best thing, but how would it sound? *Hi, Aaron, I'm only over here because Tillie thinks I should talk you out of moving to Ohio. She says it's for you, but I strongly suspect it's so I'll stay in Mississippi. How crazy is that?*

Totally cray cray.

Definitely not something that Aaron would ever say.

He came out of the barn as she pulled up. He had her horse tethered before she even crawled out of the buggy.

"Amish again?" he asked with a pointed look at her dress.

She ran her hands down herself, smoothing imaginary wrinkles. She wasn't sure why she'd donned her Amish garb. Only that she was more comfortable driving a buggy in Amish clothing.

Then why didn't you bring your car?

She pushed that voice aside and concentrated on the man before her.

"I'm here to deliver a message of sorts."

He nodded, a light of disappointment shining in his eyes for just a moment before it disappeared.

"It seems that Tillie is concerned that you will hate it in Ohio, and I needed to come tell you."

"Matchmaking again?"

She nodded. "I believe so, yes, but she was really adamant that you wouldn't like it up North."

He looked off over his field as if the answers were hidden there, positive proof of the right thing to do. "I suppose not, but the opportunity is good."

"I understand."

She made as if to get back into her buggy, but he stopped her, clasping her forearm in strong, warm fingers. "That's it?"

Hannah looked down at his hand, then back up into those smoky blue eyes. "That's it. Now I can go back and say I did the best I could."

"Best you could about what?"

"Talking to you about staying in Mississippi." She looked down at his hand once again.

He didn't remove his fingers. "You call that the best you can do?"

She shook her head and pulled her arm from his grasp. Thankfully, he let her go. If she was going to get through this, she couldn't have him touching and grabbing her all willy-nilly. "It's not about real effort. It's about making Tillie believe that I gave it real effort."

"Why the deception?"

Hannah sighed. "Because I know how much working with horses means to you. I can't stand in the way of that."

A quick light flashed in his eyes, but it was there and gone before she could figure out what it was. "But what if she's right?"

"I'm sorry?" Hannah shifted her weight and crossed her arms.

"What if she's right, and I hate Ohio?"

"You mean you haven't been there?"

He shook his head. "There never seemed to be time."

Hannah thought about it a moment. "Just when did this man contact you?"

"May," he admitted. "Just before school was out. I couldn't go then. After that, there was more planting, and the children were home. I didn't want to take them with me."

"And you didn't want to leave them here," Hannah finished for him. "Have you ever wondered that you keep making all these excuses because deep down you really don't want to go?"

"No," he said without hesitation. Almost too quickly. "Of course not."

"Then go up there."

"What?" He stopped, waiting for her reply.

"Go on up to Ohio and visit. The kids can stay with us. You already know that they like being with Mamm. It's the perfect solution."

He seemed to think about it a good long while. Then finally he gave a small nod. "I guess you're right."

"I know I'm right." She flashed him a quick smile to take the sting from her words.

Aaron watched as Hannah got into the buggy and headed for home. What had he just agreed to? Had he lost all his good sense?

He must if he was really going through with this. Taking a trip to Ohio to see what it was like. How was he really going to know? He would only be there for a little while, just a few short days, maybe a week. He couldn't know how the weather changed, how it affected the horses, if at all. But he supposed there were a few things he could learn. How the community was set up, if it was convenient or a hassle, if the folks were friendly, and if the land was good.

He couldn't go up there assuming he would be able to work with horses exclusively. It might be his dream and this might be a good starting point, but he would definitely need another trade until he could build up his training business. Farming was about the only other thing he knew.

"Dat, why are you standing there staring off at nothing?"

He pulled himself from his thoughts and centered them on Andy.

"Just thinking," he said. "Where are the girls?"

Andy gestured over his shoulder to the house. "Teacher gave them paper dolls today. They're inside coloring their clothes."

They must have been excited if they ran right past him without even stopping. Or maybe they had been so eager they didn't notice him as much as he didn't notice them.

Aaron directed him onto the porch and the plain wooden bench sitting there. "Can I talk to you about something, son?"

The words must have been exactly what Andy needed to hear. He puffed out his chest and settled down next to him. "Sure, Dat."

"I've been giving a lot of thought to Ohio."

"I know that."

"Today I came up with a new plan."

"*Jah?*"

"I'm going to go up there and see what it's like. Just stay a few days, then come home. I think I need to get a feel for the place before I commit to moving there."

Andy gave a serious nod. "That's a good idea. When are we leaving?"

"Well, that's the thing. I need you to stay with Eunice and Abner while I'm gone."

Andy's face fell. "But . . ." He stuttered, unable to express his true feelings and maintain his ingrained level of respect. "I don't want to stay with them," he finally managed.

"I thought you liked them."

"I do, but that doesn't mean I want to stay with them." He shook his head. "They don't have a lot of room, and their *mammi* has a broken hip."

"I do need to go."

Andy nodded. "I understand."

"And you can't go with me." He needed time to check things out without having his children bickering and running around. Or maybe he just needed a break. Whatever it was . . .

"Why can't we stay here? I'm old enough to stay by myself." Andy's voice was leaning very much toward a whine, but Aaron didn't mind. This was the best conversation they'd had since school let out in the summer. Aaron wasn't sure what had happened, but just after the last day of school, Andy had turned sullen and cranky. He couldn't say his son was full-fledged angry, but he was unhappy, and he didn't care to hide it.

"I know that," Aaron agreed. "But do you really want to stay here with your two sisters? All alone? With them asking you for every little thing?"

Andy's face turned from stubborn to horrified. Just the reaction that Aaron wanted. "Can someone stay with us?"

"I don't know who." All of their family, what they had left of it anyway, was back in Ethridge.

"Abner's Hannah." Andy's face lit up like the fireworks the city shot off each Fourth of July.

"I don't think—"

"She's nice, and I bet she wouldn't mind."

She probably wouldn't, but would that be asking too much from an almost-friend? "I don't know, son."

"Please, Dat."

Aaron could feel his resolve slipping despite his vow to remain strong.

"Please."

He shook his head. "You can ask her," he finally said.

Andy jumped to his feet and pumped one fist in the air.

"Hold on," Aaron said. "You can ask her, but that doesn't mean she'll say yes."

His son grinned, showing the spaces on each side of

his mouth where teeth were missing. The new adult teeth had just broken the skin, the small peaks of white barely visible. "She'll say yes," he said with supreme confidence. "I know she will."

Of course Hannah said yes, and Aaron started planning out his trip to Ohio.

"I think it's sort of romantic," Gracie said, plopping the laundry basket on the ground between them.

"There's nothing romantic about it at all," Hannah groused. Gracie had a tendency to make more out of things than needed making. "I'm going over there to stay with his children so he can go to Ohio." And decide where his life should be. Nothing romantic about that at all.

"It is." Gracie snatched up the first shirt and practically danced it around in a circle.

"Seriously, cousin." Gracie needed to get her head out of the clouds before she wound up with a broken heart. Or worse. What had happened to pragmatic Gracie?

"Oh, pooh." Gracie gave an exaggerated pout, then began to hang the clothes on the line. "The closer you are, the more chance that something can happen between the two of you."

Hannah had mulled over that very prospect. But it could only be if Aaron decided not to move to Ohio and Brandon would agree to stay in Pontotoc. She wasn't even sure that was possible. Well, he could agree to stay, but she wasn't sure what the bishop might think of that. Hannah couldn't imagine her tech-loving son being able to give up his phone and other devices to get back to basic living with her family. It just didn't seem possible. If he didn't convert, she couldn't see the bishop allowing him to stay in an Amish home indefinitely.

And so her thoughts went around in a circle. She couldn't allow Brandon to be on his own, and that left years before she could go back to the church. If she even decided that she wanted to.

"What are you thinking about?" Gracie asked.

Hannah shrugged and grabbed another shirt for the line. "Nothing really."

"That sounded like a lie if I have ever heard one."

"I think Aaron is an amazing man," Hannah started.

"I knew it." Gracie jumped up and down in place.

"I might even be in love with him." She was, no doubt about it.

"I *knew* it," Gracie squealed.

"But there are too many obstacles that stand in our way."

Gracie's jubilant mood immediately fell. "You're not even going to give this a try?"

"Just so I can get my heart broken? No, thank you."

"But . . . but . . . but . . ." Gracie sputtered.

"There are no buts."

"Then why is he going to Ohio?"

Hannah retrieved another shirt and pinned it to the line. "He's going to Ohio to see if he likes it there."

"And if he does?"

Just the thought sent Hannah's heart plummeting to her feet. "Then he'll move there."

"And if he doesn't?"

"Then he'll come back here, I guess."

"And ask you to marry him?"

Hannah shook her head. "I wish it were that simple. I really do. But even if he asked me tomorrow, I wouldn't be able to marry Aaron Zook."

"Why not?" Gracie's words were muffled around the two clothespins stuck in her mouth.

"Let's see. The biggest is I'm not a member of the

church." But she couldn't become one if Brandon wouldn't be allowed to stay with her. How could she do that to her only child? She couldn't. Plain and simple. Only her love for him could play a part in that decision.

But she had made her choice years ago. Right or wrong, she would have to stand by it now.

Chapter Sixteen

"Mamm said if we caught five fish today she would fry them up for supper."

Brandon glanced up from baiting his hook to give his cousin a questioning look. Joshua seemed serious enough. "No joke?"

"Why would I joke about something like that?"

Brandon shrugged. It wasn't like he and Joshua were friends. It wasn't like they went places together. Just fishing. But Joshua did come get him every afternoon once he had finished all his chores and Brandon was home from doing his schoolwork at the library. Brandon didn't have much to do at his grandmother's house. His mother told him if he kept complaining about not having anything to do that she would arrange for him to pick up a few chores around the house. Images of himself toting wood to heat up water to wash the dishes and the laundry flashed through his head. No, thank you. He stopped complaining, and now when he got home, he waited for Joshua to go fishing.

"Does that mean I'm invited to supper?"

Joshua grinned. "Only if we can catch five today."

"I bet we can."

"I bet I can get to three before you."

Brandon laughed. "You're on."

In the end they caught six, three each. The last two fishes were hooked almost simultaneously. Brandon's bobber went under first, but Joshua was the first to pull his onto the bank.

They strung up the fish and headed for the house, good-naturedly ribbing each other over who actually won the bet.

"Come on." Joshua loped up the steps, hooking one hand over his shoulder for Brandon to follow him inside. "Mamm's probably in the kitchen."

Brandon had never been in his uncle's house, and he wasn't sure what to expect. From the outside it was practically identical to the other houses on the property, same white siding and shutterless windows. The porch stretched all the way across the front, but unlike at his grandmother's, there was no swing hanging at one end. The inside was very much like his grandmother's house. The furniture was sturdy and wooden with only plain blue fabric-covered pillows for cushion.

There were no decorations, paintings, or pictures on the white-painted walls, and most of the light came from the many windows. A couple of oil-burning lamps sat on the side tables, much like those at his grandmother's house. For a while he had thought that maybe this was all some sort of joke, or that his grandmother was the only one who truly lived this way, but after seeing Joshua's house, the world Brandon had found himself in became all the more real.

Not that he would admit it, but for a day or two he pretended that he was a time-traveler who had been sent to the past. It amused him for a time, then he realized how lame pretending was and pushed the thoughts from his head. He would have to find something else to take up his time away from his studies. Never in his life had he been happier to go to school. And it had nothing to do with Shelly. She hadn't even been there the past two days. He wondered if her parents had found out he was talking to her and now they were keeping her away from his bad influences.

He touched his lip ring with the tip of his tongue. Maybe he had taken his rebellion a little far. His mother hadn't batted an eyelash when he came home with it. But his dad had hit the roof. Just the reaction he had been hoping for.

But Dad is gone. Dead. What use was his symbol of rebellion now?

He pushed that thought to the back of his brain and concentrated on following Joshua into the kitchen at the back of the house. They actually walked out onto the porch and into another building barely connected to the back of the house by a small stone path.

"Why is your kitchen back here?" He had never seen a kitchen outside of the house.

Joshua stopped before entering the small building. "We aren't allowed to have running water in the house. So we put it out here."

"This isn't the house?" Brandon frowned. He wasn't following this, not at all.

"Nope." His cousin grinned. "We call this the cookhouse, and since it's not attached to the main house, the bishop had a hard time telling us that we couldn't have running water back here."

Nothing like a crazy culture to make a person feel stupid. Brandon shook his head. "I don't get it."

"There's nothing to get. The *Ordnung* says we can't have running water in our house. Because this isn't the house, we can have running water."

"You mean . . . ?"

Joshua grinned, then pushed his way inside.

As far as kitchens went, it couldn't be considered modern, but when compared to what was in his grandmother's house, this one was top-of-the-line. There was an honest-to-goodness sink, in addition to the wood-burning stove and large worktable in the center of the room. Another door was set off to the left, but Brandon didn't have time to wonder about it as Brandon's mother flitted over.

"You did it, *jah*?"

Joshua grinned, obviously pleased with himself. "I had a little help." He gestured toward the door where Brandon hovered.

"You helped?" Anna asked.

He nodded.

"*Danki*," Joshua's mother said. "Then you must stay and help us eat them."

A surge of pride rose in Brandon. It was weird, really. It wasn't like she had praised him, told him how wonderful he was, but he felt like she had all the same.

"I'd love to. Thanks."

Joshua elbowed him in the ribs and gestured toward the door leading out the back of the cookhouse. "Great. But first we've got to clean them."

Brandon couldn't say that cleaning fish was the grossest thing he had ever done, but it was close. Still, somehow that didn't really matter. He had gone out with nothing more than a fishing pole and a couple of worms and because of his efforts—and Joshua's too—they would have fresh fish to eat for supper. The thought went straight to his head.

"Here." Joshua passed him a half of a lemon that had seen better days.

"What am I supposed to do with this?" The fish were

cleaned, sliced and soaking in a bowl of salted ice water. Now they were washing their hands before heading over to their grandmother's house. Brandon didn't think his mother would care if he ate with Joshua's family tonight, but he had to go make sure. And he couldn't do that with fish-smelling hands.

"Wipe it against your fingers. It'll take away the fish stink."

Brandon eyed the lemon half. "Are you joking?"

Joshua frowned at him. "Why do you think I'm always making jokes?"

"I'm not." Brandon laughed. "It's just an expression. It means . . . whatever you're telling me is hard to believe."

"Well, believe it," Joshua said. He lifted his fingers for Brandon to sniff. They smelled of soap and lemons, but there was no trace of fish.

"Cool."

"*Jah*? Wait till you taste my mother's fish."

As expected, his mother was more than happy to let him go to his cousin's for a meal. She tried not to let it show, but he could see it. He knew she wanted him to enjoy his time in Pontotoc. Fat chance, but this might be fun, just as long as she didn't know how proud he was of having helped provide the meal for so many people.

His uncle Jim and aunt Anna had five kids. Libby was the oldest, with Joshua next. Then there were twin boys, Caleb and Michael, who were ten, and a baby that toddled around the house in a dress. They told him that the baby's name was Samuel, but for the life of him Brandon didn't know why they felt the need to dress him like a girl.

"Thank you for supper," Brandon said after the table had been cleared. He had been told that it was Libby and Michael's turn at the dishes. And everyone was talking about what they wanted to do for the rest of the evening. "It was delicious."

"*Danki*," Anna replied. Brandon had learned early on that the Amish didn't use names like *Aunt* and *Uncle* as titles for their relations. They assured him that was the way, but it felt weird to refer to them by their first names only. Disrespectful somehow.

Danki. There was that word again. "Thank you, right?" he asked.

Anna smiled. "That's right."

Joshua clapped him on the shoulder. "You'll be speaking Dutch before long."

He wanted to ask if they were Dutch or German, but held his words. He was afraid they might appear disrespectful, and after the nice evening he had spent with these new family members he hadn't even known he had, he didn't want to ruin it. "Yeah." He chuckled and hoped it was appropriate.

"I want to play a game," Caleb said. "Can we play a game?"

"What kind of game?" Anna asked.

"Tell the Truth."

Libby nodded. "*Jah*. Everyone can play that."

"Tell the Truth?" Brandon asked.

"It's sort of a family game," Joshua explained.

"But it's easy to play," Michael added.

"Okay." Brandon wasn't sure what to expect, but he wasn't ready to go home yet. It was almost seven thirty, and the sun hadn't gone down. It seemed a shame to leave when they were all still having such a good time.

The thought surprised him. He was having a good time. Who would have thought? "How do you play?" he asked.

"We go around the table taking turns asking each other

questions. If you don't want to answer the question you have to do whatever the person who asked tells you to do."

Sounded a lot like Truth or Dare, but Brandon didn't say so. Something told him the game would be very different when played by the Amish. He was pretty sure no one would ask him to run down the road with no clothes on, which would have been the first dare if he had played with his friends.

Everyone except his aunt and uncle took a seat around the table. Jim and Anna settled down in the living room, him reading the Bible and her working a puzzle with little Samuel.

"Brandon, you can go first," Libby said.

He shook his head. "Nah, let someone else go first." He really wanted to see how they played it before he started in.

"I'll go," Joshua said. "Caleb, I heard you were caught slipping notes to Linda Lapp during class. Tell the truth."

Caleb turned a bright shade of pink. "What if I don't want to say?"

Joshua seemed to think about it a moment, but his expression was so practiced that Brandon suspected that he had known what he was going to have him do from the start. "If you don't want to tell the truth, then you have to go outside and kiss a chicken."

Caleb swallowed hard, the pink in his cheeks replaced by a sickly color. "A chicken?"

Joshua nodded. "That's right."

"Caleb's afraid of the chickens," Libby said where only Brandon could hear.

"How can he be afraid of chickens?" he asked.

Caleb turned serious eyes on him. "You have obviously never been around them." He shuddered.

Brandon bit back a laugh. It was true, he had never

been around chickens, but he couldn't imagine being afraid of them.

"We used to have this banty rooster," Michael explained. "He was something else."

"Chased Caleb all over the yard one day."

The mental picture was almost more than Brandon could stand. He laughed. "Why did he chase you?"

Caleb closed his eyes as if reliving the most horrible day of his life. "I spilled some of the feed on my shoes, and he wanted to peck my feet."

Must have been wintertime, Brandon thought. Since he had been in Pontotoc he hadn't seen anyone wear shoes unless they were going into town.

"What's it going to be?" Joshua asked. "Were you passing notes, or are you going to kiss a chicken?"

"*Jah*." Caleb hung his head as if in defeat. "I was passing notes."

His brothers and sister all laughed. Brandon joined in, almost disappointed. He would have loved to see Caleb kiss a chicken.

They played Tell the Truth until it was nearly dark. Joshua glanced out the window, then turned back to Brandon. "You better get on home before you can't see where you're going."

Brandon stood, surprised that he was a little stiff. He'd been sitting at the table for almost two hours straight, laughing, joking, and talking. He couldn't remember having such a fun evening in a long time. And they hadn't *done* anything. Not really. But they were together as a family. Maybe that was what it was all about. It wasn't like Brandon had much family—just him, his mom, and his dad. His dad . . . Well, Brandon had wondered oftentimes if the man had even wanted him around. He sure hadn't acted like it. But it was different here. Everyone seemed to love everybody else, and they got along, for the most part. He supposed they argued and squabbled like any siblings would do. Not having any of his own, he had to go off what he'd seen on television and at his friends' houses, but there was a peace here, a camaraderie not often found. He wanted a little piece of that for himself. Reluctantly, he stood. "I guess you're right." He looked around the table at his newfound cousins. "Thanks for letting me play tonight."

They all grinned at him.

"Thanks for catching us dinner," Libby said. She smiled, her brown eyes welcoming. And it was funny; he could see her eyes. She hadn't caked them with mascara, not like "English" girls did. Weird, but he had never noticed that until now.

"Wanna go fish again tomorrow?" Joshua asked as he followed Brandon to the door.

"That sounds good. I've got to do some schoolwork in the morning, but I'm free after that."

Joshua nodded. "*Jah*, I have some chores to do. Maybe sometime tomorrow afternoon?"

Brandon smiled. "Come and get me."

He waved goodbye to his aunt and his uncle, then headed down the porch steps. There was a spring in his stride as he walked the short distance between the houses. The evening was getting darker and darker, and soon he wouldn't be able to see his hand in front of his face. He quickened his steps even as the smile remained on his lips. It really had been a fun evening, catching dinner and cleaning fish. Well, cleaning the fish hadn't exactly been a pleasant experience, but a necessary one all the same. And what a sense of satisfaction to eat food that he had caught.

His dad had never been a hunter or a fisherman, and Brandon had never gone to do those types of things. But he could see why people liked it. There was a keen sense of pride in oneself. It was good to know that he could feed himself without a grocery store. One just never knew when the zombie apocalypse might happen.

He chuckled to himself and tripped up his grand-mother's steps.

"Mom?" he called as he walked into the house.

Tillie stuck her head out of the kitchen doorway. "She's in the *dawdihaus* talking to Mammi."

Brandon nodded, then headed for the sewing room. Talking with Mammi made him uncomfortable. She had watery blue eyes and leather skin that looked like an old saddle. She never came out of her room except to go to church. At least she had only come out that one time. Otherwise people brought in her food, people went in to visit, and she stayed put. Brandon had gone in there one time, but it had been so uncomfortable he had left first chance he got. Something about her stare seemed to go right through a person. When she looked at him, Brandon felt like she knew his every secret. Maybe even the ones he didn't know himself.

He scoffed at his own fanciful thoughts. He had been too long without television. That was what it was. There were no stories in his life, so he was making them up as he went along.

Tomorrow was Friday, and he was hoping that Shelly would be back at the library. He wanted to tell her about catching fish and playing Tell the Truth with his cousins. He thought she might get a kick out of it. It sounded so much like something her family would do.

He kicked off his shoes and laid down on his bed. Surprisingly enough, he was tired. He really hadn't done all that much, or maybe he had. And it had been so enjoyable he hadn't realized he was tired until now.

He could hardly wait to tell his mother about their after-dinner game. But he rolled onto his side and was asleep almost immediately.

Chapter Seventeen

"Did you have a good time last night?" Hannah asked as she drove Brandon into town to the library. She had gone in to visit Mammi and when she came back out she found that Brandon had returned, but had fallen asleep. He looked so peaceful and calm that she didn't want to wake him. But that wasn't the only part of his expression. He seemed almost happy. No, maybe that wasn't the right word. *Content.* Yes, that was it. He looked content, and considering everything that he had been through, it was a huge step as far as she was concerned.

"It was okay, I guess."

She chanced a quick glance in his direction. "Everything all right?"

He nodded and stared out the window. She had a feeling he wasn't telling her something. Whether it was good or bad still remained to be seen.

"I'm glad," she said. And it was sort of the truth. She was glad he had an okay time, but she had hoped he'd had more than that. There was no telling how long they would have to remain in Pontotoc, and she wanted him to have as normal a life as he could while he was there. Making friends, hanging out with his cousins, or even young people his own age, was a huge step in the right direction.

And if she could get him to hang out with people with higher values than those he had been hanging out with in Nashville, well, that would be all the better.

"Yeah," he said. He turned and stared out the window, effectively cutting off the conversation.

Hannah wouldn't allow herself to get upset about it. She knew he had to have a life that was his own. He was almost fifteen, after all. And he couldn't have had too bad of a time, considering he stayed till almost dark. If the evening had been a bust, he would've come home long before then.

She was worried over nothing, she was sure. She pulled into the library parking lot and put the car in park, but left it running. "Brandon," she started.

"Thanks for the ride." Brandon opened the car door and was out and headed for the library door before she could say any more. "I love you," she whispered to his departing back. Then she backed out the car and headed for home.

"Have you done something and then wondered later why you did it?" Brandon asked Shelly. They were sitting at their usual table, talking and doing their work, though it seemed these days he was more interested in talking than doing his work.

"Of course. Haven't we all?"

"I suppose."

"Why do you ask?" Shelly pinned him with a look.

"I don't know. It's just that . . ." He told her about his evening with his cousins and how much fun he'd had, about catching the fish, cleaning them, and eating them for supper. And the satisfaction he felt. He had been disappointed when his mom wasn't there to tell about it. This morning the excitement had dimmed, and he didn't want to talk about it anymore.

"Maybe you're a little bit jealous." Shelly bit her lip as if she regretted the words.

"Jealous? Why would I be jealous?" *And of what?*

"Well maybe, and I'm just guessing here, maybe you thought you two would have lots of time to spend together when you came here, and when you wanted to spend time with her she wasn't around."

But she was around this morning, and he didn't want to tell her then. "But—" He shook his head. "Maybe you're right."

Shelly smiled. "It wouldn't be the first time."

Brandon couldn't help it. He smiled. He really enjoyed spending time with Shelly, almost as much as he enjoyed his time with Joshua. How weird was that? Had anybody asked him two weeks ago if he thought he would find a friend here he would have told them no way. Maybe his two new friends weren't as sophisticated as his cool Nashville friends, but he enjoyed them all the same. They might not know about cars and girls and movies, but they knew how to clean fish, all about family dynamics, and a host of other things that in real life seemed much more important than cars and girls and movies.

It was an interesting thought. But one he didn't have time to mull over further. He had work to do. And he didn't want to get behind. But maybe soon, he would give that some more thought and try to figure out just when his attitude had changed.

"Hannah," Mamm called.

"In here." Hannah stood in the sewing room examining the contents of her closet. No wonder she was confused.

Amish dresses hung next to blue jeans and right beside T-shirts. But she couldn't say she preferred one style of dress over the other. After all, what did it really matter? Except that in order to return to her family fold she would have to don her Amish garb forever.

The thought wasn't completely repulsive. In fact, it wasn't repulsive at all. She had grown up wearing *fracks* and aprons. Wearing them was like wearing a small piece of her childhood.

"There you are." Mamm entered the room, a bit breathless as always, her cheeks rosy pink.

"Here I am."

Mamm nodded. "I need you and Gracie to go over to Aaron's tonight and cook."

Hannah shook her head. "Is this just another way of trying to get the two of us together? Because if it is, it won't work. We've already made up our minds."

"Hush, now, girl. This isn't about you. Mammi just reminded me that we have a doctor's appointment in town in less than an hour. And you know how they always run late. By the time we get into town and back out again, I won't have time to get over there and cook."

Well, the excuse sounded legit enough that Hannah couldn't call bunk and tell her mother she wasn't going anywhere near Aaron Zook's house.

"Can't Gracie go by herself?" Even as she said the words, her mother started shaking her head.

"Hannah Mae, there is too much work for only one person. Now promise me you'll be there at four and you won't cause any problems."

Hannah almost laughed out loud, but she knew the sound would be more sardonic that humorous. "I promise. I'll be there at four, and I won't cause any problems."

* * *

Aaron walked back into his house the following evening to the mouthwatering smell of home-fried chicken. His stomach rumbled.

"Dat Dat Dat!" Essie sprinted from the kitchen and flung herself toward him. "Gracie and Hannah let me help."

Aaron scooped his daughter into his arms, laughing at the amount of flour that covered her from head to toe. "I can see that."

He gave her a quick squeeze and set her back on her feet.

"They said I'm a good chicken fryer."

Aaron laughed. "That you are."

"Come see. Come see." She grabbed his hand and dragged him toward the kitchen. "Was Mamm a good chicken fryer?"

"Of course she was." Lizzie had been good at practically everything—another reason why it was so hard to think of marrying again.

He wasn't sure what he expected when he walked into the kitchen. Hannah was a good enough cook; Gracie too. Those skills added with the help of two little girls and he honestly anticipated a huge mess. Flour on the ceiling, egg dripping from the counter . . . but the kitchen was practically immaculate. The only thing changed were the pots now bubbling on the stove. A huge platter of chicken sat on the sidebar.

"Look, Dat!" Essie ran toward him, her smile stretching from one ear to the other. "Look what we made."

Her pride and joy were evident. Even Laura Kate seemed pleased with their accomplishments.

"It smells good," he said.

"And it's going to taste even better," Gracie confidently responded.

"When do we eat?" he asked.

Hannah replaced the lid on one of the pots and turned off the stove. "How about now?"

Aaron eyed the piled-high platter. "You don't expect us to eat all of this by ourselves."

Hannah smiled. "Put what you don't eat in the icebox. That'll give you plenty for tomorrow too."

"How about you help us eat some of it." When she opened her mouth to protest, he interrupted. "There'll still be plenty for the icebox."

"Thanks." Gracie buzzed in and flashed him a quick grin. "We'd love to stay for supper."

In the flurry of activity that followed, Aaron had a chance to watch Hannah without her being aware. Once again she was dressed in Amish clothing. He wondered if it was a voluntary act or if she had been coerced by her mother and father, or even the bishop. Either way, he loved it and hated it all at the same time. He loved seeing her the way he remembered her, but he hated how it made him feel, like they could start over. Like the last fifteen years didn't matter.

"Aaron?" Gracie called from the other room.

He shook himself from his thoughts, only then realizing that he had been staring at nothing.

"Are you coming in to eat?"

"*Jah*." Without another word he made his way to the dining table.

Hannah couldn't name a time when she'd had more fun than tonight. She had enjoyed cooking with Gracie in Aaron's kitchen, his sweet little girls helping in their own special way. Aaron eating so much he acted like he might explode. His children laughing and enjoying the meal. All in all, it was more like family than she'd had in a long time.

But it's not your family.

She shook the thought away and eased down onto the hard-backed chair on the front porch. Gracie and the girls had shooed her away so they could clean, mainly because Hannah had done the lion's share of the cooking. Aaron and Andy had headed to the barn for chores. Hannah would have much rather been inside helping and not sitting on the porch all alone.

Alone was when all the regrets came, the what-ifs and doubts and worries and fears. What happened if she didn't clear enough from the estate to start over? She had practically nothing to her name. She'd had a few hundred dollars that Mitch hadn't known about stuffed in a cookie jar and squirreled away. Good thing. Right after he died, the creditors came calling, and the lawyers froze his accounts. It seemed like every day someone new was coming in with their hand out, demanding their piece of the pie before it was all gone. Now with each passing day she worried more and more that once the dust cleared there would be nothing left. Then what would she do?

"Hannah?"

She jumped to her feet as Aaron came around the side of the house. He carried a broomstick in one hand and a frown on his face.

"What are you doing out here?" She pressed one hand to her heart to still its wild pounding as she eased back into her seat.

"I was about to ask you the same thing."

The sun hadn't completely set, though the sky was starting to show streaks of dusky purple and deep orange. It wouldn't be long now.

"I was kicked out of the kitchen."

He chuckled and climbed the porch steps to sit in the chair beside her. "Are your dishwashing skills lacking?"

"Nope. But since I did most of the cooking—"

"You did?" He raised his brow in apparent surprise.

"What? You didn't think I knew how to cook?"

He shook his head. "You could cook when you . . . well, you could cook back in the day."

She swallowed the sudden knot in her throat. "Why are you surprised that I prepared tonight's meal?"

He seemed to think about it a minute, and she wondered if he needed time to figure out his reasoning or make up something nice to tell her. "I guess I figured since you had been out there among the *Englisch* . . ."

"That I had forgotten all the Amish ways?" she asked.

"Something like that." He cleared his throat and shifted in his seat.

"It's like riding a bike," she said, using the old adage.

"What is?" Aaron frowned. "We aren't allowed to have bikes."

"No. It means you don't forget."

Aaron shook his head. "I don't understand."

Hannah smiled, his confusion so cute. "Being Amish is something you don't forget." And she hadn't—even after years away, years of living with modern conveniences, she remembered how to light the stove and the wood burner out back on the porch. How many buckets of cold to the number of heated buckets it took to produce the perfect temperature bath. She remembered it all. Just like yesterday. Just like Aaron.

"And you want to remember?" His voice was so soft, she wondered if she had only imagined it.

Did she want to remember how to be Amish? It was nothing she could ever forget. She was who she was because of the way she had grown up. And she wouldn't change that for anything. "Yeah. Sometimes."

"What about now?"

Definitely now. And yet, not. She shook her head. She couldn't get too comfortable, fall back into her old life. She had Brandon to think about. No matter how easily she could step back into the Amish ways, her son would never be able to adapt to such an austere lifestyle. After everything that had slipped from her grasp, Brandon was the one thing she couldn't stand to lose.

Chapter Eighteen

"And then Hannah let me dunk all the chicken pieces into the egg stuff. But I had to do them one at a time." Essie snuggled down into her bed as Aaron pulled the covers up to her shoulders. "If you dunk more than one at a time, then they stick together and don't get enough flour stuff on them. That's what Hannah said."

"She did?" Aaron tried his best to show genuine interest, but every time Essie said Hannah's name he thought about other things. How her eyes used to sparkle. When he had first seen her after all those years, that gleam was gone. But tonight, he swore he saw it again. It winked and twinkled, coming and going like the first star in a nighttime sky.

"Did you know that she cooked all that chicken?" Essie asked.

"I think I heard something about that." He brushed her hair back from her face and kissed her forehead.

"It was so good." Essie snuggled into the bed, her eyelids already growing heavy as Aaron stood. "That's a good trait in a wife, *jah*?" Essie asked.

Aaron chuckled. "As good as any, I suppose." He

wasn't about to debate the merits of a good wife with his daughter fifteen minutes past bedtime.

"You should marry her." Before he could answer her, Essie was asleep. That was just her way. If she was up, she was moving, but once he made her stay still she fell asleep every time.

"Good night, Laura Kate." He kissed his oldest on the cheek, pulling her covers up as well.

"Don't listen to her, Dat," Laura Kate muttered, turning onto her side to get comfortable. "I understand there's more to it than that. She's just young."

Aaron hid his smile and wiped a hand across her long, dark hair.

But they're not happy about the move.

He pushed the thought aside. He hadn't even decided yet about the move. Well, most of him hadn't.

His mind told him he needed to take the job. There were too many opportunities for him to turn it down. The kids would have more to enrich their lives. He could live out his dream of working with horses exclusively.

But his heart had other ideas. Because he really didn't want to go? Because he loved Mississippi so much? Because Lizzie was buried here? Because he had been waiting for Hannah to come back?

All that was ridiculous. He was days away from taking the trip to Ohio and finding out what it was like up there. And if he liked it at all, even a little bit, then his head needed to win out and they needed to move to Ohio as soon as they possibly could.

He snuffed out the light and made his way across the hall to Andy's room. He knew his son felt he was too old to be tucked in, but Aaron couldn't sleep unless he said good night to his children. All his children.

"Good night, Andy."

His son darted under the covers as soon as Aaron poked

his head in the door. He knew that Andy felt it was past time for him to grow up and start taking more responsibility around the farm. As far as Aaron was concerned, he did plenty. But he had a feeling Andy's attitude stemmed more from his mother's death than any need to grow up.

"Good night, Dat." He pulled the covers nearly over his mouth, his blue eyes twinkling over the edge of the sheet.

"Are you okay?" Aaron asked.

"*Jah*. Of course."

He studied his son's face for a moment, trying to figure out if he should pry or leave it alone. In the end he decided to wait, to give Andy a little more time before trying to uncover all of his secrets.

Aaron turned off the light, plunging the room into inky darkness.

"And Essie's right," Andy's voice came from out of the black. "When a lady can cook like Hannah can, a man should marry her up, and quick."

"Did you have fun tonight?" Gracie's voice floated to Hannah from across the bedroom. Tillie was on an overnight trip to Tennessee, so she had taken over her bed for the night. It sure beat the cramped sewing room she had been sharing with Brandon. Bless his heart, he hadn't complained since those first few days. Hannah was grateful. She knew he wasn't happy about being in "Amish Land," as he liked to call it. She had never expected him to accept it as a way of life, but it was a lot easier to get along when he wasn't constantly griping about one thing or another. She supposed she had Joshua to credit for that. Jim's son had taken Brandon under his wing and had shown him some of the good things about being Amish. Fishing in the middle of the afternoon, game night in a big family, and a host of other activities that were keeping

Brandon busy and, for a while, content. He didn't even mind going to school these days. If she didn't know better she would think that he was actually excited to go into the library and learn something new, but that was asking too much. As long as he wasn't complaining, that was enough for her.

"I had a wonderful time." And that was the truth. Aaron had been a wonderful host, the girls had been eager helpers, and it was a joy to cook for someone again.

Or was it just that that someone was Aaron Zook?

"Maybe we should invite Aaron to Brandon's birthday party."

Hannah nodded, even though she was lying down and the room was pitch-black. "And the kids."

"Of course," Gracie said.

"Are you sure *you're* not interested in Aaron?" Hannah's voice was half-teasing. The other half was as serious as a heart attack. Hannah herself might not be able to ever have anything with Aaron again, but the thought of him taking up with her cousin . . .

"Would it matter if I was?"

"Of course."

Gracie laughed into the darkness. "I'm not talking about you. I'm talking about him."

Hannah turned over in her bed, doubling up her pillow so she could better see across the room. Or at least try to. Only the moonlight filtered in through the windows, creating dark shadows out of everything it didn't touch. Hannah could barely make out her cousin's form just across the small room. "Me?"

Gracie's head bobbed in the shadows. "That man has a thing for you and no one else."

Hannah scoffed. "You are sadly mistaken."

"No, I'm not. I may not be married myself, but I've

traveled around enough to see couples and how they act around each other. And that man lov—"

"Don't say it." She couldn't bear to hear those words knowing they weren't true. There was too much pain, too many years, too much . . . *life* that stood between them now.

"Likes you a whole lot."

"I really appreciate you doing this." How many times had Aaron said that in the last fifteen minutes.

"It's no problem." And it wasn't. Brandon had practically moved in with Jim and Anna, preferring to spend his free time with Joshua. The fact was a comfort to Hannah. Joshua was a good kid, and she couldn't ask for a better influence on her own son.

"Are you sure?"

"Positive. Now kiss your children goodbye. Your driver is here."

He turned around so quickly she thought he might fall off the porch. "Oh."

Essie rushed forward, flinging her tiny arms around his legs. "Bye, Dat. Be good, okay?"

He chuckled and returned her embrace. "I will."

"Bye, Dat." Laura Kate stepped forward to receive a hug, while Andy hovered behind her.

"Y'all do what Hannah says, and no coming home from school for lunch. No one will be here."

"But Hannah will come back when school is out, right?" Essie asked.

"Of course." Hannah took Essie's hand into her own, giving the child the reassurance that she needed. Hannah could only guess how the children felt. They had lost their mother, and now, less than a year later, their father was taking a trip that could change their lives once again. Just thinking about it made her nervous for them.

"Have a good trip," Hannah said, placing a hand on each girl's shoulder in order to hold them in place as their father picked up his suitcase.

"I'll be home Thursday night." He waved and started toward the car waiting at the end of the drive.

Hannah stood on the porch with Andy and the girls and watched as Aaron drove away. Once the car was out of sight, she turned back to the kids. "What do you want to do now?" she asked.

Essie grinned, the gap between her teeth whistling as she did. "I want to make fried chicken again."

Aaron checked into the hotel, thankful to finally be in Ohio. Last night they had stopped somewhere in Kentucky. Two days in a car was almost more than he could stand. He was grateful to be sitting on a bed and not in a running car, even though he was miles and miles from home.

Just the distance was enough to make him second-guess this decision. It was one thing to think about moving far away, and another to put that distance into practice. He hadn't completely realized how far Ohio was from home until now. He missed his children, he missed Hannah, he missed home. But he would see this through. Who knew? Maybe tomorrow, after a good night's sleep, things would look a lot different.

Chapter Nineteen

It had perhaps been the longest week of his life. Aaron was more than excited as his mailbox and driveway came into view. Home. The one thing he had thought about most while he was gone. Home. Everything he held dear was there in that house. Everything he loved, everything he needed. Including Hannah McLean.

The driver pulled to a stop just before he got to the end of the lane.

"Do you want me to help you with your bags?" the driver asked.

Aaron stopped for just a moment longer, soaking in the beautiful sight before him. "No, *danki*." He fished his money out of his wallet to pay the man, then got out of the car. The driver popped the trunk so Aaron could get his bags. He grabbed them, shut the lid, and stopped only long enough to invite the man in. It was protocol and nothing more, and Aaron was thankful that he declined. He thanked him once again, then, with a bag in each hand, he started for the porch as the driver backed out of the drive.

Home. He'd never been so glad to be there in all his life.

He nudged open the door and pulled off his hat, hanging

it on the peg by the door. Then he followed the warmth, sounds, and smells of his house to the kitchen.

Hannah stood at the stove stirring a pot, while Essie and Laura Kate rolled out what looked to be biscuits. The girls were laughing and bickering a bit, but it seemed that Hannah had decided to allow them time to solve their own issues. Andy was nowhere to be seen, and Aaron supposed that he was bringing in wood or some other chore. It seemed as if Hannah had his household running like a clock. He was glad and maybe a little bit jealous. He had sort of wanted them to miss him, but with the way Hannah had things running, he wasn't sure anyone had noticed he was even gone.

He cleared his throat, bringing their attention around to where he stood in the doorway. "Something sure smells good."

"Dat!" His girls abandoned their biscuit dough and pushed toward him, flinging their arms around him without one thought to the flour splattered on their hands and clothes.

Not that Aaron minded. He scooped them up, loving the feel of them in his arms. How he had missed them!

"We weren't expecting you until later." Hannah dried her hands on a dish towel, her eyes unreadable.

Aaron kissed the top of Laura Kate's head, then Essie's, before setting them back on their feet. "Just anxious to get back home."

"Bad trip?" Clouds of concern crossed over her sweet face. He had missed her more than he cared to admit, and his time in Ohio had left even more questions with no clear answers.

"Not really. Just ready to be here," he said again.

"Tell me about it over supper?" Hannah asked.

Aaron looked pointedly at his daughters. "How about afterward?"

She gave him a cautious smile. "Sounds like a plan."

To be able to sit at his own table after a week away was more than heaven for Aaron. He didn't recall ever being away for so long, and if he had his way, he never would again.

And Hannah's chicken and noodles? The best, he was certain of it.

"I wanted to have fried chicken again, but Hannah said no way." Essie gave an exaggerated pout.

"Three times in one week is plenty enough for anyone," Hannah said with a smile.

"I second that," Andy said. Then quickly looked around the table. "I mean, it's delicious and everything."

Hannah laughed. "I understand what you mean."

"You've made them fried chicken three times this week?"

Hannah gave a small shrug. "They drew straws to see who got to decide what was for supper."

"And?" Aaron asked.

"Essie won three times."

Aaron shook his head. It was incredible the things she did for his children. "I really appreciate you watching after them," he said.

"It was my pleasure." And he could see the truth shining in her eyes.

"How did yours make out?"

Hannah gave a small shrug. "He spent most of the time with Joshua at Jim and Anna's, but I'm just glad he's got a friend here."

Aaron took a drink of his iced tea and nodded. "Joshua is a good kid."

"I couldn't agree more."

Hannah looked around the table, then centered her gaze on Aaron. "When are you going to tell me about the trip?"

"That depends."

"On what?"

He patted his stomach and looked at the pie she had cooling on the counter. "Is that apple or cherry?"

"Blackberry."

Even better. "Cut me a slice of that, and when the kitchen is clean, I'll tell you all about it."

It seemed to take forever before Hannah and the girls had the dishes washed and put away. Aaron finished his pie in record time, but after that each second dragged into the next.

Finally, *finally*, everything was cleaned and put away. Aaron sent the kids up to get ready for bed, and the two of them were left alone. They settled down on the bench on the front porch, allowing themselves a little more privacy than they would have in the house.

Hannah ran her hands down the front of her dress, unsure of why she had been dressing this way all week. It just felt comfortable to be in Amish clothes while taking care of Amish children as if they were her own. But now that Aaron was home, she was beginning to feel like a fraud.

She pushed those negative thoughts away and concentrated on him. "So? How was it?"

He seemed to think about it for a moment, his face pinched into an almost-frown. "Big."

Not exactly the word she had expected. "What do you mean?"

"It was big. Everything. The Amish community, all the people, the tourists."

Hannah cocked her head to one side. "Is that a good thing or a bad thing?"

"I don't know," he said with a shake of his head, but Hannah could tell that something was bothering him.

"Why don't you just tell me straight out what you thought about the place? It's not like anyone here is going to judge." Was he worried that he liked another place better than his home?

"I hated it."

"What?"

He pushed up from his seat and went to stand at the porch railing. "I hated it." He sighed, a great heaving sigh, as if a huge weight had been lifted from him. "There were so many people and horses. Tourists everywhere. There was no land for sale." He shook his head once again. "It's so quiet here you can almost hear the grass grow."

It was the truth if she had ever heard it.

"I guess I'm not used to all that commotion."

"But what about your dream of working with horses?"

He turned back to face her, propping his hip on the rail. "I'm not sure it's worth it." He stopped as if gathering his words. "I thought there would be a lot of opportunities in a place like that. And I'm sure there probably are. But the trade-off . . ."

"You're not moving?"

"I don't think so."

Hannah eyed him warily. "What's the problem?"

"Is it the right decision?"

Her heart gave a painful thud in her chest. "Why wouldn't it be?"

"Because I'm making it for all the wrong reasons."

Her mouth turned to ash. "And what reason would that be?"

"You."

"Aaron." His name quietly fell between them.

"I'm sorry."

She shook her head. "You don't have to apologize to me."

He sighed. "The entire time I was up there all I could think about was coming home. Coming back to you and the kids."

"So you didn't like it there."

"No, but did I not like it because I know you won't be there, or because it's really not for me?"

Hannah simply stared at him. Exactly what had he expected? She wouldn't sway his decision. He knew as much, but he had hoped she would give him some sort of sign, a hint as to what the future might hold for them if he remained in Mississippi.

"I can't give you that answer," she quietly said.

She rose and came to stand right next to him.

He closed his eyes, able to trace the outline of her even though he couldn't see her. He was just so *aware* of her. How she smelled, how she smiled, how she did everything so right.

He had thought that the time and distance apart had made him forget all those little things that made Hannah Hannah, but now he knew the truth. All that had been dormant inside him, waiting for the chance to come back to life once more.

How would he be able to go on if she went back to the

Englisch? How could she stay here and leave her son behind?

He reached for her hand, unable to stand so close to her and not touch her. Even if just a little.

"We went to the county fair once," he said, opening his eyes and snagging her gaze with his own. "They had this machine there, like a genie or fortune-teller or something. Anyway, you could ask it a question, and your answer would come out on this printed card. And all for a quarter."

"Oh, yeah?" Her words were breathless, and he realized that as he had been talking he was rubbing his thumb against the back of her hand.

"I wish I had something like that now. Somewhere I could go and ask what the answer is and it would shoot out on a little card for me to read."

"I guess prayers don't come with written answers." She gave him a quick smile. But in the fading light of the day, it looked a little sad.

"I've prayed and prayed about this," he admitted. "I've been hoping from the start that God would give me the answers."

"And He hasn't?"

"I'm not sure God has the answer to this."

"Aaron. You don't mean that."

He shook his head. "I don't. You're right. But I feel as if every emotion I have is wrapped up in this, and I can't clearly see the answer."

"You know what Mammi would say . . . if you can't find the answer . . ."

"Then there's your answer," Aaron finished for her. How many times had he heard her *grossmammi* say that exact phrase? More than he cared to admit.

"I'm sensing that you don't see the wisdom in those words this time."

"Unfortunately, no. But I want to." He released her hand when the urge to pull her closer still was almost more than he could resist. "I want to, but I'm still concerned. Am I trying to make God's will my own?"

"By?"

"By staying here and praying that you will stay with me too."

Any words Hannah would have said stuck in her throat. She swallowed hard, but they still wouldn't come. In the waning light, the crickets and katydids began to sing. It was a sound she would forever associate with home.

"Am I rushing things?" Aaron asked.

She shook her head. "It's not that. There are just so many things . . ."

He sighed and dropped back onto the bench. "There's a lot."

She sat down next to him, her own thoughts spinning. It was one thing to talk about the what-ifs and quite another to stare them in the face. "I need to get my mind around this."

"I guess I just thought—" He broke off, once again staring off at nothing in particular.

But he didn't need to finish. She knew what he was going to say.

"It's not that. I just keep thinking about everything else."

"The church?"

"Yes, and Brandon."

He nodded.

The church would welcome her with open arms. She would kneel and confess and all would be forgiven.

And what about your son?

"I've got to think this through."

A cloud of concern crossed his face. "I guess it's not so simple as *I love you*."

Just hearing him say those words tore her heart in two.

"I always have," he continued.

"If it was, we wouldn't have anything at all to discuss."

His face lit up with joy and hope. "You love me too?"

"I never stopped. But when Jim told me you were seeing someone else . . ."

"The mistakes we've made," he mused.

"I've got a few things to work out," she told him. To her own ears her voice sounded reluctant.

"I understand."

Sadly she watched as he stood, then made his way into the house. It was time for her to go home, before it got too dark. As it was now, she would just make it before the sun completely went down. And yet she was still hesitant.

There was no going back, only forward. And she wasn't sure that was even an option for them. Not unless she came up with some way to keep her son close to her even as she converted back into the church. It was the only way, yet from where she stood it looked more than impossible.

Hannah dragged her feet as she made her way up the steps and into her parents' house. The sun had set, night had fallen, and it was beyond dark. That was the excuse she used as to why she walked so slowly. It was definitely better than admitting that she wanted to get back in the buggy, race over to Aaron's house, and declare that nothing would stand in their way. How she wished that were true!

She collapsed onto the swing, her legs unwilling to take her farther without a rest. She fairly crumpled as she covered her face in her hands, unable to look at the bleak future.

"Hannah girl?"

She pulled her hands away from her face as her father came out onto the porch carrying a small oil lamp. His face was cast into shadows, but still showed his concern.

"Dat." She gave him a trembling smile, then scooted over a bit so he could sit down next to her.

"I would ask if everything is all right, but I have a feeling the answer to that is no." He placed the lamp on the side table and eased down beside her.

Everything wasn't all right. In fact, nothing had been all right since she had left. Tears stung at the back of her eyes, but she blinked them away. This was no time for tears.

"Want to tell me what's wrong?" he offered.

The gesture was so unlike her stern father that fresh tears threatened.

"Have you ever heard that *Englisch* expression 'You've made your bed, and now you have to lie in it'?"

Her father frowned. "Why would you make your bed and then get in it right away?"

Despite the darkness around them, Hannah hid her smile. "It's an expression. It means you've made a mess of things and now you have to live with it." The absolute truth.

"My *dawdi* used to always say, you must plow with the horse you have."

Hannah nodded. It wasn't quite the same, but close enough. But what did one do with a horse with a foot in two different worlds?

"We all made mistakes, Hannah girl."

"I know." Yet knowledge didn't change a thing. "But I've made more than my fair share."

"Maybe it's time to let God drive."

She swiveled around to look at him.

"What?" He shrugged. "I saw it on a bumper sticker at the grocery store."

Hannah couldn't hold back her chuckle. "I guess it's worth a try."

He patted her knee and stood. "With God in control, who knows what might happen?"

Let God drive.

Was it really that simple?

Hannah flipped onto her back and tried to get a handle on all the emotions zinging through her. Was it really as easy as letting God handle everything? When was the last time she had turned everything over to Him?

Never. Never in her life had she allowed God complete control. Maybe it was time to turn over the reins, so to speak.

It was well past midnight, and Brandon softly snored from the bed across the room. The room was pitch-black, not even the light from the moon enough to pierce through the veil of night in Amish country.

No one would know if she crawled out of bed, got down on her knees, and prayed. No one needed to know. It would be between her and God.

She slipped quietly from the bed and knelt beside it, bracing her hands on the mattress, much as she had when she was a child.

Lord . . .

Dear Lord, she prayed. *I have made so many mistakes in my life. So many I can't begin to name them all. Could this be because I have not let You be in charge? I don't know.*

She stopped. How long had it been since she had prayed? A long, long time. So long that she didn't feel like she was praying, but rambling on like a child in trouble might do.

But wasn't that what she was? A child of God in trouble?

All of us like sheep have gone astray, Each of us has turned to his own way; But the Lord has caused the iniquity of us all to fall on Him.

The verse popped into her head as clearly as if someone next to her had whispered it in her ear.

It didn't matter how much trouble she had caused; how much she had sinned; the mistakes and trials that she had created. God still loved her and was waiting for her to return.

I surrender all. The words were there in her heart. She remembered the song from those first couple of years when she left the Amish. She had gone to one church and then another, hoping, searching, seeking God. When He was nowhere to be found, she had stopped going. But the song had never left her.

Surrender.

Let God drive.

It sounded so very simple, and yet it might just be the most difficult thing she had ever done.

What was that popular song from a few years back?

"Jesus, Take the Wheel."

Could she do that? Hand over all control and follow what God put in her heart?

If she was being honest with herself, she had lost control a long time ago. Who was in charge of her life? It certainly wasn't her, and it most certainly wasn't God.

"I surrender all," she whispered. This time when the tears threatened, she didn't try to wipe them away. She let them fall, let them cleanse her soul, wash away the mistakes, the hurt, the bad decisions, and all the pain.

This wasn't going to be easy. But she could do it. She could be still and let go. She could be still and let God.

"Lord, I surrender," she whispered into the night. "Lead the way."

It was just a party invitation. There was no need to be nervous or anxious or any of the crazy emotions plaguing her. But she felt all of those and more as she pulled her buggy into Aaron's drive.

This morning when she woke she felt like a new person. A new person with no answers. She wasn't certain where God wanted her, but she had promised to open her heart and listen to Him. He would tell her in His own time. She just had to be listening.

The horse headed for the side yard as if she already knew which way to go. Hannah climbed down from the carriage and tethered the mare, wondering if she should start with the house or the barn. She didn't know a great deal about Aaron's work life. Did he spend most of his time in the barn? What if he was out at another farm? If he wasn't home, she would have to gather all her courage and do this a second time. She sighed. Once was already taking a toll on her heart.

Then she heard it, a faint *clink* coming from the barn. The sound was vaguely familiar, and she realized he was most likely shoeing a horse.

She started for the barn, going over the words in her head. She needed this invitation to be casual, nothing special. She needed him to know that it wasn't important, that he could come or not, but he was welcome. No big deal.

"Aaron?" she called into the cool interior of the barn.

The metallic pounding had stopped, so he must be finished with his job. All she had to do was wait it out.

"Hannah?" He came around the corner, eyes wide.

He looked good—really good. His pale blue shirt made his eyes look even bluer, his dark hair curling from under the brim of his plain straw hat. And as much as it surprised her, she loved his beard. All Amish men were supposed to grow a beard after they got married. It was more than a decree; it was a badge of honor. But just like with other men, some Amish beards were better than others. Aaron's was full and dark, not a speck of gray. It had just enough curl to it to keep it full, despite the fact that it reached toward his chest. And she found herself wanting to reach out and touch it. Simply feel it.

"What are you doing here?"

"I, uh . . ." Why was she here again? Oh. Right. "I came to invite you to Brandon's birthday party."

"*Jah*?"

"It's on Saturday." Why was she rambling? She mentally pulled herself together. "And Andy and the girls, of course. It's nothing fancy. Just family. And the four of you."

A spark shone in his eyes, but it disappeared before she had time to fully comprehend it. Maybe she didn't want to know what it meant. "That sounds like fun."

She nodded. "We're cutting the cake at three."

Aaron smiled, and it took her back fifteen years. Even with that beard and the small wrinkles that fanned out from those amazing eyes, his smile was just the same. And one flash of it could turn her knees to jelly and her insides to oatmeal. "See ya then."

Friday and one more "last chance" of seeing Shelly before the weekend.

"Mom." Brandon half turned in his seat as she drove them into town. Here lately, she had taken to dressing like his grandmother, and he wasn't sure what it all meant.

Did it have to mean anything?

He wasn't sure, but he felt positive that it had meaning to them.

When he and his mom had first arrived in Pontotoc, she had worn her jeans and her hair down. Now it seemed she had started wearing a homemade dress and apron with one of those prayer thingies on her head.

As much as he wanted to, he couldn't find fault with it. What was the old saying? When in Rome, do as the Romans. Well, this wasn't exactly Rome, but he thought it applied to other places as well.

She could go back to being Amish, but he couldn't. Well, he couldn't go *back*, because he had never been Amish to start with. But he had a feeling there was more to it than just wearing dresses and caps.

"What's up?" She still sounded like his mom, and looked like her for the most part.

"About my party tomorrow . . ."

She glanced over toward him, then turned her attention back to the road. "What about it?"

"Well, there's this girl. I've been talking to her at the library. She does her work there too. And, well, I thought I might invite her to the party."

His mother frowned, but other than that, made no reaction to his request. Was that a good thing or a bad one? He had no idea.

She didn't respond, just pulled the car into the parking lot next to the squatty brick building. She stopped in the first empty space and put the car into park.

He wasn't sure if her silence meant anything other than she was thinking about it. Hard.

"Who is this girl?"

"Her name is Shelly. She's really pretty and smart."

"Who are her parents? She's not Amish. Is she Mennonite?"

Brandon shook his head and made a face. "No. She's not Amish or Mennonite." He continued to shake his head, then realized his overreaction could be interpreted as negative. "I mean, she's English, but her parents are very conservative. They don't have a TV or a computer at home."

"And she comes to the library?"

"She's homeschooled. And like me, she has to finish her lessons at the library."

"Well, that explains a lot," she muttered.

"What?" He had no idea what that meant.

"Nothing. You want to invite this girl to your party? Does she know that you have Amish family?"

"Yeah. I don't think she cares about stuff like that. She's really cool, for a girl and all." He didn't want his mother to think he was *that* interested in Shelly. Even though he was. Kind of.

"I suppose I could talk to her mother. When she drops her off."

Brandon's heart lifted. "Yeah? That would be great." He wouldn't say anything about the way his mother was dressed. Stuff like that wasn't supposed to matter anyhow. But the longer they stayed in Mississippi, the more worried he became that they would never leave. He could put aside his electronics for a time, but he was not living his entire life without Xbox.

He just smiled and opened the car door, stepping out into the bright sun. Xbox and electronics aside, this was going to be the best birthday ever.

* * *

Hannah couldn't say that Shelly was anything like she had expected, but she was a nice girl, and her parents seemed not to be concerned about the difference in religious practices. Maybe because Brandon himself was not Amish.

You're not Amish either.

Hannah looked down at herself in her borrowed Amish *frack*. She supposed she should have worn *Englisch* clothes to drive her car into town, but she hadn't thought about it at the time.

She had begun wearing Amish clothing as a convenience. Yes, the dresses were easier, but she felt it had more to do with past traditions than anything else. It simply felt right to putter around her mother's kitchen barefoot with her skirt brushing around her ankles. Of course, wearing the dress felt completely alien without the prayer *kapp*. It didn't hurt that she saw the light of approval in her father's eyes. Approval was a far cry from forgiveness, but it was a start.

Hannah pulled her car into the bank parking lot, ignoring the curious looks she got. Aside from the fact that she was sitting alone in a parking lot she was wearing an Amish prayer *kapp* and driving a car. Of course the good citizens of Pontotoc would have questions.

She parked off to one side and plugged Brandon's cell phone into the car charger. It took a few minutes, but before long she had enough charge to make her call.

"Lipman and Qualls. How may I help you?"

"Hannah McLean for Mr. Lipman, please."

"One moment please."

Vapid elevator music was piped in from the other side of the line, and her heart pounded. Music like that was never a good thing. Something about it made her anxious. Maybe because it was the sort they played in hospital elevators. Everything about it was falsely cheery and set her teeth on edge.

"Mrs. McLean."

"Hello, Mr. Lipman. I am calling to see if there has been any resolution in my case."

She heard the sound of papers shuffling coming from his end, then he cleared his throat. "There are still a few accounts that need to be settled. So far the money is holding out, but we have come across an unexpected expense."

"Unexpected expense?"

"It seems your husband had taken out another mortgage on the house."

Hannah shook her head. "Another mortgage? But that's three loans. On the same property."

"I am aware."

Three loans meant three loans to pay off. Three loans to satisfy before she could start over. Would this nightmare ever end?

"Evidently Mr. McLean had a penchant for gambling, but not one for winning." He cleared his throat once again.

"There's not going to be anything left, is there?"

"At this point we're hoping to negotiate a settlement that will allow you to break even."

Break even. Not the words she wanted to hear. Not at all. "I guess you'll keep me apprised?"

"Do you have a new phone number or way that I can reach you?"

Those blasted tears threatened once again. "No," she whispered, not trusting her own voice to hold steady.

"I suppose I can call the number you gave me during our last call? Is it still in service?"

"Yes." She said the one clipped word, then hung up the phone. She would not cry on the phone with her attorney. She hated the condescension she heard in his tone. She might be a little sensitive to the situation, but this was not her fault. She was not to blame for her husband's infidelity, his gambling debts, and all the other expenditures he had hidden from her. She wasn't to blame for not knowing the ways of the cruel *Englisch* world, a world where she had never belonged.

It was so obvious. She had never belonged in that world. Nor would she ever. She had only been kidding herself these last fifteen years. She had no control over her life, and she had allowed her husband to take complete advantage of her naïveté.

The entire situation was her fault. If she hadn't have made so many dumb mistakes and stupid choices she wouldn't be in the situation she found herself in today.

She pounded one hand against the steering wheel and laid her forehead against it as the tears came. Sobs racked her body, shaking her shoulders as she poured out her grief. Grief for a marriage that should have never been. A son who would never really know his father. A life that was wasted.

How did she get it back? How did she right the wrongs she had created? Where were the answers she had prayed so long and hard for the night before?

My God, my God, why hast thou forsaken me? Why art thou so far from helping me, and from the words of my roaring?

She jerked upright as a knock sounded on the window next to her.

"Are you all right?" The man's face was pinched with concern.

Hannah supposed it wasn't every day he encountered an Amish woman crying her eyes out in the bank parking lot.

She rolled down the window, and a blast of heat hit her

full in the face. "I'm fine." She sniffed and tossed him a watery smile, hoping it would suffice.

"Pardon my saying so, but you look about as far from fine as one person can be."

She couldn't help the chuckle that escaped her. It started as a laugh, then quickly morphed into a sob and a hiccup. "How about, I *will be* fine?" The cry itself had done her some good.

He seemed to think about it for a moment. "Not sure I believe that either."

His eyes were clear green and full of caring and peace. How did a person walk around looking so calm like that when the world was falling apart? Oh, wait. It was just her world that was unraveling at the seams.

He handed her a tissue through the open window and waited patiently as she dried her eyes and blew her nose.

"It's just been one of those days. One of those weeks." She laughed and hiccupped once again. "One of those years."

One of those lives.

He nodded sympathetically and took a card from the pocket of his short-sleeved button-down shirt. "I don't mean to be presumptuous, but . . ." He handed it to her. "I don't know if you have anyone to talk to, but if you ever need someone." He nodded toward the card.

> *GOD IS ALWAYS LISTENING.*
> *Matthew 21:22*
> *"And whatever you ask in prayer,*
> *you will receive, if you have faith."*

The paper nearly scorched her fingers, and yet she couldn't let it go. It was the sign she had been asking for. The answer to everything. At first she had forgotten how to pray, and then she had been praying without faith. Before Jesus performed a miracle, He thanked God for it first. Faith. She had lost faith. But no more.

"Thank you," she whispered.

"There's a number on the back. You can call anytime, day or night. Someone's always monitoring the phones."

"Are you . . . ?" She craned her head back to look at him. Just a kindly man, thirtysomething, maybe a little older. He was a little on the heavy side, with rusty-colored hair and matching beard. He wore blue jeans, a plaid dress shirt, and cowboy boots. He could have been anybody. But she knew that for her he was a messenger from God.

"Jerry Adams. I'm the new preacher at the Baptist church."

"But . . ." She plucked at her dress, unsure of how to voice her question.

Jerry smiled. "There is room for all of us at God's feet."

It was a sign. She knew it. It was the answer to her prayers and everything she had been waiting for since she had returned to Pontotoc. And yet she had no idea what it really meant.

But her tears had stopped; her confusion was gone. She still didn't know exactly what she was going to do, but if she and Aaron were going to have a chance, she had to have faith. She had to believe that the answer would come to her. She only had to be patient and faithful.

She parked the car in the side yard and got out. Tomorrow was Brandon's birthday party. She could hardly believe that her baby was turning fifteen. They had been through so much together. It hardly seemed possible, and yet it felt as if they had spent a lifetime to get to where they were now.

Tillie came out onto the front porch, holding the door open as Gracie peeked out the door behind her.

"Did you get the stuff?" Tillie asked.

Hannah held up the sack from Walmart. "Got it." Balloons, streamers, a banner that proclaimed *Happy Birthday*, and a stack of matching plates and napkins. Birthdays were a special occasion, but she knew she had gone a little overboard. Still, she wanted this to be a special time for him. He had taken Mitch's death pretty hard, which was to be expected. But then, adding in the move, where they had moved, and the limbo in which they found themselves . . . well, she wanted him to know how special he was.

"What about his gift?" Hannah asked her sister. Tillie had been put in charge of securing the best birthday gift an *Englisch* boy could get in Amish country: a phone charger made from a car battery. That should put a smile on his face.

Tillie nodded. "Melvin said he would bring it by in the morning."

Tillie's unofficial boyfriend, Melvin Yoder, was something of an engine whiz. Not many farms used diesel power in the area, but if they needed an engine worked on, they called Melvin. Once upon a time, his father had been the go-to for such repairs, but Melvin had shown a natural knack that had even surpassed his father's own expertise.

Hannah wondered if his desire to work on engines was affecting Tillie's doubts over joining the church.

She hadn't mentioned it again, but Hannah knew those questions were hovering just below the surface. She could almost see them in her sister's eyes. But Hannah didn't have all the answers. And more often than not, she regretted her decision to stay with the *Englisch*. But once she had left there was no turning back. At the time, she had thought she would be able to step back into her Amish life, but in the end, she hadn't even tried. And all because of one man.

Hannah handed the sack off to Gracie and stepped into the house. The sweet scents of sugar and vanilla filled the air. "Is the cake almost done?"

"Mamm pulled it out of the oven a bit ago. Smells good, *jah*?" Tillie asked.

Hannah nodded. Their mother made the best cake in all of Northeast Mississippi.

"And guess what?" Gracie said, her voice gushing with excitement.

"What?"

Her sister and her cousin shared a look. "Leah's home!" they said together.

The words buzzed in Hannah's ears. "Leah?" How long had it been since she had seen her twin sister? Over fifteen years.

Movement caught her attention from the corner of her eye. Hannah turned to see her sister standing there. Leah had her hair pulled back, as she had when they were growing up, and wore a red, long-sleeved shirt and a denim skirt that reached her ankles.

"Leah?" she whispered again.

Tears filled Leah's eyes and a smile trembled on her lips as she rushed in to hug Hannah.

Chapter Twenty

Hannah could hardly believe it.

"When did you get back?" Leah asked.

After their initial greeting, the four of them sat around the table munching on cookies and enjoying being together.

Hannah shrugged. "A couple of weeks ago." She said the words knowing it had been too long. She should have called her sister before now. "I'm sorry," she said, even as her sister's eyes filled with pain. But hadn't it always been that way?

She was forever hurting those who loved her.

Leah had followed her out of Pontotoc to help her survive life with the *Englisch*, believing that one day they would return to their Amish home.

But before Hannah had made up her mind that she'd had enough of the world, she had learned that Aaron was seeing another. She couldn't go home if he was in love with someone else. Leah had gotten tired of being away and wanted to return to Pontotoc. Hannah had known that Leah hadn't wanted to leave to begin with, but she had talked her into it anyway. Then one horrible argument later, and she had barely seen her sister since.

How had she let her pride dictate her life?

"It's all right." Leah sniffed, then gave her a watery smile. "We're here now."

Hannah returned her smile. "It's been a little over-whelming to be home."

"But you're here, and that's all that matters."

The guests started to arrive around midday. Not that there were many guests that weren't part of the family. Aaron and his kids came first. Laura Kate and Essie raced across the yard to see who could get to her first. Andy hung back as if he still wasn't sure what her purpose was in their lives.

"*Danki, danki, danki* for inviting us to the party," Laura Kate said.

Every time Hannah had seen her, the girl had been deadly serious. Maybe the party was just what Laura Kate needed to come out of her shell. Andy too.

Essie was her typical bubbly self. "We brought Brandon a gift." She jumped up and down in place as if bringing a present was the most exciting thing she had ever done. She stopped dancing and lowered her voice to a perfect stage whisper. She leaned forward, though the gesture was not necessary. "It's a shirt. But *Dat* said that everybody needs a new shirt from time to time." She pulled herself back into place, a satisfied smile on her lips.

Laura Kate elbowed her in the ribs.

"Ouch!" Essie jumped as if she had been poked with a stick.

"You aren't supposed to tell," Laura Kate said.

Hannah grabbed Essie's arm and her attention before she could retaliate. "I'm sure it's okay this one time. Brandon's not around right now."

She wasn't sure where he'd gone, but he would turn up

sooner or later. Most likely sooner, since there was food involved.

"You're dressed funny today."

"Essie," Laura Kate admonished.

"What?"

She leaned in closer to her sister, but Hannah could still hear every word. "That's rude."

"But—" Essie tried her protest again, but Laura Kate shook her head. "Can I ask her why she's dressed like an *Englischer*?"

"No."

"But she was dressed Amish the last time we saw her. Does this mean she's leaving?"

"I don't know what it means, but you still shouldn't ask."

"How am I going to learn anything if I don't ask questions?" Essie poked out her bottom lip.

"You'll learn what you're supposed to learn when you're supposed to learn it."

Essie rolled her eyes at her sister, and Hannah had to hide her laugh.

She couldn't have answered Essie's questions even if she had wanted to. She didn't have any of those answers. She changed her dress willy-nilly depending on her mood. Today she thought she should be dressed in her own clothes. Well, the ones she had brought with her to Pontotoc—blue jeans, flip-flops, and a Tennessee Titans T-shirt.

She hadn't given her choice much thought until now. Her decision had been based more on what was clean than anything religious or spiritual.

"There's Dat." Essie took off toward her father in a dead run, with Laura Kate following behind.

Andy looked from his sisters' departing backs to Hannah. "I like your fried chicken."

Hannah blinked. Had Andy ever said one word to her?

Not that she could remember. "Th-thank you," she finally managed.

"I told my *dat* he should marry you," he said, matter-of-factly.

"You did?" *I wonder how Aaron took that.*

"You would make a good *mamm*." He nodded his head as if the matter were settled, then shoved his hands under his suspender straps and sauntered after his sisters.

As far as parties went, Brandon wouldn't call it lame, but he was certain some of his friends back in Nashville would think it was. He didn't care. He had a homemade cake that tasted like heaven on a fork—his grandmother had given him a taste the night before—his favorite girl, and his favorite cousin. What more could a guy want? Maybe one thing.

His mother dressed in regular clothes. Best. Present. Ever.

He was getting worried over the reasons why she had started dressing like the other Gingerich women, but today she looked like his mom again. Maybe she wasn't wearing any makeup, but her hair was down and her clothes were normal. And that made the day just perfect.

"Come on, Brandon," Joshua called. "It's your turn."

He started over to the flat place in the yard where they had set up the stakes to pitch horseshoes. At first Brandon hadn't wanted to play. It was his party, after all, and if he didn't want to play lame-o games then he shouldn't have to. But after watching the others carefully aim and try to ring the stake with the horseshoe, he decided to try it for himself. It was surprisingly fun. It took a lot of concentration and accuracy to make the highest points, and he found himself laughing along with his teammates, and the opposing team as well.

"Are you having fun?" he asked Shelly as he passed. She was sitting in a lawn chair, cup in one hand as she watched the others play.

She took a drink of her punch and smiled. "I'm having a great time. Tillie promised to share her quick-pickle recipe with me later."

He didn't know Shelly liked to cook, but he supposed if he'd thought about it he would have. She was so much like his mother and his aunts, and they liked all those domestic chores—canning, pickling, baking.

"Come play horseshoes with me."

She smiled and set down her cup. "You mean pitch horseshoes."

Brandon returned her grin. "Yeah, pitch them."

"One game," she said. "Then I'm going to find Tillie about that recipe before she changes her mind."

Hannah spied Tillie on the porch swing and seized the opportunity. She had been wanting to talk to her sister about her looming decision.

"Hey." She slid onto the bench seat next to her.

"Hey, yourself." Tillie scooted over to make room.

"It's a good party, yeah?"

Tillie glanced toward the yard where everyone had gathered.

Most of the guests had grouped in one place or another—the food table, the grill where her father flipped burgers and mopped his sweaty brow, the horseshoe stakes, or the impromptu game of kickball that had sprung up with the younger set. Hannah could see Essie and Laura Kate chasing after the ball, laughing the way little girls should.

"*Jah*, good," Tillie replied, but Hannah had lost the thread of the conversation.

She roused herself out of her thoughts and centered her attention on her sister. "How are things with Melvin?"

Tillie nodded. "Good. Good. He said he would be here with the present before we eat cake."

That was cutting it close, but Hannah didn't mind. As long as he got there before Brandon started opening gifts. "That's fine."

"I was hoping he would be able to come for the entire party, but his *dat* needed his help this morning." There was an unexplained wistfulness in her tone. Did it have something to do with her indecision over joining the church?

"It's okay," Hannah assured her.

Tillie nodded, but Hannah could tell that she didn't agree. Maybe whatever was standing in her way of making a decision also had something to do with Melvin.

"Have you thought any more about joining the church?" Might as well jump in with both feet.

Tillie shot her a sly smile. "What about you? Have you given it any more thought?"

Blindsided—that was the only way to describe how Hannah felt in that moment. "I—I . . . uh, I'm not thinking about joining the church," she finally managed. But the words were a lie, and she immediately regretted them. Strange the habits she had picked up in the *Englisch* world. Like withholding the truth in order to protect herself.

"Then why are you dressing Amish?"

Hannah gestured toward her *Englisch* duds. "I'm not."

"You have been."

Hannah couldn't argue with that. "It's easier," she said. "Sometimes."

"And today?"

Would Tillie understand that she had worn jeans for Brandon, or would she think it was something else? Was it? Hannah didn't know. "I thought this would be better."

"Uh-huh." Tillie's expression stated otherwise.

"What about you? Have you given your decision any more thought?"

"It's something I think about every day."

"But no answer?"

Tillie folded her fingers into the pleats in her apron. "It's complicated."

"It always is."

"How did you make your decision?"

She hadn't. The decision had been made for her. Or had she allowed the actions of others to force her decision? "I don't know. And I can't say I made the right one." There. She had said it.

"Are you saying you wish you hadn't left?"

She shook her head, unable to lie to her sister. "I don't regret leaving." There was an entire world out there that she had wanted to see—television, movies, driving cars. But once that time was up, she had wanted to come back to her life in Pontotoc. The problem was, that life hadn't waited for her. That life had continued on as if she had never been. "I can't regret leaving. It's made me who I am today." She was a much stronger person than the girl who had left Pontotoc all those years ago.

Tillie nodded. "I get it. But . . ." She stopped nodding and shook her head, her confusion evident.

"But what?"

"I think Melvin wants to leave."

Just as Hannah had thought. "And?"

"That's what's making it so hard. I mean, you made that decision all on your own."

She had.

"But I'm trying to make it knowing that Melvin feels there's more opportunities for us in the *Englisch* world."

"What about family?" That had been the hardest for her to accept, being away from her family. She wasn't shunned, not technically, but it wasn't like she could come back to

Pontotoc whenever she wanted. For a while she'd had Leah, but their differences and the stress of leaving had taken its toll. Before long they were disagreeing regularly. Then they were hardly speaking, and Hannah was all alone.

Maybe that was why she had fallen so hard for Mitch. Or she thought she had. He was good-looking, smart, funny, and so sophisticated. There had been a time when he had found her innocence of the ways of the world charming, but after a while she could tell it bothered him. She could tell that she embarrassed him, and then he started going places without her. Pretty soon, they were living different lives. But by then she had Brandon to think about.

"Just be careful," Hannah warned. "There's more out there than you know." She looked around at the camaraderie that existed so well in their community. People helping each other wasn't a phenomenon in the Amish world; it was a way of life. And one thing she had learned in all her time with the *Englisch*, there was no substitute for family.

"I will," Tillie promised. "I will."

Aaron chuckled as his girls ran through the field chasing after the kickball. They laughed and carried on and made him realize that all too often they had to be more grown-up than should be necessary. If Lizzie were still alive, he knew they would have more times like this.

Clang! Clang! Clang!

Everyone stopped as Eunice rang the triangle.

"Attention, please. It's time for Brandon to open his presents."

"What about the cake?" someone yelled.

"That too," Eunice returned. "But nothing's happening until everyone gets up here to sing him 'Happy Birthday.'"

Games were abandoned and seats vacated as the guests crowded around to sing Brandon his birthday song.

Aaron had never paid a great deal of attention to Hannah's son, but he took the time now to study the boy's features. Aaron had never met the boy's father, but as far as he could tell, there wasn't a thing of the man in the son. Brandon was the spittin' image of his mother. Same chestnut-colored hair, same hazel eyes. He had the same dimple in his chin and the same nose that turned up just a little on the end. He smiled up at his mother as she pushed the cake in front of him, candles glowing. He even had the same grin.

Everyone began to sing, and Aaron joined in. As the sound of the last word trailed off, Brandon blew out his candles while everyone cheered.

"Is that all the cake?" Caleb Gingerich, Brandon's cousin, asked.

Everyone laughed. True, the small round cake wouldn't be enough to feed even a quarter of the people there.

"Never fear," Eunice said. She moved another cake, a sheet cake, in front of Brandon. This one had no candles. On the top, someone had written *Happy 15th Birthday, Brandon*.

Hannah's son was turning fifteen. Aaron had never thought about it much. Didn't know she had a boy until she had returned home. But if Brandon was turning fifteen . . .

He did some quick calculations in his head, but didn't like the answers he came up with.

Hannah's son was turning fifteen. Which meant he had been conceived roughly nine months before. That would have been somewhere around November, almost sixteen years ago. And that would mean—

His thoughts came to a screeching halt. It couldn't

be. It just couldn't be. He didn't want it to be. Because if
it was . . .

He figured the months in his head, calculated and recal-
culated. It would have been harder if he didn't remember
the exact date when Hannah had left, but that day was forever etched into his brain. He knew it as well as he knew
his own birthday.

He turned his attention back to the party, but the ringing
in his ears prevented him from hearing what was being
said. Brandon smiled up at his mother. She squeezed his
shoulder, her pride evident. In the last week or so, the lip
earring had disappeared. The boy's hair was too long by
Englisch standards, but it was about right for Amish.

But he's not Amish.

Yet he should be.

The ringing in his ears intensified.

He didn't know for certain. He could be adding incorrectly. Or maybe he was seeing things that weren't really
there.

He sucked in a deep breath to steady himself, but his
hands trembled. He wiped shaky fingers across his face.

Brandon laughed and cocked his head to one side as he
listened to someone beside him. For Aaron it was like
looking in a mirror. He had never seen himself make that
move, but he knew what it felt like. It was his own gesture
mirror-imaged back at him. There was no denying it.

Without thinking, he pushed his way toward the crowd
until he was standing just behind Hannah. He wrapped
his fingers around her arm. She jumped, not expecting his
touch.

He bent his head to whisper in her ear. "I need to talk to
you. Now."

She started to shake her head, but he tightened his

fingers around her arm. She jerked her gaze to him, alarm flaring in her eyes.

She nodded. If she spoke, he couldn't hear her over the ringing in his ears.

He nodded toward the barn, but didn't let go of her arm as he marched her toward the open doors. This was as good a time as any. Everyone would be too busy with cake to notice if they disappeared for a spell. Though no matter how long they talked, Aaron wasn't sure he would ever feel like himself again.

What is it? she asked. He read her lips instead of hearing her words. He swallowed hard, hoping to clear his hearing.

But he didn't reply as he escorted her into the dim interior of the barn.

"Aaron?" This time her voice penetrated his stunned senses. "What's wrong?"

He shook his head and set his resolve. "Just when were you going to tell me that Brandon is my son?"

Chapter Twenty-One

Aaron watched as if in a dream. Hannah opened her mouth to speak, maybe even explain, then she closed it again with a shake of her head.

He shifted in place and waited for her to gather her thoughts. But deep inside he was afraid she was making up some wild story.

How could he believe anything else? Today she was back to being that Hannah, the one in the *Englisch* clothes who tossed her hair over her shoulder and had shiny lips.

He wanted to believe that Yesterday's Hannah was still in there somewhere, but he was certain he just didn't want to see the truth.

"Well?"

She clasped her fingers in front of her as if she suddenly didn't know what to do with her own hands. "I . . . I don't know."

"Never?" Somehow he managed to keep his tone at a normal level. God was definitely looking out for him, helping him keep his composure when he wanted to tear at his hair until it all became clear.

"It's not like that."

He shifted once again, realizing then that it was more to

keep him in place than anything else. He was an Amish man, committed to a peaceful life, turning the other cheek and all that it entailed. But right now, he didn't trust himself to be close to her. Too many emotions were flying through him, emotions he was struggling to control.

"Then tell me." His insides quaked as he waited once again for her answer. His hands trembled, and he couldn't seem to get enough air into his lungs.

"I was going to. Tell you." She shook her head as if she didn't like her own answer. Well, that made two of them.

He shifted once again. Outside the barn, the party guests had resumed their game playing. Shouts and laughter drifted in to them, teasing him with their joy. It wouldn't be long before someone missed them and came looking. "I'm waiting."

She sucked in a deep breath, then expelled it slowly. Or maybe he was just weary. "I was going to tell you when I found out. But for some reason I wrote to my brother first. He told me how you were going around with Lizzie Yoder, and I . . . Well, I figured you wouldn't care."

"I wouldn't . . . care?" Was she serious?

"I was eighteen."

"And pregnant with my baby." He shook his head. Never in his life had he had a conversation about such personal matters. But one thing was certain; they could go on like this indefinitely. And it was getting them nowhere.

"Aaron, I—"

"Does he know?"

"No."

"I want to spend some time with him. I want him to know."

"No!" The one word echoed in the rafters over their heads. "No," she repeated, softer this time. "No."

"Why not?" Aaron used every ounce of self-control to keep his tone from matching hers.

"He's been through so much this year. I can't lay that at his feet right now."

That made no sense. *Jah.* It would be hard for Brandon to understand, but certainly a living father would more than make up for it.

An Amish father.

"We can spend time together. I want to get to know him." Brandon was his son, and Aaron didn't know the most basic things about him. His favorite color, his favorite food. What did he do in his spare time? Did he like to read? Had Hannah taken him to church?

She seemed more than reluctant. "I—I guess. I mean, what are you going to tell him?"

He had no idea, but he would think of something. "Does that mean you'll let—won't try to keep me from seeing him?"

She swallowed hard and shook her head. "Just promise me you won't tell him about . . . about your relationship. That's something that should come from me. When the time is right."

But she never told him when that might be.

"You seem distracted."

Hannah jerked her gaze up to meet her sister's. Leah hovered next to the porch swing. How long had she been standing there before she spoke? How long had Hannah stared off at nothing while Leah waited for her to acknowledge her presence? "No . . . maybe . . ." She stopped pushing the swing with her heels and allowed her sister to sit next to her.

"You want to talk about it?" Leah asked.

Hannah sighed. Did she? "There's nothing to talk about." She started the swing again.

"I love you. But I don't believe that for a minute."

"Would you believe that it's nothing that I want to talk about?"

Leah flashed her a sad, understanding smile. "Aren't those the things we need to talk about the most?"

Hannah nodded. But the secret she had held for so long was jammed in her throat, refusing to budge. How could she tell her sister that she'd held this secret from her for nearly sixteen years? She hadn't told a soul. Leah had looked so hurt when she found out that Hannah had returned to Mississippi without telling her. How would she handle a secret like this? She didn't want to see the pain in Leah's eyes. They were twins, but their bond had been broken so long ago. Yet Hannah could feel Leah's pull, that sisterly magic that could only exist between two people who were born into this world together.

If Leah is going to be upset, how will Brandon handle the news?

Not good. Not good at all.

Was Hannah cursed to forever hurt those she loved?

"Aaron figured out that he's Brandon's father."

Leah stopped the swing with a jerk. "What?"

"Aaron is Brandon's father."

"I heard you." Leah shook her head. "I just wasn't sure I heard you right. I mean—" She sputtered to a stop. "You never told me that." Pain shone in her eyes.

"There was never a chance."

Leah shook her head and turned in the swing to stare at her, lips parted. "He's fifteen! You're telling me that there wasn't one time in all those years that you could have called me up and said, 'Hey, sis. Been meaning to tell you something'?"

"Really? You think it would be that easy?"

Leah's breath left her in an audible *whoosh*. "No, I suppose not, but . . ."

"But what?"

It took her so long to answer that Hannah wondered if she would respond at all. "I wish I knew. Maybe I could have—" Leah stopped again.

She didn't need to finish for Hannah to fill in the blanks. Maybe she could have helped Hannah. Maybe Hannah wouldn't have married Mitch. Maybe she would have come back. Maybe a lot of things would be different.

"It happened the way God wanted it to." The words should have felt foreign on her lips, but they came as naturally to her as they had all those years ago. There had been a time when she had believed in God's will. When she had believed that God had a plan in her life. But the more questions that stirred in her thoughts, the more that she felt God had somehow abandoned her. Or maybe He was letting her make her own way. If that was the case, she had fouled it up nicely. Maybe God having a plan wasn't such a bad thing after all.

"Do you really believe that?"

Hannah nodded, amazed at her own thoughts. "As a matter of fact, I do." A surprising weight lifted from her shoulders. Was she back in God's plan? Had she ever truly been gone? Suddenly her time in Mississippi seemed less like a last resort and more like the next step.

They fell silent for a moment, each lost in her own thoughts.

"I'm sorry about Mitch."

Hannah shook her head. "You don't have to say that."

"I never had the chance."

"Then I'm the one who's sorry."

Leah quietly studied her in the dark. "How so?"

"I should have never chosen him over you."

"I never should have made you choose."

Hannah tilted her head to one side, their differences from so long ago crowded around them. "I should have told you that I had gotten a letter from Jim."

Leah shook her head. "It wouldn't have changed anything."

And they were right back to God's plan and the night Leah had tried to talk Hannah into going back to Pontotoc. She had been thinking about going back for weeks, then she got the letter from Jim. And on the same day she discovered that she was pregnant. Leah wanted to leave, Aaron wanted Lizzie, and Hannah had no one to want her. Except Mitch McLean. She didn't choose Mitch over Leah. She chose her pride over them both.

"What do we do now?" Leah asked.

Hannah smiled and shook her head. "This isn't your problem."

"I should have made it my problem sixteen years ago. Seems like I have a lot of making up to do."

A chuckle escaped Hannah, then a sob. Leah pulled her close, pressing Hannah's head to her shoulder. Being held by her sister was like stepping back in time. All the trouble, all the hard feelings, all the mistakes just melted away. The next sob caught in her throat, but her own will mixed with Leah's strength gave her more courage than she ever knew she could have. She gave her sister one last squeeze, then lifted her head.

"I have my own share of making up."

Leah smiled and brushed two errant tears from Hannah's cheeks. "I tell you what. Why don't we call it even and let's just start again?"

"A do-over?"

"If you want to call it that."

"I'd like that." And just like that she got her sister back. Really and truly back. Tears filled her eyes once again, but these were happy tears.

"Don't cry," Leah admonished. "If you cry, then I'll want to cry. And I don't want to cry."

"I'm trying not to." But she was just so happy.

They took a minute to get themselves together.

"Now what?" Leah asked.

Hannah knew exactly what she meant. What was she going to do about Aaron? "I can't tell Brandon yet."

Leah nodded. "I understand. But you'll have to tell him eventually."

"I just want to give him a little more time," Hannah explained.

"Does he need more time? Or is it you?"

Leah's words echoed through Hannah's thoughts for the rest of the evening. Brandon had enthusiastically gone off to Joshua's for the night, allowing Leah and Hannah to have the sewing room beds. It had been so long since Hannah had shared a room with her sister that even the thought brought back more memories than she could count. They had been inseparable growing up, right until the time Hannah became interested in Aaron. Or rather, Aaron became interested in her. Neither one was baptized and therefore they couldn't officially date, but they had done more than their fair share of sneaking around.

Which is exactly how you found yourself where you are now.

"I'm glad you're here." Leah's voice drifted through the darkness.

"I'm glad you're here too."

"You're supposed to say 'me too.'"

But was she really glad that she was there? Every facet of the situation seemed at direct odds with the others. She was glad that she had come home for a time. But she was sad that her husband had to cheat and die before she did so. She was glad to see her family, but sad that Brandon had lost the only family he had ever known. She was glad that her sister was just across the room, but sad that Aaron had discovered her secret. Glad that for a time she and Aaron had almost had a second chance. Sad that he would never trust her again.

"Are you staying?" Leah's words were quietly spoken, but dropped like a bomb between them.

"I came home because—" *I had nowhere else to go.* Except she couldn't say those words. "I came here until Mitch's estate is settled."

"Then what?"

Hannah shrugged in the darkness. "Brandon and I start over. Get an apartment, go back to school." She hadn't thought about it until just that minute, but she would need to get her GED. She would need a job. And money, if there wasn't going to be any left over. She almost laughed out loud. Mitch had gone out and bought a yacht without her knowledge. She'd be lucky to get enough for a deposit on an apartment.

Then what?

"Dat thinks you're staying."

"I know."

She heard the covers rustle and could barely make out Leah's shadowy form as she pushed herself up on one elbow. "Did you tell him that?"

"I didn't tell him that I wasn't staying."

"Hannah." Her sister's tone was filled with exasperation.

Hannah sighed and flopped back onto the bed, staring up at the darkness. "You don't understand."

"Try me."

"I said you *don't* understand, not that you *won't*."

"Try me anyway."

Hannah sucked in a deep breath and shook her head, even if her sister couldn't see. "You never did anything."

"That doesn't make any sense," Leah noted.

"I mean you never got into any trouble. Mamm and Dat . . . they never had to get onto you or ground you."

"That's because they were too busy grounding you." Leah gave a small chuckle.

"Be serious," Hannah retorted.

"I am. You couldn't get away with anything, which meant I got away with everything."

That wasn't exactly how Hannah remembered it. "I just wanted to go out and look around a bit, but instead I broke everyone's heart." Including her own.

"So you came back and made Dat believe that you are staying."

"I let him believe what he wanted to believe."

"That's better." Leah's words dripped with sarcasm.

"Leah." She wanted to protest, but Hannah knew that her sister was right.

"I'm just saying. If you let Dat believe that you're staying, how is he going to feel when you leave again?"

She hadn't allowed herself to think about that. It had been easy, considering how many other things she had on her mind. And now she had to deal with Aaron and his relationship with Brandon. "I don't know," she whispered.

"You could stay." Leah's words dropped into the shadows between them.

"I can't stay." Even as she said the words, the idea of staying ran through her head. She could stay, not worry about starting over. She could go home. Hide out. Not let life get to her.

And what would that solve?

Nothing. She couldn't stay. She was just being fanciful. She had Brandon to think about. He might have been tickled with the car battery–operated phone charger that she had gotten him for his birthday, but that didn't mean he could make a life there in Plain Country, Mississippi. She herself knew how hard it was to adhere to the rules and regulations in such a conservative district. People like Gracie, they seemed to fall right into their own lives, never having to adapt. Never questioning, never wondering if there was more beyond the horizon. If Hannah herself had had all those questions, and if she had such problems adjusting after living there her entire life, she couldn't expect Brandon to be able to after being raised among the *Englisch*. It simply wasn't possible. No matter how much he enjoyed spending time with Joshua and his other cousins. This would never be home to Brandon. He would always be just a visitor. She wasn't one hundred percent convinced that she could fall back into the lifestyle once again.

But if her father thought she was staying . . .

"What are you going to do?"

Hannah fluffed her pillow and tried to get more comfortable, but the entire conversation was beginning to make her head hurt. "I'm going to go to church tomorrow and hope they don't put me under an official *Bann*. Then after church, I'm going to Aaron's house so he and I can talk about Brandon and what to do. Then I'm going to wait for my attorney to contact me about Mitch's estate."

"And that's all?" Leah asked.

"For now that's all I have."

Chapter Twenty-Two

Sunday morning dawned bright and sunny, directly at odds with her mood. The minute she thought she had it figured out, something came along and swept her feet out from under her.

God is always listening.

He knew what trials she faced. She would just have to be faithful and be patient, but honestly, both seemed in short supply these days.

"I think the bishop may want to talk to you after the service," Mamm said, as they washed the breakfast dishes.

Hannah nodded and tried not to let the pang in her belly get the best of her. Of course the bishop wanted to talk to her. She fully expected it. She had been back in Pontotoc four weeks. Four very eventful weeks. She couldn't remain there indefinitely without making a decision about where she belonged. She had known all along that this time was coming; she had just thought she would have a better idea of what to do when it got here.

"I thought as much," she managed to say.

"And what are you going to tell him?" Mamm handed her the last dish and wiped the counters down with the damp cloth.

Hannah dried the plate and stacked it in the hutch with the rest. "I don't know."

Mamm crossed her arms and eyed Hannah closely.

"What?" She really didn't want to know what was on her mother's mind, but she felt the need to say something. The look in those green eyes was too knowing for her own comfort.

"It's time, Hannah Mae."

"For what?" She was playing dumb, but she wanted to delay this as long as possible.

Mamm flicked an expressive hand toward her. "One day you're dressed in a *frack* and *kapp*, the next you're wearing your *Englisch* clothes. You can't remain with a foot in each world indefinitely."

The tension holding Hannah's shoulders stiff wilted. "I know."

"You know that, but you don't know what you want to do?"

She knew what she wanted; she just didn't see any feasible way for it to happen. Not now. Especially not now. She might have wanted, might have hoped and dreamed that there was a second chance for her and Aaron, but that had been blown apart yesterday.

She sighed. "I was hoping that Aaron and I . . ."

"*Jah?*"

Hannah shook her head. "But that's not going to happen."

"I've seen the way that boy looks at you."

Hannah couldn't stop her grin. "He's hardly a boy."

"You know what I mean."

"Yes, Mamm. I do."

"What's the problem?"

Did she really want to get into this with her mother now? No, she decided. They needed to leave for church soon, and her mother would have more questions than could be answered in fifteen minutes or less. This was a secret Hannah would have to keep for a bit longer.

"Love isn't the only thing we have to worry about."

Her mother nodded sagely. "*Jah*. There's the church, but I know they will vote to forgive you, and baptism classes start in the spring." Her mother's eyes lit up like sunshine through stained glass.

"Yes," Hannah said. "Of course."

But it was just one more lie on top of the mountain of lies she had already told.

"Hannah, a word."

She tossed the remaining cups into the trash barrel and turned to face the bishop.

Amos Raber was a tall man with an iron-gray beard and fierce eyes. To tell the truth, Hannah had always been a little frightened of him. Maybe because when she was younger she felt as if he held the keys to her redemption.

Now she believed differently, but he hadn't lost any of his intimidation. In many ways, he held the keys to her future.

"Of course." She dipped her chin and waited for him to continue.

"I'll come to your house tomorrow morning." The words held an ominous ring.

"I'll be there."

He gave a quick nod, then moved away to take care of other business, she was sure.

Hannah released a pent-up breath. She had known this was coming, but that didn't make it any easier. Just as she knew she and Aaron needed to have a long talk. She was looking forward to that even less.

"Are you about ready to go?" Tillie bounded up, her grin as infectious as always.

"I thought you were going to ride home with Mamm and Dat."

Tillie made a face. "I was supposed to ride home with Melvin." She shook her head.

"Is everything okay?" As if she could help. Hannah had her own problems with no answers. She had no business handing out advice to her sister.

Tillie shook her head, her sunny disposition disappearing in a heartbeat. She looked first one way and then the other, as if making sure no one was around to hear what she had to say. "He thinks we should go away for a little bit."

Hannah stopped. "Go away?"

"*Jah*. You know. Like take a trip."

"Like to Ethridge?" *Please, Lord, let her say yes.*

"Like to Tunica."

"Tunica!"

Tillie shushed her and glanced around again. "Not so loud."

Hannah took her sister by the arm and pulled her between two of the parked buggies. People were milling in and out. Some were getting ready to leave, but with over two hundred people wandering around, how were they supposed to get any privacy?

"Tillie, you can't go to Tunica."

Her sister pulled her arm from Hannah's grasp and sniffed. "Why not?"

"Well, there are casinos there, for one. What are you going to do in a casino?"

She shrugged. "You left and went away for years. Why shouldn't I go somewhere?"

"It's not like you think out there." How could she explain the terrible decision she had made without revealing her own secrets? She couldn't. But it wasn't like she would be able to keep her secret forever.

"I'm going to tell you something," she said, lowering her voice until it was barely above a whisper. "But you have to promise to keep it to yourself."

Something in her tone struck a chord with Tillie. Her sister's eyes widened, and she nodded.

"I would have come back a long time ago—years ago—but Jim wrote me and told me that Aaron was seeing someone else."

"Lizzie?" Tillie breathed.

"Yes. And because of that, I've not had the life I feel I should have had."

"But you could have come back," Tillie said.

"I suppose I could have, but I didn't think I could handle the rejection if he chose Lizzie over me. And Brandon."

It took a moment for what she said to sink in. "Brandon?"

Hannah nodded. "Brandon is Aaron's son."

"Does he know this?"

"He does now. And Leah knows, but no one else. I need to keep it that way until we figure out how to tell Brandon the truth."

Tillie's eyes grew even wider. "Brandon doesn't know?"

Hannah swallowed the lump in her throat. "No. It's been my secret all these years."

"Wow." Tillie's expression was one of wonder and awe. "Why are you telling me this now?"

"Because it's all about choices." She sighed. "I've made so many bad ones. Ones I can't take back. Ones that are affecting my life to this day. I just don't want the same thing to happen to you."

Her arrow hit its mark. Tillie nodded, her expression more thoughtful than Hannah had ever seen it.

"It's just for a while," Tillie protested, though her tone was weak.

Hannah shot her a sad smile. "That's exactly what I said."

In the end, Hannah had to take both Gracie and Tillie home before heading over to Aaron's. Thankfully she didn't have to answer any of Brandon's questions about her whereabouts. He had gone into town to go to church and eat with Shelly and her family. Since they knew Amish church would last over half the day, she wasn't expecting him home until after supper.

But when she pulled into the drive at Aaron's, Laura Kate and Essie immediately ran out to greet her.

"Hannah! Hannah!" they cried, "you're here!" as if she hadn't seen them less than an hour before at church.

Aaron came out onto the porch, his stance a little less enthusiastic.

"I thought we would have time to talk," Hannah said as he unhitched her horse and turned her out into the pasture. That alone made Hannah feel that she was going to be here until they worked something out. No matter how long it took.

"Girls, go find your brother and tell him it's time to go down to Nancy's."

Essie stuck out her lip in an exaggerated pout. "Do we have to?"

"*Jah*. You do."

Hannah thought they might protest further, but they didn't. With dragging footsteps, they ducked into the barn to find their brother.

"They don't like to go to Nancy's?" Hannah asked. Nancy Byler was a close neighbor to the Zooks. She was something of an odd duck, sweet as sugar, and very helpful. She didn't have any children of her own and favored baby-sitting over any other ministry to foster the community.

"They would rather stay here with you." Something in his tone seemed to accuse her. As if she were making his family care about her for some sinister reason.

Be fair.

She had lied to him about something big. Really big. And it was going to be a while before he would forgive her.

"Come on." He motioned her to follow him into the house.

They were going to sit and talk, so why did it feel as if she were headed to her doom?

Because the world as she knew it was once again coming to an end.

When will this stop, Lord? I have surrendered all to You. When will this end?

"Have a seat. Do you want a drink of water or anything?"

Hannah shook her head as she sank onto the couch. Her stomach was pitching like a ship on rough seas. She needed to get a handle on herself before she was physically ill.

Aaron sat down on the bench across from her, his eyes intense. "Why?"

The question was simple, but covered everything all at once. In order to answer she would have to tell her story from the beginning, but she supposed she owed him that much. Maybe if she told it he would understand.

She sucked in a deep breath, then let it out slowly. "When I left here, I only planned to stay gone for a couple of months. That was the agreement."

"Agreement?"

She nodded. "Between me and Leah. She never wanted to go, but she didn't want me to leave by myself."

"Go on."

"After a couple of months, I wasn't ready to come back. But Leah was. I talked her into staying a little longer. By then I had met Mitch." He was the embodiment of everything Hannah had been missing with the Amish. So sophisticated, so *Englisch*. At the time she had wondered if he held all the answers. If he could tell her what she had been missing; what she *would* be missing when she went back.

"Leah and I got into a terrible argument, and she left. I never told her, but that same day I received a letter from Jim telling me that you were seeing Lizzie Yoder."

Aaron blew out a harsh breath. "This is my fault?"

"No. I take the blame. But please understand, I couldn't come back here. I was unwed, pregnant. You were seeing someone else. What if you rejected me? What would I do then?"

"You think I wouldn't have accepted my responsibility?"

"Do you really think I wanted to be a responsibility to you?"

"I loved you!" His voice was nearing a shout, and he rose halfway out of his chair as he said the words. Then he cleared his throat and settled back into his seat.

"Then why did you start dating her?" Hannah hadn't wanted to ask that question. It was something she could live without knowing. She didn't want to hear how Aaron had fallen for Lizzie's charms. But now that the question was out and hovering between them, she needed the answer more than she needed her next breath.

"You left without one word. I had no idea where you had gone. I had no idea when you would be back." He shrugged. "I did the only thing I could. I started over."

So much pain. So many mistakes.

"I did the same." She pressed her lips together and gathered her thoughts before continuing. "Mitch was so excited."

"He thought the baby was his?" A stain of dark red flushed his cheeks.

"No. He knew from the beginning, but he said he

wanted a family. He was anxious for this immediate family." Or so he had thought. But once Brandon was born, all Mitch could see was another man's child. He had told her that very thing during one of their constant arguments. He had thought he could look past Brandon's parentage, but he wasn't able. And Hannah was stuck in a marriage to a man she had nothing in common with, a man who tossed her over the first chance he got.

But now Mitch was gone, and the man sitting across from her deserved a chance to be a father to the son he had never known he had.

"I might be able to understand why you kept this from me when he was alive, but why didn't you tell me this when you came back into town?"

Hannah clasped her hands in her lap, unsure of what to do with them. "I guess I had been lying about it for so long that it never occurred to me to tell the truth." She hadn't thought of Aaron as Brandon's father . . . ever.

She choked back a sob. "That was so unfair of me. And I know that you'll forgive me." It was simply the Amish way. "But I can't ask for it." She shook her head. Maybe she had been living with the *Englisch* for too long, but as much as she needed Aaron's forgiveness, what she had done was simply unforgiveable.

"I want to spend some time with him."

Hannah's heart sank. What had she expected? For him to demand her to ask him for forgiveness? Would she be absolved if he had? "He can't know."

"Hannah." The one word was loaded with anger, hurt, and disbelief.

She put her hands to her ears to stop the buzzing that had taken up there. She had started this, and she had to see it through. "Just give me a minute to think, Aaron."

"What's there to think about? You've had him and

hidden him from me for the last fifteen years. An afternoon at the farm is the least you could do."

Her hands fell to her lap. "He can't know," she said, hoping her tone was as emphatic as she intended. She couldn't be sure; everything she said tended to sound like a question.

Because you know you are wrong. You have wronged this man, you've wronged your son, and now you have to do whatever it takes to make things right.

"I don't want to tell him yet. He just lost his father—"

"*I* am his father."

She shook her head. "Mitch has been the only father he's known. I'll tell him, just not right now. There's a time and a place. I'll find it, but I'll only tell him then."

She could see that Aaron wanted to protest, but he held his tongue. Finally he gave a stern nod. "You have two weeks. After that, I'll tell him myself."

Somehow Aaron made it through the next hour without losing what control he had over his temper. He had never known that he had a temper until today. He had managed not to shake Hannah until she changed her mind. He hadn't raised his fist to the sky and railed to the heavens for the injustices that he had been served. Not just him, but Brandon as well. Brandon. His son.

Hannah had promised that he could spend time with Brandon tomorrow. She needed tonight to figure out a way to arrange it so that Brandon wouldn't be suspicious, but Aaron was to come over tomorrow and work with Abner's mare, and she would take care of everything from there.

"Dat! Dat!" Essie dashed into the house, one hand on her head to hold her prayer *kapp* in place as she ran. "Look what Nancy gave us." She whirled around, but no one was there. "Laura Kate," she yelled. "Hurry up!"

Laura Kate finally came through the door toting a large sack filled with jars of pickles, two loaves of bread, and two new dresses for the girls.

"Look at them!" Essie danced in place as she held the dark green dress in front of her. "It's so pretty. And Laura Kate has one just like it. Now we can be twins like Hannah and Leah."

And to think he'd almost pushed her from his mind.

"And she made Andy a shirt too," Essie said.

Just then her brother came in, shutting the door behind him. Until that moment, Aaron hadn't given any thought as to how Brandon and his newly uncovered relationship with him would change the dynamics of his family.

Andy would go from being the oldest to being in the middle and from being the only boy to one of two.

And what were they going to do?

"She wanted to know if we made any decisions about Ohio." Andy made a face as he sat down at the kitchen table across from Aaron.

Ohio. "What did you tell her?" he asked.

Andy shrugged one shoulder. "That we don't know yet." He sighed. "We don't, do we?"

Aaron shook his head. "No," he choked out. "Not yet." But he knew: a move now was completely out of the question.

Chapter Twenty-Three

When Hannah pulled her car to a stop in the side yard at her parents' house, she was faced with the last thing she wanted to see: the bishop's buggy parked near the barn and the bishop himself waiting in the drive. Her father hovered nearby.

She cut the engine, grabbed her purse, and got out of the car.

"Hello," she called in greeting.

The bishop nodded, his unsmiling expression unreadable. Honestly, the man always looked that way. How was she supposed to know what he was thinking if he always looked the same?

"I think you should join us, Abner," the bishop said as Hannah drew near.

Great. That was just what she needed. She and her father had barely gotten back on speaking terms. She didn't need him to turn against her again.

"As you wish." Dat nodded toward the work shed. "Let me go tell the boys, and I'll meet you inside."

Her father headed off toward the shed, and Hannah was left alone with Amos.

"Let's go inside," she suggested, suddenly more nervous than she had ever been in her life. She knew what was about to come, had known it for weeks. So why did she feel like the world had just been jerked from underneath her feet?

He cleared his throat and held his ground. "I would like to ask you about the uh, car."

A small, non-humorous laugh escaped her. "It's not mine."

"But you're driving it."

She nodded. "It's my son's. He has to go to school in town, and I have to take him."

"And you can't take him in a proper carriage?"

All the excuses that popped to her lips were weak at best. The car was quicker. Her son would have a fit if he had to ride in a buggy. "It just seems easier . . . ?"

"And dressed like that?" He gave a scalding look to her Amish *frack*, apron, and prayer *kapp*. She would have thought her manner of dress might make him happy, but she could see now that she was wrong. Though she wasn't sure if she had been dressed in blue jeans and a T-shirt that it would have made any difference to him at all.

"I'm sorry," she managed.

"It's unacceptable." He looked down his nose at her, but Hannah couldn't find fault with his disapproval. His job was to keep everything running smooth in the church, and she was nothing less than a jagged pothole mucking up the road.

"I—I—" But she had no words to defend her behavior. She had gotten up, not with this meeting in mind, but the one to come—the one with Aaron—even more prominent in her thoughts. She hadn't been thinking about what she was wearing when she drove to town.

But you knew what you were doing at Brandon's party.

So she was confused. How could she not be? She had a foot in each world and no clear direction. No matter how many times she had asked God, she still had no answer.

"You didn't have to wait." Her father came out of the barn, and Hannah was saved having to reply.

The men turned and made their way toward the house, leaving Hannah to trail behind.

Lord, take this decision from me, she prayed. *I have surrendered it to You. I don't have the answer on my own. I need Your help.*

But she still didn't know what to do as she made her way into the house.

Her mother cast them all a cautious glance, then bustled into the kitchen to warm up the coffee and find them a mid-morning snack.

"Now," the bishop said once Mamm had poured everyone a cup and slid into the chair next to Hannah. "I feel we've let this go on long enough." He shot Hannah a pointed look. "We are very glad to have you back in the community, but we have rules, as you know. I need to know your intentions."

Where's my answer, Lord? I want to stay.

Until that moment she hadn't realized that it was true. She did want to stay with her family. She wanted to join the church, reconnect with everyone, especially Aaron, but there was one big problem standing in her way. Brandon.

How could she have both? How could she rejoin her Amish roots and raise her *Englisch* son?

The son who should have been Amish.

She shook her head at herself. Wasn't it all part of God's will? Did she even know what God's will was anymore? She had prayed and prayed the other night. Prayed harder than she had prayed in years. And yet she was no closer to an answer now than she had been then.

"Hannah?"

She jerked her attention to her mother.

"Are you okay?" Mamm asked.

Hannah nodded, even though it was a lie. What was one more?

"I don't know," she whispered.

"I'm sorry?" the bishop asked.

"I don't know," she repeated, louder this time.

Her mother and father sat in stunned silence. They had been hopeful that she would somehow make her way back into the fold. She had been hopeful too, but the answer wasn't there. She didn't know how to make it work. She had asked for answers, but she hadn't received even one. Where was God when she needed Him?

God is always listening.

Why wasn't He listening now?

"I'm sorry." She shook her head. Her heart pounded in her throat. She could practically hear the blood rushing through her ears. There were too many decisions to make. She needed help, and yet there was none.

"This is not an acceptable answer," the bishop said with a frown. At least this time his expression and his words matched. She knew exactly what he was thinking.

"I know." Hannah clasped her hands around her coffee mug. "I don't have the answers."

My God, my God, why hast thou forsaken me?

I just need to know what to do. How can I have all that I need? How can I become Amish again and take care of my Englisch son?

"I cannot allow this to go on indefinitely," Amos said. "You have two weeks to make a decision. That is more than enough time."

He didn't need to say what would happen if she didn't

decide. She would have to leave, and an official *Bann* would begin. The time of reckoning was near.

The bishop stood, and her father quickly followed.

"The most important thing is that you're home," Amos said. "That's a big step in the right direction. I'm sure the answers are closer than you think."

She wished.

He nodded toward Mamm, then headed for the door, her father on his heels.

"I thought you were going to stay," her mother whispered, eyes focused on the table in front of her.

"I never said that." If Hannah had known how cold the words would actually sound, she never would have said them. "I'm sorry."

"You don't have to leave," Mamm continued.

Hannah shook her head. "I don't see how I can stay."

"There's a way," Mamm said.

But how can you leave?

Aaron deserved a chance to know his son. Brandon deserved to know his real father. Yet, what kind of relationship could they have if she remained out of the church? What would the bishop allow?

And what about Aaron? They had almost reached a new point of understanding. She loved him. And he loved her, or so he had said. But now she suspected that everything he felt for her was buried underneath the lies of the last fifteen years.

Overwhelmed was not quite the word for what she felt when Aaron pulled his buggy into the drive less than two hours later.

She had gone into town to pick up Brandon, so very aware of driving the car and everyone's stares. She had

to endure stares from her family when she changed into
Englisch clothes, though she left her hair pulled back in its
tight bob. She was certain everyone in town was staring at
her as she drove to the library. And then Brandon cast
curious glances at her all the way home.

"Brandon," she called. "Aaron is here."

Brandon came out of the kitchen, a sandwich in one
hand and a glass of water in the other. "So?"

Hannah shrugged nonchalantly. "I thought you might
want to go watch him work with the mare today."

His eyes lit up, but he shrugged his shoulders and took
a bite of the sandwich as if it were no big deal. "I guess.
Maybe."

She stepped out onto the porch and motioned for Brandon to follow. Thankfully he did, stopping next to her as
Aaron let himself into the corral.

"Have you known him for a long time?" Brandon asked.

If she said the question surprised her, it would be a
gross understatement. "Yes. Why?"

Brandon cocked his head to one side in lieu of a shrug.
"I dunno. It seems like you know him pretty good."

You could say that.

"Aaron and I grew up here together."

"Is that all?"

Hannah eyed him curiously. "Are you asking me if he
was my boyfriend?"

Brandon had the grace to turn pink even though he
maintained his cool attitude. "Maybe. The two of you
seem . . ." He trailed off, and she was glad he did. Was it
so obvious that even a self-absorbed fifteen-year-old boy
could see what simmered between them?

"Well, that was a long time ago," Hannah said primly.
Her tone was one her mother had used a hundred times.

"So there is something between you two." Brandon chuckled.

"Was," she corrected. "Are you going to go watch him?"

"I dunno."

"I thought you were interested in how he works with the horses. I'm sure he would tell you about it if you asked."

"I suppose." He loped down the steps and started for the corral.

Hannah watched him, her heart in her throat. She knew in that moment she couldn't keep father and son apart. She had to do whatever it took. She owed them both that much.

Was this really Hannah's idea of spending time together? Aaron glanced over to where Brandon had climbed up on the slatted wooden gate to watch. If he had been Amish, Aaron would have asked for the boy to come stay with him, help with farm chores and the like. But he wasn't Amish, and Aaron didn't have the first clue as to what he liked.

Andy was into kickball and going fishing when he wasn't at school or doing chores. But Aaron had a feeling that kickball would seem juvenile to Brandon. If Aaron remembered right, he had seen Brandon pitch horseshoes at his party, but Aaron's attention had been torn between the party itself and the truth about the boy.

Aaron grabbed Star's reins and gently tugged her toward him. He released them and took a step back, hoping she would follow. He smiled when she did. He repeated the exercise until they were on the other side of the corral where Brandon sat.

Knowing she had done what he wanted, Star butted her head against his chest.

He laughed and retrieved the two sugar cubes he had put there for her.

"Why did you do that?" Brandon asked.

Aaron turned his attention to the boy. "Because she did what I wanted."

"You wanted her to follow you across the pen?"

Aaron rubbed the horse's soft nose, and she blew out a snorting *thanks*. "*Jah*."

Brandon shook his head. "Why?"

Aaron gathered the reins once more and tugged the horse close. He patted her neck, giving her the love and attention he knew she had lacked with her previous owners. "It's about trust. She needs to know that I won't hurt her. That I care about her and love her. That I will uphold my promise to care for her."

The parallels between his relationship with the horse and his fledgling relationship with Brandon slammed into him. He would have to take this slow, build trust.

Last night he had listened to the things Hannah *hadn't* said. If her late husband hadn't been able to look past Brandon's parentage . . . Aaron could easily suppose that they didn't have the best relationship. And, like Star, he would be leery of others, protective of his heart, withholding of his affections.

As much as Aaron wanted to run headlong into this new realm of fatherhood, he had to go slow, for all their sakes—his, Hannah's, and Brandon's as well as Andy's, Laura Kate's, and Essie's.

A family. They could all be a family. He nearly staggered with the thought. Never in his wildest dreams had he imagined he would have a second chance with Hannah, and even though he needed a little more time before the forgiveness would come, he would forgive her. And if she stayed . . . if Brandon stayed . . . Aaron would stay, and the six of them could be a family.

It was more than he could have ever prayed for.

And what of the church?

How would the church handle the situation with Brandon? It was unusual, to be certain, but Amos Raber was a fair man. He might be harder than most, but he cared about family and keeping the community as one. Aaron was confident that they could figure out a solution that would suit them all. They had to. They simply had to.

"Can I ask you a question?"

Aaron shifted his attention to the boy sitting on the gate. Until then, he hadn't been aware that he had been staring at the ground, a thousand thoughts swirling around his head. "*Jah*. Sure."

"And you won't get mad or all offended?"

Aaron's heart gave a hard pound in his chest. He wasn't sure he could honestly say, but this was about trust. "Okay."

"Why does everyone's hair look like they had a bowl plopped on their head before they got it cut? All the guys, I mean."

Aaron bit back a laugh. "I never thought about it much. That's just how we do it."

"Is that why everyone dresses the same too?"

"It's about community and God."

Brandon frowned. "Why does God care what you wear?"

"God cares about everything."

He seemed to think about it a moment. "You think?"

"I know."

Brandon fell quiet.

"If you're curious about the Amish, maybe you should talk to your mother about it."

The boy nodded, but he still wore that contemplative look. "Is that bad? To be curious?"

Aaron shook his head. "Not at all. It's only natural, since your mother grew up here."

"I suppose." Brandon hopped down from the gate and gave him a quick wave. "Thanks for letting me watch you." He turned to leave, but Aaron stopped him.

"Brandon?"

"Yeah?"

"How would you and your mother like to come to my house for supper tonight?"

"I dunno. I'll have to ask Mom."

"That's all right. I can ask her."

Brandon nodded. "If she says yes, then I guess that would be okay."

"*Jah*," Aaron agreed. It would be okay. And a small, small start.

"Let me get this straight. You invited me to supper tonight at your house, but I'm going to have to cook?"

Aaron rubbed the back of his neck and shot her a sheepish grin. "Something like that. *Jah*. Are you mad?"

Hannah chuckled. How could she be upset with him? After only a day he had seemed to forgive her. Or at least to try. Now it was up to her. "No."

"I thought it would be a good idea for the kids to spend a little time together before we tell them."

Hannah hadn't thought about that. She had only been concerned with telling Brandon, but Aaron was going to have to tell his children too. How would they handle the news? "That's probably a good idea."

"Have you thought any more about talking to Brandon?"

She shook her head. She hadn't been able to think of anything other than the bishop's ultimatum and her unanswered prayers. When she hadn't been able to commit one hundred percent she had been afraid that her father would revert back to ignoring her. So far that hadn't happened. "No," she finally said.

Disappointment scarred his features. "He's a good kid, Hannah."

A lump of mixed emotions clogged her throat.

"I just want a chance to get to know him."

"I know," she whispered. "And you'll get that chance. I promise."

"What do you think is going on?" Shelly asked.

It had been almost a week since Brandon's birthday party, and his mom was acting weirder every day.

"I don't know," he whispered in return. He propped up the large book in front of him to help hide from the watchful eyes of the librarian. She was nice enough, but if he spent too much time talking to Shelly, he knew she would tell her mother. Other than Joshua, Shelly was the only friend he had here, and he surely didn't want to blow it.

"No idea at all?"

He shook his head. "I mean, she started acting strange at the party, but I figured it was just 'Oh, my baby's turning fifteen' crap. You know how moms are. But she's just been acting weirder and weirder."

"Okay. Tell me what she's doing, and I'll see if I can find a pattern." That was his Shelly, always with a plan.

He smiled at her, so thankful that he had met her. He'd heard people talking about serendipity and kismet—even the Amish talked about God's will. He supposed it was all about the same thing. What was meant to be would be, and being in the right place at the right time. He was just glad he had come into the library at the right time that first day.

"Well, every night this week we've either gone over

to Aaron's house or he's come over to ours. Well, my grandmother's, you know."

She nodded. "And are they spending a lot of time alone?"

"Not really. I mean, that was what I was thinking too. Like maybe she has a thing for this guy. But they aren't holding hands or making goo-goo eyes at each other." The thought was a little sickening. Another reason to be glad it wasn't happening. Thinking about it was bad enough. But to actually see it? He shuddered.

"The Amish are different," Shelly explained. "They don't hold hands and things like that. I mean, not when other people are around."

Brandon frowned. "Do you think she has a thing for this guy?"

Shelly shrugged. "It's possible, I guess. Didn't you say that they knew each other before?"

"Yeah." He leaned back in his chair, then sat forward when he realized he was clearly in the librarian's sight. "But if she has a thing for this guy . . ." His dad had only been gone a couple of months. Could she be ready to move on and get married again?

"If they are serious about each other, I think your mom has to join the Amish church."

"Is that a big deal?" Something in Shelly's tone told him it was.

"Yeah." She shook her head. "I'll see what I can find out, okay?"

"Yeah, okay." But he felt anything but satisfied. "If she joins the church, does that mean I do too?"

Shelly pulled a face. "I think so. But I'm not sure."

Everyone he knew who was Amish dressed the same and lived in plain white houses and went to church for three hours every other Sunday. No one had electricity or indoor toilets or phones. He might could do that for a time, but that didn't mean he would want to live that way for the rest of his life. The last few weeks had been hard enough. And he had been willing to give it a try to take some of that stress from his mom's eyes, but he couldn't live like this forever! He wouldn't even do it for another three years.

One more week, he told himself. When they had first arrived in Pontotoc he had vowed three weeks. It had been over a month. He'd give her one more week, and after that, something was going to change.

Chapter Twenty-Four

"You haven't heard a word I've said," Leah complained, crossing her arms and shooting Hannah a look she knew all too well.

"Sorry." She hadn't been listening. She had been lost in her own thoughts.

She had one more week to make her decision. Seven days, and yet she was no closer to an answer than she had been the day she drove into Pontotoc. Every night she had prayed. Every night she asked God to give her an answer. Every night she told Him that she surrendered all unto Him. But every morning, the same problems were still there.

"Tell me again," Hannah asked.

They were sitting on the porch enjoying an afternoon away from canning. It wouldn't be long until there were no quiet days, just hours measured in how many quarts of tomatoes they had put up.

"Have you seen that empty shop downtown, there on Main?"

"The one next to the new Chinese place?"

"That's it."

"What about it?" Hannah asked.

"I'm thinking about opening a shop."

Hannah blinked, unsure that she had heard her sister correctly. "A shop?"

"Yeah." Leah nodded. "A resale shop."

"There are three or four of those on Main already."

"There are two, and mine will be different." Leah raised one brow as if daring Hannah to contradict her.

"How so?" Discussing Leah's new idea might be a fine distraction from her own life. How many times did she have to ask God for an answer before she got one? She was running out of time.

"I'm going to gear it toward Plain people."

Hannah shook her head. "You lost me."

"I'm only going to take in clothing suitable for Mennonite men and women to wear. And then housewares and that sort of thing."

"What about commissions?"

"I haven't decided yet."

"And the Amish?"

Leah's face lit up. "That's the biggie. I want to set up a swap in the back for the Amish community."

Hannah thought about it a moment. "Are you going to charge?"

"No, that'll be my offering to the community."

"I see." Hannah gave an exaggerated nod. "You're trying to get in good with the bishop."

Leah laughed. "You should try it sometime."

"Just because you hadn't joined the Amish church before you hooked up with the Mennonites is no reason for him to give you a clean slate."

"Jealous much?"

It had nothing to do with jealousy. And everything to do with Aaron and Brandon.

Leah grew quiet, as if sensing Hannah's thoughts. "The Mennonites are great people. I think you would like the church."

"And you're going to drive to Southaven every Sunday in order to go to church?" She would if she rented the store in town.

"There's a Mennonite church in town."

"In Pontotoc?" Hannah didn't bother to hide her surprise.

"On Second Street. You could come with me." But becoming Mennonite would not solve her problems. It would only shift them to a new religion.

"What are you going to do?" Leah asked.

Hannah blew out a frustrated breath and went to stand by the porch railing. She leaned against it, her back to the yard. "There's no answer." She threw her hands into the air and let them fall back against her thighs. "I've prayed and prayed, but there is no answer."

"There's always an answer."

God is always listening.

"Then what is it?"

She could join the church, but what about Brandon? She still had to tell him that Aaron was his father. It wasn't like the bishop would allow him to stay in the community and drive a car and do all the other things she knew he had been waiting for half his life.

"Do you want to join the church?" Leah asked.

"Yes. I mean, I think so."

"You either do, or you don't."

What did she want?

A time machine to go back and make different choices. But since that wasn't an option . . .

"I guess so. I mean, I—Aaron—"

"Spit it out, sister."

Hannah shook her head and gathered her thoughts.

"Aaron and I might have a second chance together. But not unless I join the church."

"So I'll ask again. Do you want to join the church or not?"

"It's not that simple."

"It never is." Leah swung one leg up into the swing and used the other to push herself back and forth. "What happens if you join the church?"

"I'm afraid I'll alienate Brandon completely. He's going to be upset enough when the truth comes out." She lowered her voice even though she had just seen him disappear over the ridge with Joshua, fishing poles in hand.

"And the bishop?"

"I don't know." Hannah bit her lip and shook her head. "I just don't know. I don't think he'll let him live with me with the Amish and carry on like an *Englischer*."

"And he's not going to want to join the church."

Hannah shot her a look. "You didn't even join the church."

Leah grinned. "But you're thinking about it, and that just goes to prove miracles are still alive and well."

"Ha. Ha."

"I'm serious."

Hannah wished she could agree. She could use one of those miracles right about now.

"Are you really going to join the church?"

Hannah pushed off the railing and nudged Leah's leg out of the swing before returning to her place beside her sister. "I called my attorney the other day. When this whole thing started I thought I would have enough to start over. Now that's not looking good for me."

"Is that what this is?" Leah asked. "A do-over?"

Hannah shook her head. "I've thought about that too, but I've so enjoyed being back here. It's so quiet and peaceful. The only thing you have to worry about is what's for supper."

"And heating water, and cleaning the outhouse. Face it; this is a hard life. You and I both know that."

"But there's something beautiful about it. Its simplicity, I guess."

"And that's what you want? Simplicity?"

"I just never noticed it before."

"Maybe because you were too busy trying to find out everything you could about the *Englisch* world."

"Maybe." Or maybe she had been too young to appreciate it. Or perhaps she had to live the life she had lived in order to see what she had left behind. "But I want a piece of it now."

"Forever?"

The thought didn't send her stomach plummeting to the floor. "Yeah. I think I do."

"Then isn't that your answer?"

"Brandon," she said.

"Basically you have to choose between your son and the man you love."

"Now you understand why I'm having such a hard time. I mean, I know I can't leave Brandon, but there's this part of me . . ."

Leah nodded. "I get it. You're a mother, but you're a woman too."

A mother who kept hoping for a miracle. An answer in God's promise. An answer that was not forthcoming.

Hannah pulled into Aaron's drive and shut off the engine. But she didn't get out of the car. This . . . this was the last thing she wanted to do. But it was over. She had searched and prayed, begged, then searched and prayed some more, but there was no answer from God or anyone else. She was in charge of this, and she had to see it through.

She blew out a heavy breath and got out of the car. It was two o'clock, and Aaron's kids would still be at school. That was good. She needed to talk to him all alone.

He came around the side of the house, a bag of clothespins swinging from one hand.

"Hannah?"

"Hi."

He squinted as if he didn't recognize her. She supposed to him she looked so different than the Hannah she had been portraying these last few weeks. But it was her in her *Englisch* clothes, driving her beat-up clunker of a car, no longer pretending that any of this could work itself out.

"What are you doing here?"

At least he didn't ask her about her clothes, but they would get to all that soon enough.

"I need to talk to you."

He swallowed hard, but nodded. They both knew; this was a conversation they'd rather not have.

"Want to come in the house?"

She shook her head and nodded toward the bag he carried. "Doing laundry?"

"Just a random load. Essie slipped and fell into a cow patty yesterday."

Hannah laughed. "Poor Essie."

"Poor Aaron. She's off at school, and I'm left to clean up the mess."

How did he manage to get everything done as both mother and father? The responsibility was staggering, much more than an *Englisch* single parent would face. Hannah knew he had help, and yet deep down, she suspected it wouldn't be long before he married again. His year of mourning was almost over. Three kids and a farm were more than one man could handle alone.

There had been that small window of time when she had allowed herself to believe she might be that woman. But now she could see clearly. They hadn't stood a chance. Not with everything they faced.

"Come around back?" He didn't wait for her to respond, just spun on his heel and led the way to the backyard.

Like most Amish houses in the area, Aaron's had a laundry wheel attached to the back-porch post. The line itself stretched toward the upper level of the barn and ran perpendicular to the wire laden with martin bird-gourds. The homemade birdhouses swayed in the warm breeze.

"So," Aaron said, pulling another dress from the basket near the porch's edge. "What do you want to talk about?"

"I think you know."

He looked back at her even as he pinned the dress to the line. There was no mistaking with the way she was dressed. There was no mistaking her intentions.

"Just let me finish this . . ." He trailed off and hung another dress on the line.

Hannah shifted from one foot to the other, waiting as patiently as she could. It was not easy, knowing what needed to be said and having to wait to actually get the words out. But she would do this, for him.

"Okay." When the last dress was on the line, Aaron grabbed his basket and made his way to the back door. "Are you coming?"

She started up the steps after him. "Don't you have someone to help with the laundry?"

He nodded and set the basket in the small mudroom at the back of the house. "The bishop's wife comes once a week, but if something happens in the meantime . . ."

"Like Essie falls into a cow patty?"

"Exactly. Then I'm stuck doing a load in between."

How long would that last? How long before he remarried? How was she going to stand by and watch him reach for a happiness that might have been theirs?

He led the way into the kitchen, and they sat down at the table, facing each other but silent. Not the best way to talk, but really? What needed to be said was so hard she wasn't sure she could get the words out.

"Say it," he quietly commanded.

"I'm not joining the church." But that was just the tip of the iceberg, as they say. "I'm so very, very sorry." Tears rose into her eyes, but she wiped them away with the back of one hand. The time for crying had long since passed.

"I understand."

"Do you?" she cried. "Because I'm not sure I do."

There was so much at stake. She knew she hadn't lived the life she had been raised to live, but she had worked hard her entire life. Why was God abandoning her now when she needed Him the most?

Aaron took her hands into his own. "You're a good mother, Hannah. I knew you would do what was best for your child, above anything you wanted for yourself. I would have done the same."

She shook her head, but didn't pull away. "Why isn't there a way that everyone can get what they need?"

"That's for God to know."

"Ugh!" She growled and pulled her hands away. She scrubbed them over her face, smearing her tears in the process. "It's not fair."

"But it's the way it is."

She stopped, wiped at her tears once again, and eyed him. "You knew all along."

He shrugged one shoulder. "I had my suspicions."

"Why did you let me go on like that?"

"Hope. Faith. I wanted to believe that there was an

answer as badly as you did. That if we both believed hard enough and long enough, it might just come true."

"Aren't we a pair?"

"I love you," he said quietly. "I have always loved you and I believe that I always will, but I understand. The choices we've made have led us here. We can't go back. We can only go forward."

And right now *forward* meant "alone."

"Are you moving to Ohio?"

He shook his head. "I would like to be close to Brandon. See him from time to time. I know he may never accept me as his father, but I would like to spend time with him occasionally."

"We can tell him tonight. Maybe we could come over for supper . . ."

But Aaron shook his head. "No. I've been thinking about it. It's unfair for him to spend fifteen years of his life believing one man was his father only to find out that another is. And then to have that other in a situation such as this . . . Maybe it's better if he doesn't know."

The quiet words nearly broke her heart. "Aaron."

"I have a beautiful family. And I have loved two beautiful women. Sometimes things just don't work out the way we think they might. God's plan is different for us all."

Anger rose inside her, and she did her best to tamp it down. "You really think God had a hand in this?"

"God has a hand in everything."

Hannah jumped up from her seat and paced around the kitchen. "I find that hard to believe."

"You don't mean that."

She whirled on him. "Don't I?"

"Sit down, Hannah." He nudged her chair with one foot.

She didn't want to, but she slid back in her seat and

propped her chin in one hand. "I think you should tell Brandon. Isn't that what you wanted?"

"It was." He nodded. "But it'll just confuse him. I think it's better we just leave it for now."

She didn't want to give up, but she didn't want to continue to argue with him about it. A time would come, and they would tell Brandon. Until then, they would live. Just live.

"What are you going to do now?" he asked.

She peeled up the edge of the plastic place mat and smoothed it back into place. "Leah is talking about opening a store in town. I think maybe I'll stay and help her." There was nothing for her to return to in Tennessee. She might not be able to rejoin her community, but she could stay close this time. Spend time with her family, not be so removed.

"Have you talked to the bishop?"

She shook her head. "I'm not sure how he's going to take it." The bishop seemed sure that she would come back into the fold, but there were too many other factors involved. She had to do what was best for Brandon. She could only hope that the bishop and the other elders would understand. They could easily put her under a *Bann* whether she had joined the church or not. Or they could decide to allow her to remain close and keep a relationship with her Amish family. But she knew what would happen. There would be a shunning, and she would continue on, forever in the fringes.

Oh, the choices she had made.

She looked up and met Aaron's steady blue gaze. "I'm sorry."

"For what?"

She shot him a trembling smile. "For everything. For keeping Brandon from you. For not coming home all those years ago. For not telling you sooner." She shook her head. "I've made so many mistakes. So many. I would give anything to go back and correct them."

"We can only go forward."

She nodded. "I know. And I am sorry." Once again she had hurt all the people she loved. Maybe one day she would learn her lesson.

It was more than strange to pull her car into the bishop's drive. She didn't mean any disrespect, but it was better to go in honest. She wasn't staying. She couldn't stay. She wasn't joining the church. She had a son to raise.

The bishop stepped out of the barn and made his way across the yard toward her. "Hannah Gingerich, I wasn't expecting to see you today."

"Sorry. Is this a bad time?"

He shook his head, his beard brushing against his chest with the motion. "Come sit on the porch in the shade." He gestured toward the house, and Hannah eased up the steps and took a seat in one of the rocking chairs there.

"I see you're dressed a bit differently today. I assume this is the answer to my question about you staying."

"Yes." Simple and direct.

"I'm sorry to hear that. I suppose you know what this means."

She nodded. "I wish it could be different," she said. "But there's no other way."

He smiled gently at her. "There's always a way."

Everyone kept saying that to her, and she was about tired of it. She had given herself headaches racking her brain for an answer. She had surrendered the problem to God, but He hadn't answered. She had no choice but do right by her son. It was all anyone should expect from her. "So I've been told," she managed.

"You have to have faith, Hannah."

Faith. Now she needed faith.

"I'm sorry." She stood and went to move past him and down the steps.

"You know we will always welcome you back to the church. All you have to do is say the word."

"Thank you." She made her way to her car. She would be shunned, but welcomed back if she ever changed her mind. Maybe when Brandon graduated; maybe after his college. If she could wait that long. By then Aaron would most likely be remarried. Who knew if her parents would still be around. The thought was sobering. So much wasted time, and only herself to blame.

"Are you really not joining the church?" Tillie bounded into the sewing room, pinning Hannah with a quick look.

"No, I'm really not. And I don't want to talk about this now." Not where Brandon might overhear.

But her sister seemed to know what she was talking about. "Brandon's over at Jimmy's." Tillie hopped onto the bed and sat with her legs crisscrossed. "And you, my dear sister, are a hypocrite."

She should have known this was coming. And there would be more to endure before it was all said and done. "It's complicated," Hannah said, placing a stack of underwear in the basket that served as a dresser.

"It always is. Isn't that what you told me?"

"Tillie."

"Seriously, Hannah. How can you encourage me to join the church when you aren't doing that yourself?"

"I'm trying to save you from making the same mistakes that I made."

Tillie shook her head. "Try again."

"I have Brandon to think about."

"Do you really think the bishop would make you abandon your son for the church?"

When she put it like that . . . "It's better this way."

"It's easier."

Hannah propped her hands on her hips and eyed her sister. "There's nothing about this that's been easy." Once again she was walking away from those she loved. She was hurting her family and Aaron and all because of one stupid, prideful decision she'd made over fifteen years ago.

"Maybe you're making it hard."

"It is hard."

"Do you want to join the church or not?"

"What?" Hannah shook her head at the shift in the conversation.

"Do you want to join the church?"

She wanted to be with Aaron. She wanted to be close to her family. And in order to do that she had to rejoin the church. It was as simple as that.

"You're taking way too long to answer."

"There's more to it than you know, Til."

Her sister shook her head. "No there's not. Church isn't about being with family or being able to date. Not really. Church is about God. And you have to ask yourself, *If I don't join the church, am I being obedient to God?*"

The words sent a pang through her belly, but she waved them away with one hand. That was Tillie, always dramatic, always playing for show. Well, Hannah wasn't falling for it. This was about her, as a mother, doing what was best for her child. And there was nothing more to it than that. And the only role God had played was to not answer her prayers, not give her the direction that she needed. Surely He couldn't find fault with her in that.

"I'm staying in Mississippi, but I'm not joining the church. I'm going to help Leah with this store she wants to open, and I'm going to . . . I'm going to get my GED. Maybe even go to college." What a riot that would be. Her and Brandon in college at the same time. But the idea made her heart sink in her chest. She had so much catching up to do. Especially now that she wouldn't have any means of support.

"Is that what you want to do?" Tillie pinned her with another knowing stare.

"Of course." But she almost choked on the words. She didn't know what she wanted anymore. She had thought and prayed and thought and prayed until she couldn't keep anything straight. Life shouldn't be that confusing.

"So when I decide that I want to go with Melvin to work on car engines, you can't fuss at me for that."

"Tillie, that's different. Don't make the same mistakes I have." And then there were their parents to think about. How would they feel with all three of their daughters *out of the church?*

Chapter Twenty-Five

"Now, where are we going again?" Brandon looked to his cousin, who sat next to him driving the boxy, horse-pulled buggy down the dusty road.

"A volleyball game."

Brandon tilted his head to one side. "And y'all do this often?"

Joshua shrugged one shoulder, hands still loosely grasping the reins that came right through the front window. "Every other Saturday or so."

If someone had told him that he would be lumbering down the road in a conveyance that resembled a black cracker box he would have called them a liar straight to their face. Yet here he was. And though the mode of transportation was slow, it was kinda cool at the same time. Not that he would ever admit that to anyone. Not even his best friend/cousin.

"And how many people are going to be there?"

"Thirty or so."

"Any girls?" Brandon asked with a grin.

Joshua elbowed him lightly in the ribs. "I thought you already had a girlfriend."

"Dude, we're just friends."

"*Jah*. Sure."

Okay, so he talked about Shelly a lot, but that didn't mean anything. She was the only other true friend he had in Pontotoc, and he enjoyed sharing his study time with her. But that didn't mean anything else was going on. She was pretty enough, he supposed, but he had a feeling that her parents wouldn't let her date anyone even if he and Shelly decided they wanted to go out. They might not be Amish, or Mennonite like his aunt Leah, but they were just about as conservative.

"No, really."

Joshua shot him another look, then turned his attention back to the road. "The girls who are there are going to be Amish."

And even more conservative than Shelly.

"That doesn't mean that I can't talk to them."

"No, but you have to be . . . be . . ."

"Be what?"

"Less *Englisch*."

Brandon rolled his eyes. "Like they're not going to know that I'm English since I'm wearing this?" He plucked at his shirt and gave a wave toward his jeans. He had wanted to wear shorts since it was so hot, but his mother had told him that was a little too risqué even for a volleyball game. Whatever that meant.

"*Jah*. But I'm talking about how you talk. Dude and all that."

"You don't want me to embarrass you."

"I don't want you to embarrass yourself."

Fair enough. "Anything I can't talk about?"

Joshua shook his head. "Stick to safe topics."

"Like the weather and . . ." He couldn't talk about baseball scores, or the NFL draft, or how the Titans might do this year, or where he was thinking about going to school after he graduated. Or any of the things that he might talk to English girls about.

"The weather's good," Joshua said with a laugh. And Brandon knew right then it was going to be one long afternoon.

The volleyball "court" was basically a flat place in someone's pasture with a portable net and a large rectangle spray-painted on the grass. But everyone seemed to be having a really fun time. The game itself hadn't started yet, and like them, a few were still arriving. Someone had set up a couple of tables, and the girls were arranging snacks. A large cooler sat at one end.

"Hand me that bag." Joshua pointed to the brown paper grocery sack sitting on the back floor of the buggy.

"What's in it?"

Joshua grinned. "My mother's seasoned pretzels." He shook the sack so that the pretzels rattled in their container.

"Should I have brought something?"

He shook his head. "Nah. This is fine. Come on. I'll introduce you around."

Joshua led Brandon into the crowd of teens. According to his cousin, all of the kids in attendance were over sixteen and in their run-around time. Once Brandon had heard that Amish kids were allowed to do whatever they wanted during this time of their life, but Joshua assured him that wasn't the case. They might be able to attend singings and ball games like this one, but they were still very much under the supervision of their parents.

He received a few strange looks, but not as many as he had expected. He supposed Joshua had already told most of them about his odd *Englisch* cousin.

"Are you going to play?" Joshua asked.

Brandon shook his head. "I think I'll sit it out." He

didn't want to come on too strong. He was a visitor here, and though most of the teens seemed to accept him readily enough, he certainly didn't want to push his welcome. Plus, he wasn't sure he wanted to run and jump in this oppressive heat. He would end up smelling like the wrong end of a goat. And that wasn't a good impression at all.

The kids divided up into teams, three in all if he was correct. The plan was simple: the first two teams would play, then the third team would play the winner. Brandon hung out on the fringes while Joshua took the field with one of the first teams.

Brandon could honestly say that he had never seen anything like it. For sure he had never seen girls play sports in dresses. But they played as hard as the boys, laughing and running after the ball, seemingly not bothered at all by their skirts as they ran.

Most of the guys wore some shade of blue shirt. Even Joshua's shirt was a light blue. But the girls wore all sorts of colors and of an odd mix. He saw burgundy-colored dresses with green aprons, blue with purple, brown with green and endless combinations with gray and black. Every one of them was barefoot, a fact he found fascinating.

"Hi."

He turned as a girl sauntered up beside him. She was dressed much the same as the other girls, though her dress was purple with a brown apron on top. Brandon wanted to ask why they wore aprons when they weren't cooking, but he was afraid he would embarrass his cousin, so he tucked that question away until he could ask his grandmother or one of his aunts.

"Hey," he returned, noting that like the rest of the kids, she was barefoot too.

"I'm Katy Ann." She stuck out a hand to shake.

Brandon took it, surprised at the gesture.

"Joe Daniel said you used to live in Nashville. Is that

true?" Her blue eyes sparkled with excitement. She was pretty, he decided. Dark blond hair, lightly tanned cheeks, and eyes the color of the sky. He was beginning to get used to the fact that Amish girls didn't wear makeup. In fact, he thought he kinda liked it.

"Yeah. I was born there."

"I've been there, you know."

She seemed so proud of herself that he nodded. "That's cool."

"*Jah*." She tossed her head as if trying to get her chin at just the right angle. "I was in Ethridge visiting some family, and my aunt got really sick. She had to be taken to the hospital there."

"That's too bad."

"Oh, she's okay now. But it's so big there."

"It is big."

"A lot bigger than here for sure." She laughed, a sweet sound, and he realized that she was trying to flirt with him. He wasn't sure if he was creeped out or flattered. Flattered, he decided. "We must seem like country bumpkins to you."

Well, yeah, but he wasn't about to say so. "It's charming here." Best word ever. Thankfully he'd heard someone in town say that very thing. It seemed to work, for Katy Ann smiled, revealing twin dimples in her cheeks.

"Your *mamm*'s Amish?"

He nodded.

"How does that work?"

"It's complicated." He wasn't sure he understood it all himself. His mom had seemed happy to be back with her family. Happy enough that she started dressing like them, but then yesterday something had changed. He wasn't sure what it was. She didn't seem as happy any longer, and she had gone back to wearing her jeans.

"Are you staying here? In Pontotoc?"

He laughed. "You sure ask a lot of questions."

"Sorry." She ducked her head. "It's just we don't get a lot of visitors around here."

"It's all right. I don't mind."

Her chin shot up, and she flashed him another sweet smile.

"Hey. What are you doing?" A tall, older-looking Amish guy walked up, his tone anything but friendly.

"I'm talking to Brandon," she retorted.

The guy propped his hands on his hips, clearly unimpressed with Katy Ann's stern tone. "And I told you not to come over here."

Brandon took a step forward, preparing to defend Katy Ann. She wasn't doing anything wrong. They were just talking. No laws against that.

"Ray, you may be my brother, but you are not my keeper."

"Dat would tan your hide if he knew you were over here flirting with an *Englischer*."

Family feud. Count him out. "It's okay, Katy Ann."

Ray turned her by the shoulders and nudged her in the direction of a cluster of girls who were watching the game. "Stay with your friends." His tone brooked no argument.

Once Katy Ann was out of hearing range, Ray whirled on Brandon. "And you need to stay away from my sister."

As much as he hated being told what to do and Ray's surly tone, this wasn't a fight he wanted to have. He held up his hands as if in surrender. "No harm."

"Keep it that way." Ray spun on his heel and walked away.

Maybe it was a mistake to come. If the guys didn't want him to talk to the girls, then he was stuck talking to no one until Joshua's game was over. With any luck, they wouldn't win, and Brandon could beg a ride home. It seemed not all of the Amish were as welcoming as his family had been. Understandable, he supposed, but it still stung.

Just another reason to leave. And soon.

Joshua's team won, and Brandon spent the next hour sitting by himself on a milk crate he found in the back of the buggy. Chalk this one up to "lesson learned."

And as if sitting by himself wasn't enough, he could feel their eyes on him. The guys seemed to glare. Brandon supposed Ray had told them all that he was trying to hit on his sister. It would do no good to explain that she had come up to him first. They would believe what they wanted to believe. He had learned that the hard way when his dad died.

On the other hand, the girls seemed to take turns staring at him, talking among themselves and giggling behind their hands. There was no way he was the only Englisher they had ever seen. He knew for a fact the Amish went into town and shopped at Walmart like everyone else. But he supposed that he might be the only non-Amish to come to one of these get-togethers. Never again.

The game ended in a tie, and they wanted to play a tiebreaker. Brandon figured everyone was having such a good time that no one was ready to go home. Everyone but him.

He was going to wait by the buggy. Surely they couldn't play much longer, and the stares were beginning to get on his nerves. If he knew the way home, he would walk it. But he hadn't been paying close enough attention on the drive over.

He stood and picked up the milk crate, motioning toward the buggies to tell Joshua where he was going.

His cousin gave a nod and turned his attention back to the game.

"I'm sorry about my brother." Suddenly, Katy Ann was there again. How she snuck up on him, Brandon didn't know. He was sitting all by himself with not one Amish person around. He should have seen her coming, because everyone else did. He could feel all eyes on the two of them.

"No big." He gave a quick shrug and moved as if to walk away.

"It's not okay." She stopped him with one hand on his arm.

He looked down at her fingers.

She jerked them away. "I'm sorry. I just—" She shook her head.

"You better do what your brother says. I don't want any trouble." He'd already had enough of that.

"It's not like he's going to come fight you."

"I don't want any trouble," he repeated. Maybe he should head on down the road and let Joshua catch up with him once the game was over.

"Talking isn't hurting anyone, and I'm tired of my brother bossing me around."

"I'm sure you are, but I'm not getting in the middle of this."

"You already are." Ray spoke from behind him.

Great. Just great.

Brandon turned, preparing to be decked in the face regardless of the rumor that Amish were pacifists. Not everything floating around was true, that much he knew for certain. "I was just leaving," he said.

To his left, the volleyball game had stopped. He wasn't sure if it was over, or if they were taking a break to see how this was going to turn out. He figured it was the second one, considering that everyone was standing stock-still and watching them like the latest blockbuster movie.

"*Jah*. You're not wanted here."

His tone alone raised the hair on the back of Brandon's neck, but the last thing he wanted was a fight. He took one step back and toward the buggy.

"Even if your *dat* is Amish."

"Ray," Katy Ann protested.

"Stay out of this, Kate." He spoke to his sister, but he didn't take his gaze from Brandon.

Brandon rolled his eyes. "My *dat* isn't Amish."

"Shows what you know. I heard some people talking. Seems everyone's saying that Aaron Zook is your *dat.*"

Aaron Zook? Wasn't that his mom's friend? "Mitchell Alan McLean was my dad." He turned to leave. He needed to get out of there before he busted a gasket.

"You keep telling yourself that," Ray sneered.

Do not turn around. Just keep walking. Stiff-legged, Brandon made his way to Joshua's buggy and started to climb in. After all that, Joshua would want to leave as well. He hadn't meant to, but he had embarrassed his cousin all the same.

"Hey," Joshua called. "Over here."

Okay, so he wasn't at the right buggy. How was he supposed to tell them apart? They all looked just alike.

He stomped over to where his cousin stood. "Can you believe that guy?" Brandon pulled himself into the buggy and settled in for the ride home. But his skin itched. He wanted to go back and tell that guy off but good. Who did he think he was, talking to Brandon like that? It wasn't like he had done anything to the guy.

"Ray's a little protective of Katy Ann," Joshua said as he pulled the buggy out onto the main road.

"You think?"

"He's always been like that. A little hotheaded."

"I was just talking to her." He shook his head. "And she came up to me first. Both times."

"*Jah.* She likes to rile him up."

"What does that mean?"

Joshua took his gaze from the road for a moment. "If she can get him to act up at an event, then she'll get to come to the next one by herself."

"Now I'm really confused."

"It's simple, really. She gets him upset, and he makes a fool of himself. His parents ground him, and she gets to come alone."

"And that way she can talk to boys without him around." Now he saw what had happened. He'd been used. Straight up.

"You got it."

"But why would he say those other things?"

Joshua coughed. "What things?"

"About my dad. Was he trying to get me to hit him? I don't understand."

"Who knows?" But something in his tone had Brandon studying his profile.

"Who would tell him such a thing?" And why were they even talking about it? No. It all had to be lies, straight from Ray's imagination.

"Maybe you should talk to your mother about it." Joshua's gaze stayed glued to the front.

"Talk to my mother?" He shook his head. Why would he want to do that? Ask her about a bunch of lies?

Unless they weren't lies.

His stomach pitched like he'd gone over the top of a steep roller coaster. "Are you telling me that what he said was true?"

"No."

But the one word didn't make Brandon feel any better. "What are you saying?"

"You might should talk to your mother."

"I don't want to talk to my mother." It didn't take a

genius to figure it out. If Aaron was his father, then that meant she was already pregnant when she got married to his dad—er, Mitch. He didn't have to grow up in Amish Land to know that sex before marriage was a no-no. He didn't want to accuse his mother of such things. Plus he would be calling her a liar. "Pull over."

"Brandon."

"Pull over!"

Joshua sighed, but did as Brandon demanded. Once the carriage had stopped, Brandon turned to his cousin. "Have people been saying this about me and my mom?"

His cousin's gaze flicked away, then settled on his own lap. "*Jah.*"

Just because they were talking didn't mean it was true. And just because it was a rumor didn't make it a lie.

"Who did you hear it from?"

"My *mamm* and *dat.*"

The words dropped like a bag of manure between them. "Your mom and dad? Anna and Jim?"

Joshua nodded.

And if they were talking . . . It wasn't like strangers or people who barely knew them. It wasn't like they wouldn't know.

"Take me home."

The front door slammed. "Mom!" Brandon hollered from the front room, his voice getting louder as he moved toward the kitchen.

"In here," she called in return. She had promised her mother that she would wash the jars for tomorrow's canning session. They had more tomatoes than they knew what to do with. More than even the *Englisch* visitors would want.

He stormed into the room, eyes blazing and cheeks ruddy. "Is Mitch McLean my dad?"

The jar slipped from her grasp and fell harmlessly back into the pan of dishwater. She retrieved it and gave a small laugh. "Why would you ask such a thing?"

She was not ready to have this conversation. Once Aaron told her that he didn't want to tell Brandon, she had stopped practicing the dialogue in her mind.

"Is he my father or not?"

Hannah left the last jar in the pan and turned to face him. She dried her hands on a dish towel as she contemplated the best way to answer.

"Why are you asking?" Where had he heard the truth? Did he even know all of it?

"This guy at the game, Ray Somebody, he told me that Aaron Zook is my father. Now I'm asking you for the truth."

Never before had she so wished that the floor would open up and swallow her whole. "Brandon—"

He stared at her, eyes wide. "When were you going to tell me?"

"Come sit down."

"No." He shook his head and started to back up toward the door. "You've lied to me all this time?"

"Brandon—"

"For fifteen years. My entire life!"

"If you'll sit down, I'll explain."

"No," he said again. "The time for explanations is over." And with that he spun on one heel and stalked out. Seconds later the front door slammed behind him.

Hannah sank into the nearest chair, her legs trembling too badly to hold her up any longer. She folded her arms on the table, laid her head down, and let the tears go.

* * *

"Hannah? Aaron's here."

Hannah removed the wet rag from her face and pushed up from the bed. After Brandon had stormed away, she'd had herself a good long cry, then sent Gracie after Aaron, sent Joshua to look for Brandon, and laid down to ease the pounding in her head.

She might have thought that the revelation would take a burden off her. And it might—just not today.

"Thanks."

Gracie shot her a sympathetic smile and stood to one side so Hannah could make her way out of the room.

"What's wrong?" Aaron asked the moment he saw her puffy eyes and red cheeks.

"Someone told Brandon." She didn't have to say more. He knew.

"Where is he?"

She waved him out onto the porch, needing to sit while they covered all the details. "He stormed out, and I sent Joshua to find him," she said after they had settled down in the porch swing. So many moments of her life had happened right here. Some good, some bad.

"He's probably down at the pond." Aaron stood as if to go after him, but Hannah stopped him.

"Let him have some time."

Reluctantly, Aaron eased back down. "We need to talk to him."

"I agree, but he's embarrassed and angry. Give him some time to work through that. He won't be able to listen to any sort of reason until he gets his head clear."

"That could take months."

"I don't have anything else to do. What about you?"

"Hannah, we can't let this drag on any longer."

She nodded. "We won't, but give Joshua some time to find him and bring him back. Maybe then he'll be up for hearing our explanation."

"And what are *we* going to tell him?"

She didn't miss the emphasis on the word *we*. "The truth."

"All of it?"

"All of it. I've lied to him too much." It was time to come clean.

Unbelievable.

Brandon wanted to run. And run. And run. And run.

Instead he stumbled up the incline behind his uncle's house, the roaring in his ears blocking out the sounds he knew were around him. The crashing of his feet against the ground, the birds in the trees, the bleat of the sheep, and the occasional plop of a fish in the pond.

His entire life had been a lie.

The one person he had always trusted had betrayed him.

He lost his footing and slid halfway down to the pond. It didn't matter. Nothing mattered. Not until he could sort this out.

He pushed back to his feet and stopped at the water's edge, his breathing ragged. His thoughts were turbulent, spinning out of control. He couldn't grab ahold of one and focus, so he just stood there, hands on his hips, as he tried to calm his breathing.

He sucked in a breath. *Inhale, exhale. Inhale, exhale.* And life went on.

"Brandon?"

He didn't turn as Joshua came over the incline and started down the slope toward the pond. He wasn't sure he was ready to see anyone just yet, especially not his cousin. "Go away."

"Your *mamm* sent me."

"I don't care. Go away."

"Brandon—"

He whirled around then, his temper flaring. "You knew." He glared at his cousin. "You knew all along, and you didn't bother to tell me. I thought you were my friend."

"I am."

"Yeah? Well, friends don't do that to other friends."

"Your *mamm* is worried about you."

"She should be." He was angry and out of control. He wanted to hit something, break something, curse the sky. This was unfair. So unfair.

"You don't mean that."

Brandon shook his head. "She lied to me. How could she lie to me? For years?"

Joshua eased forward until they were nearly standing side by side. "I don't know. *Mamm*s can do weird things. But I do know that she loves you."

"What? So she was trying to protect me?" He slammed his hands on his hips and stared up at the sky. It was a clear, impossible blue, mocking his turmoil. "I have spent my entire life thinking my father didn't like me." He scoffed. "I never questioned his love, but the man did not like me. What had I ever done to him to make him despise me so? Well, now I know."

"If you come back to the house, she will have a chance to explain."

"So she can tell me more lies? No, thank you."

Joshua picked up a rock and skimmed it across the water. It jumped twice before sinking beneath the surface. "I won't pretend that I understand all of this, but it seems to me that your *mamm* had her reasons. And now you know the truth."

"Yeah. The truth." Brandon picked up his own rock, but his angle was off. It barely touched the water before sinking to the bottom. He started searching the ground at his feet for another, flatter rock.

"It seems to me that you gained a father today."

He stopped, still stooped at the waist. He had gained a father? "How so?"

"Your one father died, right?"

Brandon picked up another stone and frowned. "He wasn't my father, remember?"

"You thought he was."

"Yeah." He skipped the rock, this time getting three good bounces out of his toss.

"Now he's gone, and you have Aaron."

Did he?

"He's Amish." It could have been the dumbest thing Brandon had ever said.

Joshua laughed and selected his own rock. "Amish make good *dat*s."

"But . . ." This was just more for him to try to get his mind around. He had a dad, then he didn't. Now he had a dad that he didn't even know. How was he supposed to make peace with all that?

"Listen, I know it sounds like a lot, but I think if you give it some time, it'll be easier to accept."

Get used to the idea. Like he had any choice. "Tell me something."

"*Jah*?"

"You knew all along, and yet you never told me."

Joshua shook his head. "I only found out after your birthday. I think that's when your *mamm* told Aaron."

Aaron hadn't known about him either. Whoa, his mom had some stuff to explain.

"And I wasn't even supposed to know. I just happened to hear my *mamm* and *dat* talking about it."

"How did that Ray guy find out?"

Joshua shrugged. "Amish people talk."

"You mean gossip." Had everyone in the community known but him?

"Call it what you want, but we talk about each other and what we can do to help."

It sounded like a lame excuse to gab behind someone's back, but Brandon wasn't going to point that out. He had more important things to worry about.

"Are you going to come back to the house now?"

He'd have to go back eventually. He didn't want to go back now, but he couldn't stay out here all afternoon. "I guess." He picked up another rock and skimmed it across the water. One, two, three, four. His personal best, and on a day that could easily be considered the worst. Oh, the irony.

Chapter Twenty-Six

As far as family meetings went, this one left a lot to be desired.

Aaron looked from Hannah to Brandon and back again. She looked ready to burst into tears at any moment, but she was managing to keep it together.

Brandon was another story. Aaron could feel the animosity coming off of him like waves of heat rising in the summer. But he couldn't say he blamed the boy. Aaron honestly couldn't say how he would feel if he'd found himself in Brandon's position. He would like to think that he would be happy to learn that he still had a father, alive and breathing, but it had to be a shock. Maybe with time . . .

"I know you have a lot of questions," Hannah said by way of a starting point.

Brandon snorted.

It was on the tip of Aaron's tongue to tell the boy to sit up and respect his mother, but he was pretty sure that directive wouldn't be followed, or even accepted well. He sat back in his seat and waited for Hannah to continue.

"Like why I didn't tell you."

"Something like that." Brandon's tone grew even surlier.

"Listen," Hannah started, reaching across the table toward him.

Brandon crossed his arms and slouched in his seat, effectively getting as far away from her as possible without moving his chair.

"I know you're angry, and I'm not even going to pretend that you don't have the right."

"Why?" he asked.

He didn't have to explain; Hannah understood.

"It's complicated."

Brandon shook his head. "That just means *I don't want to tell you.*"

Hannah sucked in a deep breath and squared her shoulders. "Okay. When I was eighteen, I decided that I wanted to know more about the *Englisch* world. You know, non-Amish."

"Okay."

"Well, I guess I really wanted to know more long before then. When I was eighteen, I decided to act on it."

Brandon stared at the table as his mother spoke.

Once again Aaron had to bite back instructions for Brandon to sit up, listen, and show some respect. He'd let him have tonight, but after that . . .

"I decided to leave. Your aunt Leah didn't want me to go alone, but she didn't want to leave. In the end, she went with me, but only for me. And I knew that if I told Aaron what I had planned, he would never let me leave."

Brandon finally looked up and caught his mother's gaze. "You didn't tell him?"

"No."

"What about me? Why didn't you tell him that you were pregnant with me?"

Aaron had to hand it to the boy. Those couldn't be the easiest words to say, but he managed them without so much as a crack in his voice.

"I didn't know."

Aaron could tell from the light in Brandon's eyes it was a scenario that he hadn't considered.

"I wasn't going to be gone forever, just a couple of months. I just wanted to see what I was missing."

"How does Dad . . . Mitch figure in?"

"Well." Hannah sucked in a deep breath as if preparing herself for a long battle. "When I found out that I was pregnant, I had been seeing your dad for a couple of weeks."

"Mitch," Brandon corrected.

"Yeah." Hannah nodded. "We had been seeing each other for a little while. When I told him that I was pregnant, I figured he'd run for the hills."

"But he didn't?" Brandon asked.

"No."

The one word was hard for Aaron to hear. Mitch had had fifteen years with Hannah and hadn't appreciated them at all. How cheated they had all been.

"He told me that he had always wanted a family and right then was a great time to start."

"Why did he act like he hated me?"

"Oh, Brandon." She reached for him again, and this time he allowed her to take his hands. "He never hated you, but he could never get over the fact that you weren't his. Biologically speaking."

Aaron couldn't imagine what sort of man Hannah had tied herself to.

"He resented me."

"I guess that's as good a way to put it as any."

Aaron could see the thoughts churning in Brandon's head. They reflected in his eyes: fear, confusion, his own resentment.

"Now what do we do? I mean, it's not like we can be

one big happy family. Can we?" Brandon looked at each of them in turn.

Hannah's expression clouded over. "No. We can't."

"Why not?" The yearning on his face was almost more than Aaron could bear. The son he had never known was starved for love and acceptance by a man who had never known what he had. The thought sickened him. And yet there was nothing he could do about it.

"The Amish church has certain rules and regulations. I can't follow those, and therefore I can't join the church."

"It's not like the two of you are going to go get married or anything."

"No."

The word pierced Aaron's heart. He wanted that more than he wanted his next breath. He wanted Hannah to finally be his. He wanted Brandon to know a father's love. And yet . . .

The only way they could all be together would be for him to leave the Amish. And that was just something he couldn't do.

They talked until Brandon couldn't talk anymore. He was exhausted, all talked out, and yet he still had a hundred questions floating around his brain.

He flopped over and stared at the ceiling. He was alone in the sewing room. His mom hadn't come to bed yet, and for that he was grateful. He needed a little alone time.

There had been a moment or two during their talk when Brandon had thought for a brief time that the three of them might form a family. How great would that be?

But no.

How dumb that he even thought about it. That was a kid's dream, and this was a grown-up situation. Things just didn't work out like that. Life didn't have a Hallmark ending.

What would happen now? Would they stay in Pontotoc? Maybe. Go back to Nashville? Probably not. They couldn't remain with the Amish, at least that was what he thought they had said. He would have to start over once again.

He was fifteen years old and so very tired.

Brandon rolled onto his side, pounded his pillow into submission, and did his best to fall asleep. But oblivion was a long time in coming.

She should be at church.

Hannah couldn't shake the feeling that something was terribly wrong, and the only thing she could think of was that she should have gone to church. Maybe she couldn't attend the Amish church, but she could have gone into town or attended the Mennonite church with Leah. It wouldn't be the same as church in the house of one of her neighbors, but at least she would have been closer to God.

She looked out over the yard and prayed for peace. It was just another unfulfilled request.

Brandon had gotten up and walked down to the pond just after breakfast. Hannah didn't blame him for needing space, but she wished with all her might that she could take some of the confusion and anger from him. He had every right to be mad at her, even though it killed her inside. She could only hope that one day very soon, he would find it in his heart to completely forgive her. Until then, she vowed to give him love and space and pray for the best.

A car engine drew her attention. Leah's car puttered down the drive. Hannah was a bit jealous of her sister.

Leah had such a sense of peace about her life decisions. For someone who hadn't wanted to leave their conservative Amish community, she had adjusted comfortably into her new Mennonite life.

Hannah figured that it wouldn't be long until the bishop came to Leah about her place in the church, but until then she would come and go as she pleased. And if they were really lucky, the bishop wouldn't get involved at all unless someone in the district complained.

One thing was certain: Hannah couldn't stay there indefinitely with no plans.

Leah got out of her car and made her way toward the house, her long skirt swinging around her ankles. She waved to Hannah as she approached.

"Is everyone still at church?"

Hannah nodded.

"Where's Brandon?"

"He's at the pond."

"Still?" Leah slid into the porch swing next to Hannah.

"I guess he's got some things to work out."

Leah gave a quick dip of her chin. "Like his *mamm*."

"There's nothing more to work out."

"You're not fooling anyone but yourself. And maybe Mamm, because you know, she sees only what she wants to see."

"What's that supposed to mean?"

"It means our mother—"

"Not what I was talking about."

Leah shot her an innocent smile. "You love Aaron."

"Not that it matters."

"You're wrong. It matters a great deal."

Only to the two of them. "What's your point, Leah?"

"I want you to be happy."

"You know, when I found out that Aaron was seeing

Lizzie Yoder, I stopped praying. I figured God wasn't listening anymore. I guess I was too far away from the church to believe that He cared about me."

"You don't really believe that. Do you?"

"My list of unanswered prayers would reach from here to Memphis."

"You think He has forsaken you?"

Hannah spread her hands before her, their emptiness a reflection of how she felt inside. "He's not listening. If He is, then He's not answering. I'm navigating this all by myself when I need Him more than ever." Again she envied her sister for finding her own place with God. "I can only suspect that I'm not supposed to have what I've been asking for." It was a bitter pill to swallow. Was she really asking for so much? She wanted to rejoin the church. She wanted to spend her life with Aaron. But she wanted— no, *needed*—to raise the son who meant so much to her. Why would God give her those desires only to make them impossible to achieve?

"Maybe it's not what you're asking for, but how you're asking."

"Maybe," Hannah murmured. But she had prayed, she had surrendered, she had made vow after vow. What else was a woman to do?

"What do you think?" Leah's voice echoed inside the empty shop.

First thing Monday morning, Leah had invited Hannah to come check out the space. In support of her sister, Hannah readily agreed. They dropped a sullen Brandon off at the library to do his schoolwork while they went down the street to check out the store space together.

"It's . . ." Hannah had no idea what to say about the

blank space. The only thing the shop had in it right then was a wall of empty shelves and a small counter made of glass. The top panel was cracked.

"I know it doesn't look like much, but I can see it." Leah whirled around toward the shelves. "The shoes could go there. Housewares in the front window, clothes in the middle, and the Amish stuff in the very back."

"Have you talked to the bishop about it?"

"*Mamm* mentioned it to him. He seemed to like the idea. Well, as much as Amos Raber likes anything." Leah chuckled. "He didn't veto it, so I consider that a positive response."

"And you think the Amish are going to come down Main." Hannah shook her head. Unlike some of the other, larger Amish communities across the country, the Amish in Pontotoc kept to themselves as much as possible. A horse and buggy on Main Street would garner way too much attention for most of the community to be comfortable with the idea.

"That's the beauty of it. The Amish customers can come in through the back. Then they won't have to deal with gawkers. Perfect."

"It does sound like a good plan."

Leah crossed her arms and squinted at her. "Then why do you sound so down?"

Hannah sighed. "I'm sorry. It's . . ." She shook her head.

"Have you even talked to Aaron?"

She shook her head. "There's nothing left to say."

"He's staying here to be closer to Brandon, but the two of you—"

"Are history, as they say." The defeat in her voice was as thick as stew.

"You're giving up."

"There's nothing to keep going."

Leah shook her head. "I think you're missing something."

"Like what?"

"I don't know, but it wouldn't do any good for me to tell you. This is something you have to work out for yourself."

She might be only eight minutes older, but Hannah hated when her baby sister was right. The only problem, there was nothing else to figure out.

"Come on." Leah hooked one hand over her shoulder. "I'll show you the upstairs. There's the cutest little apartment up there."

"Are you serious?" Shelly leaned across the table, her eyes wide. "What did you do?"

Brandon shrugged as if it were no big deal. "I asked her."

"And she said?"

"That it was true."

"Wow." Shelly leaned back and exhaled heavily. "Just wow."

"Yeah."

"Now what?"

"I don't know."

"What do you mean you don't know?"

"It's not like I can live with him or anything. It's not like I'll spend my weekends there, like my friends with divorced parents do. I mean, he's Amish."

"What a mess."

"You can say that again. Don't," he continued when she opened her mouth to do just that.

Shelly shot him a sympathetic smile. "I know you're upset, but this has some good aspects, don't you think?"

That was Shelly, always looking at the bright side of

everything. "Like what?" From where he stood, all he could see were the people who had lied to him his entire life.

"You have a father."

"That I don't know."

"You're living close to him. And he seems like a nice man."

Brandon had almost forgotten that she had met him at the party.

"And you have a brother and two sisters."

That was definitely something he hadn't thought about. "And that's a good thing?"

"Of course it is. I mean, it's not like you'll be living together, but brothers and sisters are the best." Family was very important to Shelly. Through her eyes, he had started to view his newly found family a bit differently. It had just been the three of them when they had lived in Nashville—him, his mom, and his dad, Mitch. But now he had a grandmother, a great-grandmother, aunts, uncles, and all sorts of cousins.

"I'm just saying, you should give it all a chance. You might find out you like having an Amish father."

Brandon laughed, and Shelly joined in. The librarian shushed them, and they ducked back behind their books.

Somehow Shelly knew just the right thing to say.

Maybe he would give this all a chance. After all, going around mad at everyone was beginning to get exhausting.

His aunt Leah picked him up and drove him back to his grandmother's house. All the way, she chatted about her new store.

"People want to buy things that other people have already owned?"

"Of course. Look at all the thrift stores and antique stores."

"And a secondhand store is about the same thing?"

"It's exactly the same thing," his aunt said.

Leah Gingerich was a little odd as far as he was concerned, and he meant that in the best possible way. She dressed a lot like a hippie, and a lot like Shelly, in long shirts and loose tops. She wore her hair pulled back much like the Amish women did. Most days she wore a small black doily-looking thing pinned to her bun instead of one of those white caps his grandmother preferred. Today, however, Leah wore a triangle bandanna over her hair and tied at the nape of her neck.

"Why do Amish women cover their hair?"

She looked over at him, her eyes curious. "What makes you ask that?"

He shrugged. "I've just noticed that all of you cover up your hair. My friend Shelly doesn't do that, and her family is really conservative."

"Well, the Amish and the Mennonite both believe that in order to properly respect God when we pray, our heads should be covered."

"What about now? Why are you wearing one of those in the car?"

"I might decide to start praying."

"And you pray outside of church?"

Leah cast him another quick glance. "Your mother didn't take you to church very often, did she?"

"No. I mean, we went a couple of times, but not regular."

"Would you like to go with me?"

"To the Mennonite church? Am I allowed?"

"Of course." Leah laughed. "Everyone is welcome."

"And I don't have to be Mennonite?"

"Not at all."

He half turned in his seat. "But you have to be Amish in order to go to the Amish church."

"That's right."

"And it's not easy being Amish."

She shrugged one shoulder, but kept her hands loosely on the wheel. "Most people don't want to convert. It's not an easy life."

"Tell me about it," he grumbled. A month plus without video games and cell phones had made him appreciate them more, but that long without electricity and indoor plumbing had about driven him crazy. "I don't understand why anyone would want to live that way. No offense to Mammi or anything."

"When you're born Amish, it's different."

"But my mother didn't want to stay."

"That's a hard one," Leah finally said. "Your mother did want to stay. She wanted to explore a bit and then come back."

"Why didn't she?"

Leah shot him a quick smile. She and his mother might be twins, but they looked nothing alike. Leah's eyes were a true green, and her hair was dark like tar. But when she smiled she looked just like Mom. Weird. "You're going to have to ask her about that."

Yet another mystery.

Leah pulled the car into the drive and parked it next to his. Well, one day it was going to be his. Now that he was fifteen he could get his license in Mississippi. It seemed they were staying, and that would suit him just fine.

"What's going on?"

His mother was standing in the middle of the yard, hands on her hips as she turned in a circle. She looked almost lost.

"I don't know. Hannah?" Leah called.

"It's Samuel," Mom said. "He's gone."

* * *

"Gone?" Leah asked. "What do you mean 'gone'?"

"Gone." Hannah wanted to scream. Didn't her sister understand? "First he was here, and now he's not. Jim's baby is gone!"

Leah shoved her keys into her purse. "He has to be around here somewhere."

"Did you check down by the pond?"

Hannah's stomach dropped at Brandon's question. "No." That was dangerous, so, so dangerous.

"I'll go." He took off through the pasture and over the top of the small incline.

"Where is everybody?"

Hannah shook her head. "Jim and Anna are over at the school. David went with Dat and Mamm is searching the barn."

"He's got to be around here somewhere," Leah said. "He's got little legs. He can't have gotten far."

Hannah wrung her hands together. "He was with Mamm, and then he just disappeared. What if he gets in the road?"

Leah shook her head. "We just came from that way. I think we would have seen him."

"Help me find him," Hannah begged. How could they just lose him?

"Of course," Leah said. "You check in the house, and I'll check over at Jim's. Maybe Samuel decided to go back home."

Hannah nodded as Mamm came out of the barn. "He's not in there."

"Brandon went to check at the pond," Leah said.

Mamm's eyes widened with fear.

Please, God, don't let him be in the pond. Please, please, please.

"I'm going to check Jim's." Leah took off in the direction

of Anna and Jim's, her purse swinging against her hip as she hurried away.

"I'm going to look around back again. Maybe he wandered off into the woods." Mamm started around the back of the house. She had been hanging up laundry while Samuel played nearby. Then the next thing they knew, he was nowhere in sight.

"I'm going to check in the house again." Hannah started for the porch, each step ringing out a prayer.

I know You haven't been listening to me. And I understand. But this isn't about me. This is about an innocent little boy. Please, please, hear my prayers. Let us find Samuel. Please let him be okay. Unharmed. Please.

She had been taught her entire life to pray for God's will, but she couldn't say those words. She needed Samuel to be all right. So much had gone wrong these last few weeks. She wasn't sure she could take another tragedy.

The house was so quiet when she stepped inside. If Samuel was in there, he would be making noise, right? Unless he was asleep. Wouldn't that be a hoot? They were out looking for him, and he was curled up asleep in Mamm's extra laundry basket.

Lord, please let him be curled up asleep in the extra laundry basket.

But the laundry room off the back porch was empty. She checked everywhere in the house she thought a toddler could fit, calling his name as she opened closets and pantry doors, and even looked under the beds.

"Eunice, is that you?" Mammi's voice carried in from the adjacent *dawdihaus*.

"It's me," she called in return. "Hannah." She moved closer to the door that led to the space that Mammi claimed as her own.

Hannah's voice was raw from yelling Samuel's name. She was worn out from all the hollering.

"Why are you screaming so?" Mammi asked.

Hannah stepped through the curtain that separated the two "houses."

Mammi's quarters were dark and quiet. They had moved her bed into the living room when she fell and broke her hip to help her get around easier. She could get out of bed when she wanted, but not be far from it when she needed to lie down again.

Hannah's grandmother was nearing her nineties, and every minute of her hard life was etched into her face. She had more wrinkles and creases than an old weathered cowboy, but Hannah loved every one of them. She had missed her *mammi* when she was gone and was so glad to be able to connect with her grandmother once again. If only for a little while.

"Now tell me why you're hollering again?" Mammi's lips protruded a bit, her teeth soaking in a glass at her bedside. She was sitting in a chair near the window working the crossword puzzle from the paper.

"Samuel's missing. I need to go . . ." Hannah trailed off as Mammi pointed to her bed.

Samuel lay curled up on one side, sound asleep. His cheeks were pink and angelic. Tears rose into Hannah's eyes. She rushed to his side and scooped him into her arms, kissing him repeatedly as if she needed the connection to convince herself that he was indeed whole and fine.

"Hannah Mae, you're going to wake him up," Mammi admonished, but Hannah was too grateful.

Samuel started to cry, startled awake by all the jostling.

"Thank you, Mammi."

"You're welcome . . ." Mammi's voice trailed behind her as Hannah rushed back into the main part of the house. "I tried to holler for you, but no one answered. I didn't know you were looking for him."

"It's okay," Hannah called over the sound of Samuel's wails. "He's fine, and that's the main thing."

Hannah rushed out of the house and back into the yard, the crying Samuel cradled to her chest. She bounced him up and down to comfort him, but he just cried harder.

"What happened?" Mamm rushed around the side of the house as Brandon came back through the pasture.

"You found him?" Brandon took off running toward them, his own relief shining on his face.

"Hannah?"

She barely heard her sister's call over Samuel's cries.

"Is he okay?"

They all three ran toward her as she stood bouncing Samuel and shedding tears of her own. He was fine. She could hardly believe that he was okay.

She raised her face to the heavens even as her mother rushed in and scooped Samuel into her arms. Hannah clasped her hands together and raised them toward the sky. "Thank you, Lord. I know that You are listening. I'm so sorry for ever doubting. Thank you, thank you, Lord, for answering my prayers. Amen."

"I've never seen anything like it before," Brandon said, checking his bait and tossing his hook back into the water. He and Joshua were stretched out on the mossy banks of the pond, pretending to be fishing. Brandon just needed a little quiet time. Everyone had been so happy that Samuel was found, that a quiet moment couldn't be found between the two houses.

"You've never seen anyone pray before?" Joshua frowned.

"I've never seen her pray before. At least not that I can remember."

Joshua tilted his head to one side and chewed on the

inside of his cheek. He had his back propped up against a fallen tree, his legs stretched out in front of him. "You didn't go to church?"

"A couple of times. Sometimes on Easter. But never all the time."

Joshua shook his head as if the concept of only going to church occasionally was the oddest thing he had ever heard. "You never learned to pray?"

"Nope. Not really."

"Do you ever pray?"

"I dunno. Maybe."

Joshua continued to stare as if he couldn't believe his ears. "Do you believe in God?"

"Of course." How could a person not believe in God?

"What good is believing in God if you don't take the time to pray to Him?"

His mother believed in God, but he had never seen her pray, not until today.

What good is believing in God if you don't pray to Him?

He remembered all the things his mother had told him about the Amish church. He wished he had paid better attention. They prayed all the time here. Before they ate, after they ate—though the prayers were all silent. There was no way to know if a person was really praying or sitting there with their head bowed waiting for time to eat.

But she had prayed today.

"Do you think my mother thought God had given up on her?"

"What do you mean?"

Brandon thought about the question again. "Why was it such a big deal that my mom left the Amish?"

"When she went to the *Englisch* world, she couldn't be compliant to the ways she had been taught. There are too many distractions in the *Englisch* world. Most believe that the distractions alone can cause a person to fall from grace."

"'Fall from grace'," Brandon repeated. "Why doesn't she join the church now?"

"You."

Brandon jerked into a sitting position, whirling around to face his cousin. "Me? What do I have to do with it?"

Joshua seemed to think about it a minute, then a minute more, and again, until Brandon knew he was taking way too long to answer.

"Tell me," he quietly demanded.

His cousin nodded. "I will, but you have to know that I am telling you this because of what happened the other day. I don't want you mad at me because you think I'm withholding information."

At Joshua's words Brandon's stomach fell into his lap. "What?"

"Your mother and Aaron love each other."

The words shouldn't have been such a shock, but now that it was brought to his attention, he knew that was the truth. His mother had been happy for the first time in a long while. She had been wearing Amish clothes and hanging out with Aaron and his kids.

But then his conversation with Aaron and his mom came back to him. She told him that she and Aaron weren't getting married because there were rules of the Amish church that she couldn't follow.

"What rules of the church would keep her from marrying him?"

Joshua shook his head. "It has more to do with you."

He had said that once before. "How do I fit into all this? I'm not going to join the Amish church."

"Exactly. And you surely don't want to live without your cell phone and computer."

"I have to use the computer for school." His tone was more than defensive.

"You're missing the point."

"Then tell me what you're trying to say." He hadn't meant to raise his voice, but this conversation was getting beyond annoying.

"A person can be *Englisch* and live in an Amish house."

Brandon nodded. "That's what we're doing now."

"But an Amish person can't live in an *Englisch* house and stay in good standing with the church."

Brandon rolled those words around in his head, sorting through them to the meaning inside. "Are you saying that because I want electricity and a car, that my mother is not marrying the man she loves?"

"That's exactly what I'm saying."

But that couldn't be true.

Maybe it wasn't. Maybe his mother wasn't really in love with Aaron. Maybe he wasn't what was keeping them apart. After all, Brandon didn't know for a fact that his mother wanted to join the church.

How many times had those words been thrown around, and he wasn't even sure exactly what they meant? He was certain it had something to do with wearing those plain dresses and the white caps on their heads. Well, that might be part of it. Somehow he knew there had to be more.

Did his mother want to marry Aaron? Did Aaron want to marry her? Did she want to join the church? There was only one way to find out for sure.

Hannah eased down onto the porch steps, thankful that life had returned to normal. Anna, Jim, and the kids had returned from the school and gathered Samuel up to take him home, unconcerned that he had been missing for a good fifteen minutes that afternoon. It might not seem like a long time, but when she was living it, it felt like an eternity.

Dat and David had also come home. They had gone into the barn with some new tool, grinning like kids at having a new "toy" to play with.

Mamm had gone back to hanging up the clothes, and Leah had gone in to get a snack.

And all was quiet for a time.

She heard the rattle before she saw the buggy. Buggies, she corrected herself. Two carriages pulled down the lane, the first one pulled by the bishop's gelding.

"What does Amos want?" Leah's question reached her ears a split second before the screen door slammed behind her.

"You know what I do."

Leah moved down the steps, then eased in next to Hannah. "You think he's coming for another reckoning?"

"Please." She said the word, but her heart panged in her chest.

The bishop pulled to a stop, tethered his horse, and gave them a quick wave before ducking into the barn after her *dat* and brother.

"Dat got a new tool today."

Leah nodded sagely. "That sounds about right." She flicked a hand toward the second buggy. "What's Aaron doing here?"

She wanted, more than anything, to tell her sister that Aaron had come for her, but as much as she wanted that to be true, she knew it wasn't. There was nothing left for them. Not any longer. Probably not ever.

"He's working with a new mare Dat bought."

"Huh."

As they watched, Aaron followed much the same routine as the bishop, giving them a wave, then heading for the horse barn.

"And that's it?" Leah asked.

"Looks that way." Life had settled back into its quiet rhythm.

After the excitement of the afternoon, that was A-okay with Hannah.

"Have you talked to your attorney?" Leah asked.

"Not this week." Normally, Hannah called him every Monday, but she had missed today, instead touring Leah's new store with her sister. Not that she thought she was missing any good news. Mr. Lipman had seemed pretty sure that there wasn't going to be much, if anything, left of Mitch's estate. There was no start-over money. No money for her to go back to school. "You don't happen to need any help in that store of yours, do you?"

Leah shot her that smug sister look that clearly said *I told you so*. "I might. You looking?"

Hannah sighed. "I'm going to have to do something. I'm not qualified for much else."

"You could go back and get your GED."

Hannah nodded. She probably would—but she still had to have groceries until then.

"Mom." Brandon came over the hill, fishing pole in one hand as he hurried toward her.

"Oh no." She stood and started across the yard, her heart in her throat at his urgent tone. "What's wrong?"

He shook his head and kept coming.

Lord, she couldn't take this. "Brandon?"

But he refused to answer until he was standing just a few feet from her.

"Are you in love with Aaron Zook?"

Her heart stuttered in her chest. "It doesn't matter."

"If it doesn't matter, then answer the question."

She didn't have an answer that she wanted to give her son. Movement caught her attention out of the corner of

her eye. Her father and the bishop had come to the door
of the barn, alerted by Brandon's loud tone. Even Aaron
had stopped his training and stood stock-still as Star
nudged her broad forehead against his chest.

"Are you in love with Aaron Zook?"

"Yes," she finally managed.

"Do you want to marry him?"

She shook her head. "Brandon—"

"Answer the question. Do you want to marry him?"

"Aaron and I can't get married." It hurt to even say the
words, but she knew from past experience that pain would
dull with time.

"That's not what I asked." Brandon propped his hands
on his hips, the manner so much like Aaron's it nearly took
her breath away. He might look just like her physically,
but he was still Aaron's boy through and through. "Do you
want to marry him? Yes or no."

"Yes." It wasn't like it was a big secret. Aaron knew as
well as she did the obstacles that stood in their way.

"One more question."

Good. Hannah wasn't sure her heart could take much
more.

"Why didn't you come back here when you knew that
you were pregnant with me?"

There were a hundred white lies she wanted to tell him,
but she knew the truth was the only way to go. Brandon
needed to know that his father—his real father—was a
good man. She had made the mistakes that had kept them
all apart.

"After I had been gone a couple of months—"

"After you left here," he clarified.

Hannah nodded. "I got a letter from your uncle Jimmy
about how Aaron had started to see someone else. I wanted
to come back. I'd just found out that I was pregnant, and I

wanted to share that news with him. But he was already dating another. What if he rejected me?"

Aaron coughed. Somehow during Brandon's questions, Aaron had moved closer. He now stood only a few feet away.

Hannah looked up and snagged his gaze. "It was a terrifying thought."

"But—" Aaron started.

Hannah cut him off. "I couldn't risk it." She shifted her attention back to her son. *Their* son. "I would be shamed and Aaron would be forced to marry me, and I couldn't stand the thought of him loving another and having to be married to me forever."

"And now?" Brandon asked. "What about now?"

She shook her head. "I thought you were only asking one last question."

"I lied."

"Brandon, I—"

"Are the two of you in love but not getting married because of me?" He laughed. "That's weird to say. Don't most couples get married because they have a child?"

"There's more to it than that," Hannah said. She wanted to turn to Aaron, have him help her explain, but this was a mess of her making, and she had to see it through.

"What?" he asked. "Joining the church?"

"There's more to it than that."

"Me." His tone was matter-of-fact.

"Yes," she finally admitted. "I can't join the church, because I know that you don't want to live in an Amish house. I can't ask you to do that. It's hard enough when you're born into it."

"And if you don't join the church . . ."

"Then I can't marry Aaron. Or any Amish man, for that matter."

"Do you want to join the church? I mean, I saw you pray."

He saw her prayers answered.

"Mom?"

Did she want to join the church? "Yes." Whether she and Aaron ever found their way together, she knew that it was time for her to be back with her people. And God. Past time.

"Then I give you permission to join your family in the Amish church."

Tears stung her eyes, and she shook her head. "I can't do that." She was a mother, and her first responsibility was to Brandon. She could connect with God on a different level. Maybe take Leah up on the invitation to the Mennonite church. God would understand. She knew that now.

"You can," Brandon said.

"No." He was so sweet to worry about her. She trailed her fingers down one of his cheeks. He had grown up these last few weeks. He wasn't perfect. His hair was still a bit too long, and he still had a sassy mouth, but he was going to be just fine.

"Yes."

She shook her head. "I prayed and prayed about this. And there is no answer that will make everyone happy. I gave everything to God, and there is no answer."

"You have to have faith."

Hannah blinked at his wise words. "What?"

"You have to have faith. You have to put it into motion. You have to surrender it all to God, and then the prayers will be answered."

"You were listening."

Hannah half spun to look at her sister. Leah was beaming like a proud mother.

"That was the sermon," Leah explained. "One we were listening to in the car."

Hannah turned back to Brandon.

He smiled. "You have to let go."

Could she do that?

"I want you to," Brandon continued. "I want you to be happy. If that means you need to become Amish again, then that's what you should do."

Her head spun with the idea. "What about you?"

He shook his head. "You've spent my entire life worrying about me."

"I'm your mother. That's my job."

"God will take care of things."

"Oh yeah?" She smiled through her tears.

"Well, that's what Leah says. So go ahead and say that you'll join the church, and let God take care of the rest."

She could say it now, and then if something happened, she didn't have to go through with it. The bishop would understand. Aaron would underst—

She was doing it again. She had thought that she was turning all her problems over to God, but she hadn't been. She had been fighting for control, trying to do what she knew God wanted her to do, but unable to relinquish that control.

She said she had surrendered all, but she hadn't. And that was why she never got her answer.

"Okay." She felt as if a weight had been taken from her.

Brandon smiled, the greatest and most genuine smile she had seen from him in a long time.

She took Brandon's hands into her own and turned toward the bishop. "I want to join the church."

Amos smiled. "We'll get started on that next service."

"And you can live with me, Brandon." Leah stepped forward. "I have plenty of room in my apartment. You'll be within walking distance of the library to get your work done. And I could use the help in the shop."

"I thought that was my job," Hannah protested.

Leah shook her head. "You've got a house to keep."

Did she?

Aaron took a step toward her. Suddenly they were all in the middle of the yard, standing in a large circle. "Hannah Gingerich, I know you have to still join the church. But I pledge my love to you. And soon, I hope you'll be my wife."

There came the tears again. She wanted to fling her arms around him and press her lips to his, but that could wait until they didn't have an audience. Hopefully that wouldn't be too long away.

"I love you, Aaron." She gazed into his beautiful blue eyes, then turned to Brandon. "And I love you."

"I love you too, Mom."

Leah threw one arm across his shoulders and pulled him into a one-armed hug. "And I love you, roomie."

Brandon grinned and wiped the tears from his own cheeks.

She was becoming Amish again and marrying Aaron. Their *Englisch* son would live with his Mennonite aunt so he could attend school. It was a strange situation to be sure.

"What is the district going to think?" she asked.

The bishop grinned. "They'll think that we made the best of the situation that God handed us. *For I know the thoughts that I think toward you, saith the Lord, thoughts of peace, and not of evil, to give you an expected end.*"

God's will was done. They couldn't hope for more.

The screen door slammed, and Mamm stepped out onto the porch.

"What's everyone doing in the middle of the yard?" She squinted at them as if that would help her better understand. "What did I miss?"

Connect with Us

Visit us online at
KensingtonBooks.com
to read more from your favorite authors, see books
by series, view reading group guides, and more.

Join us on social media

for sneak peeks, chances to win books and prize packs,
and to share your thoughts with other readers.

facebook.com/kensingtonpublishing
twitter.com/kensingtonbooks

Tell us what you think!

To share your thoughts, submit a review,
or sign up for our eNewsletters, please visit:
KensingtonBooks.com/TellUs.

There's one more Belle who needs to find her beau...
Read Skylar's story, SKYLAR'S OUTLAW
coming January 2010, only from
Harlequin Superromance®.